THE DEVIL'S CHIMNEY

THE DEVIL'S CHIMNEY

a novel

Anne Landsman

While *The Devil's Chimney* is a work of the imagination, some locations
and characters in the novel are based on real places, people, and events in
South Africa.

The prologue in this novel appeared in slightly different form in *The
American Poetry Review*, May/June 1994.

An excerpt from the poem "The Recall" by Rudyard Kipling is published
by permission from Bantam Doubleday Dell Publishing Group, Inc.

The lyrics from "A Scottish Soldier" are used by permission of Kerr
Music Corporation Ltd., Glasgow

The lyrics from "The Skye Boat Song" are used by permission from
Middle Eight Music, Ltd., London

An excerpt from the poem "R.L.S" from *The Collected Poems of A.E.
Housman* by A.E. Housman, copyright 1939, 1940 by Henry Holt &
Co., Inc., © 1967, 1968 by Robert E. Symons. Reprinted by permission
of Henry Holt & Co., Inc.

Library of Congress Cataloging-in-Publication Data
Landsman, Anne
The devil's chimney : a novel / Anne Landsman
p.   cm.
ISBN 1-56947-101-0 (alk. paper)
I. Title.
PS3562.A4832D4   1997
813'.54—dc21
97-18951
CIP

Published by
Soho Press, Inc.
853 Broadway
New York, New York 10003

for James

and for our daughter,

Tess

Acknowledgments

Many of the Afrikaans and Xhosa words in this novel appear in a glossary at the back of the book. I relied on *Home Life on an Ostrich Farm* by Annie Martin and *Ostrich Farming in South Africa* by Arthur Douglass for many of the details of the ostrich feather industry and Laurens van der Post's *The Heart of the Hunter* for the San explanation of why the ostrich doesn't fly.

For their careful and generous readings of my manuscript, I would like to thank Shelley Stenhouse, Judith Estrine, Naomi Rand and David Tomere.

I would also like to thank Stephen Berg, Renée Shafransky, the late Frank Daniel, the MacDowell Colony, the Corporation of Yaddo and the Writers Room, Inc.

Thank you to my editor at Soho, Melanie Fleishman, for working with me so passionately and so well, and thank you to Anthony Gardner, my agent, for his sound advice. And to my family for their support, especially Fredrica Wagman and Nela Wagman.

And finally, thank you to my parents, Ruth and Gerry Landsman, for your love of words and your faith in me.

Prologue

Ever since Pauline Cupido's disappearance during the Christmas holidays in 1955, I have been trying to remember things. Nobody made much of a fuss about it, really, and nor did we. But around that time, I started to think what it would be like if I just disappeared suddenly like that, or died. Of course it's not the same thing when you're non-White. She probably just went back to her people on the farm, the way everyone said. I don't think there's any reason to believe that something bad happened to her, even though the Coloured tour guides won't go into the cave where she was last seen, or anywhere near the Devil's Chimney. They've closed up that whole area anyway because the air quality is very thin. It's for purely scientific reasons and has nothing to do with ghosts or anything superstitious like that.

Everything was fine before it happened. How could you complain about a job with the South African Tourist Board, with a four-bedroom house thrown in and a swimming pool in the yard? I keep thinking that if I find Pauline everything will go back to the way it was before. No more bad dreams at night, no more *skollies* under the bed with knives, no more fights with my husband, Jack.

Shaka, our German shepherd, was part of the search party that went to look for Pauline. At night, he sometimes goes back into the Caves. He's not the sort of dog who gives up easily. The next morning you can smell the caves on him. He wears the darkness in his wet coat like the smell of sex. I often watch him licking himself afterwards. His tongue pulls at the soft white hair around his penis until it stands up in little peaks. Jack hates me talking like this, or even thinking it. He says I'm part dog, that I make up stories about Shaka just to make him angry. He says Shaka sleeps in his kennel at night, like all the other dogs.

Where does the smell come from? I always want to know.

What smell? That's when he bangs things and I don't know whether to laugh or hide.

The family Pauline worked for, the Steenkamps, had a black Schipperke called Smiley because he had a habit of pulling his lips back and showing his teeth when he wanted to please you. Smiley almost became a boarder, while they were looking for Pauline, so I had some time to get to know him. He was stocky, with thick black fur and a ruff around his neck, like a small lion. His face was pure Schipperke, all fox and bat with coal black eyes.

He seemed starved for affection although I could see that the Steenkamps were good owners. He came sidling up to me right away, his ears pressed close to his head, his lips curled back in that funny grimace. I've never seen a dog cringe like that and it made me uncomfortable. Before you could say "disappear", Smiley was eating dog biscuits out of my mouth and lying on his back, his little stick legs pawing at the air, his rib-cage arched, waiting to be stroked.

Smiley came from quite a respectable family. The husband was a doctor, the wife was very well dressed and they had three children. The youngest, Marie-Louise, was about six. When they came to the Cango Caves that day, they all seemed very excited, except Pauline, the maid, who was very quiet. She wasn't a Bantu, like the girl who works for me. She was a Coloured.

The Steenkamps left Smiley with us and then went into the main building, where they bought their tickets. Barbara was on duty that day although she doesn't remember them at all. The Steenkamps took the tour at ten and Pauline went at eleven, with the other non-Europeans. John Malan was the tour guide for the Steenkamps, and Pauline's guide was an old man the Coloureds call Oom Piet, who still remembers when you would go into the Caves with ropes and candles, in the old days, before they had all those fancy lights.

I often think about all the things that happened that day, the way you do when you're looking for something. Where did I see it last? Is it hidden inside an armchair or did it fall behind the bed? Is it lost or staring me in the face? Most people have forgotten about Pauline. But I'm the one who has to live here, right at the spot where she vanished. The kennels are not far from the entrance to the Caves, so that it's convenient for people who want to leave their dogs with us. People walk in and out of this place as if it is nothing. I'm stuck here, with the ghost of someone else's maid roaming around. (She probably did it on purpose, to scare me. She's probably laughing at me right now, like Jack.)

Pauline must have a been a little chilly in the Caves,

because she had left her nylon cardigan in the car. This came out later. Oom Piet led her and her people past the tableau, right up front, of a Bushman family doing their daily chores the way they did them thousands of years ago. Then Oom Piet led them into Van Zyl's Hall which is more than fifty feet high and hundreds of feet long. I wonder what she was thinking while she stood there surrounded by all those gigantic stalactites and stalagmites lit up in all the colours of the rainbow.

That's when they usually switch off the lights and start playing the tape. It's pitch-dark and very quiet and you're underground in this enormous cave, like Jonah in the belly of the whale. You hear voices high up near the ceiling. You see a few bobbing lights, as small as stars in the sky. It's supposed to be van Zyl, the man who came into the cave for the first time with Klaas, his slave, and saw everything the way it was then, without the coloured lights, in tiny black-and-white patches. You can hear their axes hitting rock and then something that sounds like a whip or a scream, followed by van Zyl growling Klaas . . . ! as if the slave boy didn't want to go any further.

The tape goes on for a few minutes, with all those chopping, squeaking and whipping noises, the footsteps of the men, more grunts and shouts of Klaas! and *Baas!* That's when children in the tour group start to cry. Sometimes on the non-European tour the Coloured maids scream. Maybe that's what happened to Pauline. The tape could have scared her and she could have run away.

Oom Piet says he remembers Pauline going deeper into the caves so she must have gone beyond Van Zyl's Hall which is really just the very beginning. But if she screamed then, I wonder how she felt at the Devil's Chimney. All Oom Piet says when you ask him about Pauline is, *Sy was 'n mooi vrou.* She was a pretty woman. When I think about that, it makes me short of breath. Why did Oom Piet say she was pretty? I've never seen a pretty Coloured woman. The strange thing with Pauline is that all the men say that when they think about her, even Jack. Jack says he remembers her which is impossible. How could he? He says that she reminded him of a deer, with big, scared eyes and soft features. One man even says that she had long, thin legs!

She's probably laughing at me now, thinking all these things. She's probably a vandal and is sitting with her people on the farm showing off all the stalactites and stalagmites she stole. It takes millions of years to make a stalactite, millions of years of water dripping, water becoming rock, and then vandals go in and spoil it by breaking off big pieces. They should get killed for that.

Not long after Pauline disappeared, I was having a drink before supper when Jack came in holding up a long stalactite, like an icicle, and put it on the mantelpiece. My heart nearly stopped. I said nothing which was just as bad as saying something, because he knew what I was thinking. He could see it on my face. I knew I was pursing up my lips but I couldn't help it. Then he started to play with the damn thing. He acted as if it was a sword and started coming towards me, laughing and taunting.

I sat there, with the ice-cubes in my drink melting away. Jack started poking at my drink with his spear, shouting horrible things about me being an alcoholic. That's when something broke loose inside me and Look who's talking! came out of my throat, like a gurgle almost. I just remember my drink landing on the floor, thinking about the carpet and then his hands were around my neck, squeezing. I don't know where the stalactite went. Then Flo, our basset hound, came in and started barking her head off. It was all mixed up somehow, the way things go when you put them in the blender. I started to see patches of hot purple and black and then Jack let go.

Suddenly it was all quiet. Then there were some soft sounds which sounded like they were coming from Flo but were actually coming from me. Jack was in an armchair staring at the ceiling. My drink was lying on the carpet, Flo had climbed onto me and the stalactite was gone. I have never seen it again and I hope I never will.

After Van Zyl's Hall, there's another big cave called Botha's Hall. After Botha's Hall comes the Vestry, Catacombs, Temple and Crypt. Then there's the Rainbow Chamber, the Bridal Chamber and Fairy Land. Maybe she stopped right next to the formation that looks like a four-poster bed, in the Bridal Chamber. I could imagine a young woman like her climbing into that bed waiting for Prince Charming. It's quiet there, just the drip-drip sound, the glow of the lights and all those beautiful, shining stalactites and stalagmites. Maybe she took a little nap there and woke up and everyone was gone. Fairy Land is right there, with its baby stalactites on the ceiling and curly ones called helictites. That's where I would get lost. It's the way the world is in a fairy tale.

After Fairy Land comes the Drum Room. The tour stops here and people get a chance to bang the stalagmite that looks and sounds just like a drum. Maybe this is where the two tours got mixed up. Sometimes that happens. The non-European tour catches up with the whites and then they have to wait behind those metal chains until the white tour has moved on. Pauline might have slipped through and joined the white group.

After the Drum Room, you go down Jacob's Ladder, which has fifty steps, and then you end up in the Grand Hall, which is even bigger than Van Zyl's Hall. There are huge formations on the ceiling that look like giant chunks of meat. This room always scares me. I imagine a black man hiding in there somewhere waiting to get me and hang me up from the ceiling. Maybe Pauline is up there, turned into rock.

Then there's the Sand Rooms, Lot's Chamber, the Labyrinth. After that comes Lumbago Walk, Crystal Chamber, Crystal Palace, Crystal Forest, Ice Chamber. Around here, the air starts to get thin, especially towards the end of the day when all the tourists have used it up. The Crystal Forest has a Japanese garden with a stalagmite tree. The top of it is all covered with crystals. I nearly left out King Solomon's Mines which is one of my favourites. It has frozen waterfalls coming down from the ceiling. Some pieces are so delicate that it looks like they froze in mid-air, as if a piece of washing in the breeze suddenly iced up.

By this time you've walked across a few pools and even a little stream so it feels like you're at the bottom of the world. And they start telling you about the Devil's Workshop, which is the last section, to make you really frightened. That's the part that's closed up now. When Pauline took the tour forty years ago, it was still open. Being scared doesn't help with the air problem especially if you get asthma the way I do sometimes. This is where the group splits up into those who want to go through the Devil's Chimney and those who are too scared or too fat or get asthma. Jack always goes with the first group and I'm always in the second. He loves to tell people about all the things I'm afraid of. Heights, going across bridges, the Devil's Chimney, sailing, the water, crayfish, monkeys, speaking in front of people.

Barbara, who works in the office, says it's not that bad. The Devil's Chimney is just an opening between rocks. You crawl through it on your stomach. The last part is the Devil's Letterbox which you have to wiggle out of. What I don't like about the whole thing is that people get stuck in there, in the shaft. Once someone was in there for nearly an hour, and they had to rub grease on him to slide him out. His face was bluish from not breathing and trying to make himself thinner. You finally come out and everybody's laughing their heads off. It's not worth it as far as I'm concerned, although Jack seems to be very proud of the way he can crawl in and out of there. Maybe it reminds him of the Army. I'd like to see him do it these days, with all that extra weight he has on him. I'd like to be the one laughing for a change.

Jack says right in my ear that Pauline got lost there, at the Devil's Chimney. He puts his arm around my titties and says that Oom Piet made a pact with the Devil. I can't imagine him involved with the Devil in any way. He showed me a picture of his grandchildren once. One of them is very clever and got a scholarship to study in America even though he is a Coloured. When I say this to Jack he gets furious and pushes me away. He says that Oom Piet's grandson probably made a pact with the Devil as well. They just say that he went overseas when he's probably in the Caves somewhere doing torture on someone.

But then Jack always comes back and his hand struggles to get right into my shirt. Pauline was sacrificed to the Devil, he says. He knows how I hate stories about the Devil. Every few years, Oom Piet would bring the Devil a nice, young woman with long legs and firm breasts, preferably Coloured, and the

Devil would make sure that another grandchild could go to school. When the Devil saw Pauline, he whispered in Oom Piet's ear, saying that he wanted her. When they got to the Devil's Chimney, Oom Piet made sure that the others went ahead of her, squeezing and pushing themselves through the narrow opening. Pauline didn't want to go but he forced her, taking out a knife and pushing her into the shaft. She was terrified but he made sure she kept moving. He even put his hand up her dress and cut off her panties with his knife. She was sobbing now, but she kept going. When she squeezed through the Letterbox, she came out into another cave which wasn't the Ice Chamber, the way it's supposed to be. It was all black, and the stalactites and stalagmites were alive. There were huge bats the size of people. They surrounded her and took off her clothes. Then the Devil came in, with his skin and hair on fire. He took Pauline into his arms and she started to burn. He did awful things to her while she was burning, like putting his hand inside her which made her burn on the inside too. Finally she disappeared in a puff of black smoke which stuck to the top of the cave like a piece of skin.

I'm trying to do up my bra and tell Jack that's why I refuse to go into the Caves. Whenever I look up and see patches of black or even colours like red or brown, it all comes back to me.

The part I remember as if it was yesterday is about the Steenkamps. When the Steenkamps came out of the Caves and Pauline didn't show up, Marie-Louise, the little girl, threw a fit. I have never seen anything like it. They came to fetch Smiley but ended up leaving him there. Marie-Louise was lying on the ground, screaming and kicking as if the Devil got hold of her, not Pauline. You couldn't go near her.

Mrs. Steenkamp looked like she needed a stiff drink. Her husband, the doctor, was just standing there taking some film out of his camera as if nothing was going on. The other children went to get a cool drink. It was all very embarrassing for the parents. They had to get a search party to go look for their maid.

The search party looked through the caves for a while, even Oom Piet, calling Pauline, Pauline! She never answered. Jack went in there with them and took Shaka, who can sniff out anything, even if it's covered in plastic. That's when Mrs. Steenkamp gave us Pauline's cardigan. It smelled like Vaseline and Sunlight soap. Maybe it was hard for Shaka to find her smell because of the smell in the Caves. It's the kind of smell that you can taste because it's damp and waxy and old. Also the sound is confusing underground because there's all that dripping and soft echoing as if you're in a giant stomach and the juices are working.

After a few hours, they stopped looking because there were more tours coming in the next day and you can't make the whole world stop because of one screaming little girl who misses her maid. Dr. Steenkamp came to fetch Smiley. Apparently Mrs. Steenkamp was in the car with Marie-Louise because they had given her a shot to calm her down. Dr. Steenkamp was polite and cool in that way doctors are when they wash their hands and look at some part of your body. He had his camera around his neck and said something about letting the light in by mistake and ruining the roll of film. Smiley was pleased to see him at any rate and jumped up and down like someone trying to land a plane in the desert. I wasn't sorry to see him go because of all the trouble even though it wasn't his fault.

I think Pauline didn't go on the tour at all. I think she

walked back down to the parking lot and got a lift with some Coloured people to the main road. She started walking along the Outeniqua Pass like those Coloured men and women you see walking for miles and miles in the middle of nowhere. Sometimes they have a bicycle but usually they walk. Sometimes, when I take the dogs out, I see her in the distance with those long, thin legs. She turns around and I wave at her but she doesn't wave back. She just keeps walking.

ONE

An ostrich can split you in half with the nail on his big toe. Kobus Visser, who also works at the Cango Caves, knew a little girl who ran into her father's ostrich *kraal* by mistake and was kicked to death by the males. So many people in Oudtshoorn have stories like this because of all the ostrich farms. There are not so many left, mind you. Just two, really, for tourists. People come here to go to the Caves and see the ostriches. There's also a crocodile farm now although I haven't been there yet. Crocodiles are much worse than lizards and I am afraid of lizards.

My older sister, Gerda, is visiting with Flippie, her husband. They live in Ashton where they have a furniture shop. Flippie makes yellowwood tables and chairs and Gerda does the *riempie* work. Gerda and Flippie celebrated their silver wedding anniversary five years ago.

Jack and I got married in 1951 because we had to. It was a shotgun. The funny part about it is that I didn't even know I was expecting until the very end. I kept getting fatter and fatter and eating more and more. So I thought it was the food. My mom used to say, Connie, my girl, if you fall pregnant, I'm sending you to the Magdalena Tehuis. That's where they make the girls wear maids' dresses and scrub the floors. It's run by the Dutch Reformed Church. You stay there until the baby is born and then they give your baby away. That's when you can come home.

Jack told me not to worry about the Magdalena Tehuis. He told me to forget about what my mom and dad said. I listened to him because he was twenty-five and his hair was pitch-black. I was only eighteen. He had Simba and Hotnot then, two Dobermans, and he showed me how to train them. At first I was scared and then I liked it. We were out on the veld together a lot with the dogs. My dad said I was turning into a *hotnot* myself I was getting so dark.

One day I fell over and they had to take me to the hospital. The doctor looked at me and said, *God, meisie, jy verwag!* Good God, girl, you're pregnant! My mom's side teeth suddenly got very long, the way they do when she gets furious. I was terribly scared of her. I remember throwing myself on the floor and crying and begging her not to send me to the Magdalena Tehuis. It sounded so horrible. The doctor told her I must stay calm because of the baby. So she picked me up and told me I was going to get married and that it was a shame I was getting married before Gerda.

Your poor sister is deaf and how would you like that, she said. The wedding would be next week so that I wouldn't show too much. I was laughing through my tears because I always wanted to be a bride. So what if Gerda is older.

We got married in the Magistrate's Court, right next to the office where you pay your speeding fines. I wore a yellow dress of my mom's and I had a bouquet of *vygies* which I picked myself. I don't remember anything else except that Jack was mad as a snake. He wasn't planning on getting married to a Poor White he said. That wasn't fair of him. My mom and dad are very respectable. Two months after the wedding, the baby came. It was a still-born. I think Jack was even more furious because he didn't have to marry me after all. But he was sad when we buried the baby in the yard under the lemon tree, between Simba's mother and Dandy, the fox terrier. I didn't want to know whether it was a boy or girl because sometimes the less you know the better.

Gerda wants to go to the Oudtshoorn Museum. There is a storm coming and the wind is blowing very hard. *Ag no*, I say, let's stay at home with the boys, and have a *dop*. She has her fingers on my arm and it feels like I'm having my blood pressure taken.

I have a *dop* anyway when she isn't looking and off we go to the *blerrie* Museum. I think I must have put my lipstick on skew or my hair is coming loose because the *tannie* at the desk stares at me as if I was that woman in the Bible with horns and a terrible red dress. Or maybe she is staring at Gerda. You never know.

I am thinking the *tannie* is my Primary School principal and then suddenly I see Gerda's grey hair and realize we are old. Her hair is short and she looks like Oom Paul Kruger. I have mine in a *bolla* just like my *ouma*. Jack watches me when I let it down and brush it. It's almost white now.

The *tannie* is wearing a hair-net with tiny stones that twinkle. I am watching how the light dances in her hair when Gerda takes my arm again. The deaf leading the blind, or is it the blind leading the deaf? Or just a bad storm?

Gerda takes me to a glass display box and there are ladies in there, made of pink plastic, wearing grey and black dresses from the olden days. On their heads are big flat hats stacked high with feathers. It looks like water spilling over the edge except it's feathers. Of course the Oudtshoorn ladies wouldn't wear them. It was just overseas. Here every *kaffir* could pick up an ostrich feather and stick it in his dirty hat.

The box is wrong, I want to say, but it comes out like *fok* and now that *tannie* thinks I'm swearing. I see that fat Voortrekker Bible and it's scaring me and those stones in the *tannie's* hair aren't stones anymore, they're *miggies* and they're coming to get us.

So I go into the toilet for a *dop* and Gerda is standing there by the ostrich feather cabinet staring at more feather hats and feather fans and so on.

I come back and I'm feeling better now and she's pointing at a railway ticket that says 1910. It's the story about Miss Beatrice and Mr. Henry who came here so long ago when everything was different. Someone left their things to the Museum after they were dead and you can see an old green dress that looks like rotting seaweed.

Gerda and I are both staring at the dress thinking of poor Miss Beatrice when the *tannie* comes back in, her thighs rubbing against each other like two hissing snakes. I hope my legs don't sound like that. I try to wear slacks. Gerda is wearing Flippie's track suit and if it wasn't for her bosom sticking out like a tray you'd think she was Flippie's twin brother.

I don't want the *tannie* to *skel* so we go into the kitchen which is done exactly like a kitchen in the olden days. A lot of things came from Highlands, which is Miss Beatrice's and Mr. Henry's farm. There is a big open fireplace and one of those three-legged pots that you make *potjiekos* in. Gerda is talking and it's very loud and unless you know her it sounds like something an animal makes. She picks up an iron with a place in the bottom for the coals and I tell her to put it down but she won't. *Ag* no man, I say, but she doesn't listen.

I try to stop her by telling her the story of Miss Beatrice but the *tannie* is right there again, with those hissing legs and she *skels* us out, just what I was afraid of. Gerda puts down the iron, and I know the *tannie* is glad. She probably thought Gerda was going to throw it at her.

When we leave the Museum, it's pouring with rain outside. I say, Let's go to the Ladies' Bar. The wind is blowing so hard I don't know if the sound is coming out of Gerda or out of me or out of the lamp post. The Hotel is quiet and the bar smells of old cigarettes and dirty velvet and just looking at the bottles makes me happy. Gerda has a Fanta and I have a gin.

I'm glad it's empty because Gerda likes to put her hand on your throat when she gets tired of lip reading and people always stare.

I start talking about Miss Beatrice. This is her story and I have to do all the parts myself.

Miss Beatrice had a maid called Nomsa. People say Nomsa was a witch or a witch doctor or whatever it is they call those women who throw bones and make small fires. Mr. Henry and Miss Beatrice weren't scared of her because they were English people, real English people straight from England, not the ones you get nowadays, *Rooinekke* and *Boers* mixed up together like different meats in *boerewors*. Some people even said that Henry Chapman, the *baas*, was a baronet or a marquis. He certainly acted like one. Miss Beatrice, his wife, was another kettle of fish.

Nomsa worked at Highlands for a long time. She started there when she was just sixteen, during the Boom. In those days, Oudtshoorn was the world capital of ostrich feathers. There were feather palaces and feather barons and lots of people who fancied themselves.

They even had special dogs from the steppes of Russia. I wouldn't mind having a dog like that although my dogs, Skollie and Miss Esther Bester van Worcester, would probably get jealous. But there is always room in my heart for another one. I have a very big heart when it comes to dogs.

Gerda is barking now or is she laughing and that's when we have more drinks. How much Fanta can one person drink I ask her but she's not looking at my mouth and her hands are sitting quietly around her cooldrink.

* * *

Nomsa used to make special *muti*. All the Bantu people used to go to her with their problems. Some say she could make people fall in love, or die. I'm surprised *Baas* Chapman and Miss Beatrice kept her for so long. Some people say she made *muti* for them too. They didn't understand how to live here which was why they made such a mess. Mr. Henry had hands that were as soft as a baby's and he always wore white. None of the farmers wore white. They always wore khaki and *veldskoene* like they still do.

Mr. Henry was a gambler which was why they came here in the first place, in 1910. I heard that he spent everybody's money in England, including his mom and dad's. It was either jail or a workhouse or Highlands. He liked to tell people that he and Miss Beatrice came here because of the climate. He said he had TB. He always had a hanky near his mouth, as if he was about to cough up some blood.

He upset everyone, and so did his wife. They brought things here that nobody had ever dreamed of. They had strange medicines and electric bells. Mr. Henry even had an easel and would stand in the veld, drawing on it, as if it was nothing, with a big white hat on his head, like a girl. They say he drew demons and monsters crawling out of the mountains and the sky. Some people have a terrible imagination. Look at those broken faces and stick legs you see on paintings. They scare me. Ordinary diseases are bad enough.

Mr. Henry and Miss Beatrice had the whole thing upside down. He wore floppy hats and she wore pants, although she only put on the pants when he took his big walk which was in the winter of 1911. Some people say he was trying to get to Cape Town and that he started off on horseback. I don't know. Coloured people found him at the top of the Swartberg Pass.

I went once with Jack just after we got married and I swore I would never go back again. I can't look down because of the drop and looking around, at the side of the road with the black rocks and bushes and ruins, is almost worse because it's so empty. And it's windy. You have to button up your cardigan.

We had some brandy in the car which we drank on the way down to Prince Albert. It's a fancy name for a place that isn't there. I think there's one shop, a general dealer, and it was closed because it was Sunday. So we went back over the pass again and this time it was even worse. It was getting dark, and Jack kept pretending that he was going to drive over the edge, which isn't hard to do because there are so many hairpin bends. I kept drinking, and praying, drinking and praying. By the time we got to the bottom, I was seeing herds of baboons jumping over the car. I had this terrible fear that we were going to knock one down. They look like people, old people with lots of hair. Jack was laughing at me until he saw a few of them himself. By the time we got back to Oudtshoorn, I was already *babbelas*. That's the Swartberg Pass for you.

Oupa would always say it's not good to get on the wrong side of an ostrich. Well, Mr. Henry never knew any of this. He never wanted to learn either. September ran the farm. The people in Oudtshoorn said it was a disgrace to watch a Coloured man come into town and order things and drive around as if he was the *baas*. When Mr. Henry took his big walk, it was Miss Beatrice and September driving around together. That's when she started dressing like a *klonkie*. *Veldskoene* on her feet, and those shirts the convicts wear. Nobody could believe it. I once told the whole story to Jack and said he would give me such a *klap* if I did something like that. But he liked it when I told him everything that happened at Highlands. He likes it when I tell him stories. He says it's better than the radio. He's not as bad as you think.

A pound of ostrich feathers used to cost ninety pounds. That was donkeys' years ago. When we were girls, it was only fifty shillings a pound. So you can see why everyone was so upset. I wish I was here before everyone left Oudtshoorn. Gerda even left but at least it was because of the School for the Deaf.

I like company. The more the merrier. When I am alone too much, I drink. The bottle keeps me company. I look at those pictures on the labels of vineyards and people carrying baskets on the shoulders and everyone looks like they have a song in their heart. Jack hates it when I get happy, when I get a song in my heart like those people on the labels.

The first time I ever heard the word alcoholic was when we were parked on the national road, having a picnic watching all the cars go by on their way to Johannesburg. Ma pointed to a lady and her husband sitting under a blue gum tree with their sandwiches and she said, You see her, that's Mrs. de Waal. She's an Alcoholic. I thought it was a religion like the Jews or the Jehovah's Witnesses. She looked like a nice lady. She was quiet, her hair was dyed black and her skin was very white and puffy. Her eyes and cheeks fell down, what you usually see on bulldogs. I saw her another time, and I noticed that everything wobbled a little. Just a little, the way a leaf trembles in a small wind. She drinks like a fish, Ma said, and I saw Mrs. de Waal swimming with those round dark eyes, her mouth wide open, all the water rushing into her. She looked like she had a secret although everyone seemed to think they knew what it was.

My dogs, Skollie and Miss Esther Bester, could care less. Skollie is Shaka's great grand-cousin and Esther is another liver-and-white basset.

The dogs love me no matter what. That's what I say to Jack when he goes on about my drinking. As if he should talk. I'd like to see him try to sit down at the table without the brandy bottle next to him. And everyone else here. They all like a *dop*, especially in the evenings. You never know what goes on inside peoples' houses. Mr. Henry and Miss Beatrice acted as if they were the King and the Queen and look what went on there.

Miss Beatrice was the thinnest person you have ever seen in your life. And she was very tall. Everyone thought she was the mad one, not Henry. They say she had lice because she kept cutting her hair shorter and shorter. She broke her sister's arm once. She walked with a *knobkierie*, but her legs were fine. Someone said they saw her kill a *boomslang* once, with the *knobkierie*. She wasn't scared of snakes. How can that be? Everyone, since the Bible, hates snakes, especially the *boomslang*.

That's the kind of person Miss Beatrice was. Fearless. I would like to have met her to see if they were telling the truth. Seeing is believing. I also heard that she had a meerkat called Scorpion.

I don't understand that. Real scorpions are bad enough. Sometimes we find them in the bath and Jack has to bang on them with a broom or something to squash them. The worst is when they escape and go down the plug. Sometimes when I sit on the toilet I worry that that same scorpion is now in the toilet and is going to sting me with his tail on my tail and kill me.

Meerkats aren't so friendly either although they say Scorpion used to eat out of Miss Beatrice's hand. They don't just lie in the sun like *dassies* and get fat. When you're out on the veld, you look up at Pienaar's Koppie and sometimes there's a *dassie* lying on every rock. They can't be bothered with you, those *dassies*. They're too busy getting a tan. Meerkats make me nervous. But there's less of them.

Scorpion must have lived in the house. I am sure you could still find some of his droppings under the bed, if you looked. He had a collar with rubies. I would like to have a ruby myself. When we got married, Jack gave me a ring out of a Lucky Packet which was red but it broke. I still feel like I'm eighteen inside only when I look in the mirror I see an old woman there. I get a shock and then I think, she's not so ugly for an old bag. She still has her own teeth and look, her eyes are nice if you look into the middle part, which is greenish-brown. It reminds you of a river. Not the frogs but the moss and the light on the water. That lasts for a split-second, the way the sun sinks. Then I see the old bag again and I have to have a *dop*.

Gerda doesn't like the mirror. She never has. She looks at me *skeef* when I talk like this. She's banging her feet under the table and maybe she wants to go. Just one more, I say. Flippie and Jack won't mind.

There was trouble even before Mr. Henry's big walk. There was a palaver about the branding. September and some other Coloureds who worked on the farm had driven the ostriches from the big *kraal* into the smaller one. They were chasing the ostriches with mimosa sticks with thorns on the end. They were cramming them into the small *kraal* so that the males didn't have room to kick. It was like a sea of birds, their wings being the waves. The males are so pretty, with their black and white feathers so big and fluffy. The females are too plain, all grey and small with no make-up. They were all squashed in like that and one of the Coloureds was catching them one by one and taking them over to the plucking box. The plucking box is another squash. There they put a sock over the ostrich's head and then they brand him. September had a branding-iron and he was branding them on the thigh, which is the best part, while a Coloured held up the wings. Of course the ostriches don't like it and they make a horrible noise like lions with asthma. September was putting HC on them, and then a star for the prettiest ones and a black spot for the ugly ones, who get used for feather dusters and so on.

That's when Mr. Henry came along and started shouting about the stink and the noise. He was on horseback and all the animals got very upset. I think the horse reared and something happened and the fire for the branding fell over, which was like one of those grills you use for *braaivleis*. The next minute one of the males was on fire and the Coloureds were jumping all over him to get the fire out. Everyone was worried because he was one of the biggest birds. They wouldn't have jumped like that for one of the females. They would have thrown her onto the *braai* with some peri-peri sauce. Mr. Henry didn't help. He just stood there and then he left. September sent the men home which was the first mistake. Some were kicked and burned.

The ostrich who caught on fire was also the fastest racer, they said. They had ostrich races even in those days.

I remember when Ma and Pa took us and Gerda rode on the ostrich. We all laughed when she fell off.

Mr. Henry must have felt like a fool because it was all his fault. They say he pretended it wasn't and blamed September although everybody knew how many ostriches September had branded. September was married to Nomsa, even though she was a Xhosa and he was a Coloured. I think her father was a Bushman because she had such a small face. When I saw her, she must have been over a hundred. She looked like one of those dried monkeys you see in *muti* shops hanging upside down from the ceiling. She was talking, though, and called me madam. I thought of Pauline and it made my hands go cold.

They had a party then, with a big race, although the favourite was growing his feathers back. Mr. Henry organised the whole thing. He took everyone's bets and gave the ostriches names like Corkie and Sunshine and Flapjack. They had tables outside with umbrellas like you see at the beach and everyone was dressed up in their frills and finery. Miss Beatrice was still wearing frocks in those days.

I would like to have been there. I like parties and I like punch. Ma could of helped me make a dress. I have some white cotton with tiny spots which was going to be for the christening. I got it at the OK Bazaars. It just sits in the cupboard now and gets yellow. They even invited some Jewish people—the old doctor and his wife. His father was a *smous*, you know, and he used to go everywhere with his cart even in the rain selling buttons and dried fruit and forks. People laughed at him and some of the boys would even throw stones at him when they saw him coming down the road. But now his son is Doctor Fox.

Somebody stole all the money from the race. It was probably one of the Coloureds although they never found out where the money was. Mr. Henry had to promise to pay everyone back. The money was outside in a box and a baboon could of run off with it. Maybe somebody *skopped* it into a hole by mistake and the hole was part of the Cango

Caves and now that money is sitting somewhere turning into a stalagmite.

Mr. Henry was in quite a pickle because he had to pay the Landbank his monthly payment for the farm as well as all the people who came to his party. He was in a big rush to make some money quickly and so he put up all his paintings inside his house and invited everyone to come and see. Of course everyone had just lost their money on the race so why did they want to buy a painting especially one that looked like the Devil himself had painted it. Eggs with legs and giant *goggas* not to mention lizards and fish without eyes that he said lived in the Cango Caves although no one has seen them. They were albino on top of it. Can you imagine such a thing? A dead-white lizard with blanks where his eyes are supposed to be and an ugly white fish with a smooth face? It's too revolting for words.

Gerda makes pictures with her hands that look rude and she wants me to tell her about the fight and what happened after that but now I'm the one getting worried. It's late and who will feed the dogs?

She puts her hand on my throat the way she used to when I was little to hear the vibrations of a person's voice and so I go on anyway. Never mind the dogs.

You can't say happily ever after, even when you have a big farm, hundreds of ostriches, and a chimney that came in a boat. Mr. Henry packed up and left just after the ostrich race. He and Miss Beatrice must have had words. I know what Jack would have been like if no one liked his paintings.

I can just see her sitting there, minding her own business and he comes in screaming about how stupid everyone is and starts throwing things around. First it's small things, like the sewing-table and the pins and needles go everywhere and she's on the floor trying to pick them all up so that the dog or the cat doesn't swallow them and then he starts with her, telling her it's all her fault because her family sent them to Oudtshoorn and did she remember how sick he was, vomiting all the time on the boat, because he really loves England and England is his soul. England is cool and damp and green and there are no bad animals, no scorpions, not even the tiniest threat of a scorpion. Ah! And that's when he sees something slithering on the floor. Is it a snake or is he dreaming? Did Beatrice put it there just to drive him mad? September told him there was a *tokolosh* in the house and is it one of those? Goddamn September for telling him in the first place. That's when the lamp crashes down and there's glass on the floor. Beatrice is now in a corner and Wait! She's got something. She's going to throw an iron. She broke her sister's arm and now she's going straight for Mr. Henry. He's cutting himself somehow, and starting to whine, running into the bedroom. He's the one packing, mind you. He's going back to mother except there is no mother because he stole her last penny. He's going somewhere. Somewhere out of here, with the pins and the glass and the snakes and the *tokolosh*, with Beatrice tall and thin, glittering like a knife and coming at him. He's packing and she's unpacking and the clothes are going around the room in circles and the suit-case is up and then it's down, up and down, and finally, so higgledy piggledy, he's at the front door. And he's going.

He's going. She's crawling now, and crying and saying she's sorry but it's too late.

She stays there, lying by the door, while the black horse, Dingaan, and Mr. Henry fly into the mountains. She doesn't know how long it is but when she gets up and sees the blood on the side of her hand and bits of lamp caught in her skirt and the broken chair, the one with the embroidery on the seat, she wants to believe that it was the wind, the South-easter, the Northwester, the Berg wind, but not Henry and especially not her. Her auntie was the one they locked up, the one who cried when she looked at her own shoes, who cried when she put on her hat, the one who couldn't stop crying.

I was a shoe myself. I came into this world too soon and so they put me in a shoebox. I'm not sure if I was a man's shoe or a woman's, if I was leather or plastic, if I laced up or buckled or slipped on. I just know that ma took a shoebox out of her cupboard, filled it with cotton wool and made a bed for me. I'm not sure if she punched holes in the lid the way they do with silkworms but I know that the box was my bed, until I was big enough for Gerda's cradle. Maybe Miss Beatrice's auntie had the same thing and so her shoes made her cry. Perhaps she went from a shoebox to a hatbox to a cradle and that's why the hats made her cry too.

Mr. Henry galloped and galloped and galloped until he had a whole new set of problems. It was getting dark and he didn't know where he was. Which pass was this? Was it the Montagu Pass or the Outeniqua Pass or, heaven forbid, the Swartberg Pass? The land was open and dry, and there were mountains to the left and mountains to the right. Behind him, in the far, far distance were mountains too. The names spun around in his head like *goggas* and that over there, was it the Kamanassie Dam? For once, just once, he would like to have run into a Voortrekker, with his big fat wife and big fat Bible, maybe a slave or two and some white-haired children struggling north with their ox-wagon on their way to God knows where. But the Voortrekkers were gone. They had been gone since the Great Trek and that was a long time ago.

But look. He sees a grave and a cross and something written. And yes, there was a Voortrekker here but all he left was his wife and some words on the stone which you can't see anymore. All you can read is her name—Johanna Jacoba. Johanna Jacoba could have died of so many things.

Now he knows it's the Swartberg. He knows in front of him is the Great Karoo. He can't go back because you can never go back and he can't go forward because it's too far from the sea, too far from Cape Town, from boats and ships and ways to get somewhere else. The Great Karoo is bigger and emptier and harder than most places. It's where the ground cracks and the oxen die. It's where the Voortrekkers fought with the Natives, where they drew up their *laagers* and loaded their shotguns while the women prayed like mad and handed them ammunition. The babies sleeping and the young boys shooting next to the men. The black bodies and *assegaais* coming at them, the armies of Satan coming to get them and their wives and their children.

Mr. Henry sits down. He has to think. Next to his foot is a

patch of white and he picks it up and it's cold. He doesn't know why but he licks it. He's back in England and it's December and outside it's snowing and the world is becoming something else. This miracle in his hand is snow. There is more of it on the other side of the rock. He runs over there and he sees a huge patch of it, which goes up, up, to the top of the mountain. He's scooping it up and rolling it and patting it like it was ice cream. There. He has made a snow dog and a snow house. The house is a little crooked but that's all right. He's not an Eskimo.

He forgot about his hands and he forgot about Dingaan. His hands are wet and numb and no matter where he puts them—in his shirt, down his pants, under his bum—they stay wet and numb. Then he notices that his feet are no longer feet. They're wooden shoes. He calls for Dingaan but Dingaan's no fool. He's going home. Mr. Henry looks down the mountain and he sees a black spot kicking up dust in the distance. And then the black spot disappears.

Mr. Henry is all alone. And it's clouding over. The wind is blowing his hair into his eyes and his jacket and his pants are flapping like sails. So he curls up, next to the rock, under the rock, forgetting for once about the scorpions and *goggas* and snakes that live there where it's dark and warm and soft. He sings for a while. "Speed bonnie boat like a bird on the wing" and "There was a soldier, a Scottish soldier, who wandered far away and soldiered far away." He's singing "For these green hills are not my land's hills, they're the island's hills . . ." when the cloud wraps itself around the mountain so tightly that you can't see anything. Mr. Henry tries holding up his hand to his face but he doesn't know where it is anymore since he can't see it and he can't feel it.

This wooden stump bumps his eyebrow and he's not sure if it belongs to him or is part of a tree.

His mother—or is it the nanny?—is smacking him and his bum is wet and cold and bare and a leather belt—or is it a snake?—is hanging in the air, behind his left eye. The back of his head tenses like a piece of leather shrinking and then she's laughing like a hyena and her side teeth are long, so long. It can't be nanny because nanny's lips are small and sealed tight, as tight as the lid on the can of golden syrup. Mother is growing, like a storm that's about to break right over his head, on top of the mountain, which is where he is right now with water pelting him and darkness in his ears. He's screaming and sinking and he's not sure which comes first, the screaming or the sinking but the walls are falling and the hole is closing and soon he will be buried alive.

He blinks and he looks around and people like sticks covered with rags are making three fires and working with the earth. The fire melts the ice on his eyebrows and the water runs into his eyes and makes him furious. Who are these brown shadows, like *knobkieries* with arms and legs? Where is my mother? Where is my nanny? A man with pinholes for eyes touches him on the arm and hands him an ostrich shell filled with juice, a dark brown juice of some sort that looks like a melted piece of the Swartberg Mountains. He wants to tell the man that he's had enough of melting, thank you very much, but his tongue is like a small dead mouse and won't move. His arms are reaching forwards. He can see them as they take the ostrich shell. He can feel the dark brown in his throat as it runs past the dead mouse, down his gullet. He knows he is drinking the soil and the ugly trees and probably the dung but he just keeps drinking, hoping he is going back.

They wrap his feet with feathers and thongs and rags and

now he is walking. But he is not going back the way he had hoped. He is still on top of the mountain, screaming and sinking, his voice echoing all the way to Prince Albert. He shuffles along, crying for his mother, his heart left under the rock for a hawk to find, in that soft place where the scorpions live.

We stay up late, talking. I forget what time it is. I still feel Gerda's hand on my throat when I go to bed. There's Jack and while he's sleeping I put his hand right there, where her hand was. My bonnie lies over the ocean, my bonnie lies over the sea, my bonnie lies over the ocean, oh bring back my bonnie to me, to me.

How can you sleep?

TWO

What is Miss Beatrice doing? What happens when she finds out that she's alone on the farm, with the *volkies*? Mr. Henry was the one who wanted to leave, who wanted to drink coffee in Paris, who wanted to eat olives and swim in a green sea. Miss Beatrice is the one who stays, who takes off her blouse and puts on a khaki shirt the convicts wear. She is scared because she has to do everything by herself. She doesn't know how to tie a knot or saddle a horse or fix a waterpump. The metal cuts her hands and the sun burns the top of her head. She shouts at Mr. Henry and blames him for everything. She is writing a letter to her father, when suddenly the pen stops in her hand and she finds herself throwing the paper away. On the page on the ground, so that the ants can read, it says, Papa, I am writing because. "Because" is half-scratched out.

She stares at the sky, as the light slowly fades into pink

and the mountains bloom like purple flowers. There is woodsmoke curling up from the *pondokkies* and a woman shouts—is it Nomsa?—and laughs.

She can see the ostriches in the *kraal*, the black and white plumes of the males, the brown-grey feathers of the females. She knows that she is the female ostrich, dressed in the colours of the earth, set here, on this piece of land, to belong. In a split-second, everything is different. She cannot live here with Henry. She no longer wants to lick that envelope like a good girl. She will not go back to England. This land is hers. She is the Queen Bee.

The air is strong with the smell of animals and iron, plants cooling, low fires. Miss Beatrice floats into the evening. She sails to the ostrich *kraal*, her shoes behind her, left on the *stoep*. She looks into the eyes of a male, those enormous pretty eyes with long lashes. It looks like he's hanging his head and blushing and she bends down in front of the fence and digs in the ground with her hands. She comes up with a pile of small stones which she offers to the ostrich. He snakes his head through a gap in the fence and one, two, three, the stones go down his throat, joining the marbles and watches and pebbles that help him to digest the lucerne he eats all day long. He doesn't say thank you. He just stands there, his white feathers gleaming against the black ones. She looks at the length and shape of his feathers, thinking business now, and when to clip.

She keeps walking, from one *kraal* to another, counting each bird, noticing who's been fighting, who's thin and who's fat. Burrs get caught in her skirt and her hair, and the soles of her feet get pricked and scratched but all she can feel is the Farm. There must be a full moon in the sky because it's night and she sees everything, every bale of lucerne, every shed, every tool. Even the mountains are lit up, the way they light up the Cango Caves, except there are no bright colours, they are rhinoceros grey.

I was afraid once, when I saw a page in a children's book with a picture of a backyard by night, all the animals stalking, the cat on the fence, the dogs' eyes like lamps, and moles and mice awake and busy.

This was more than somebody's backyard. It was a whole farm in the Little Karoo with the chance of snakes and vermin and night scorpions and everything else that hops around when it's pitch-dark. Not to mention the *volkies*, who were in their tin huts, making fires and telling stories and sleeping ten to a bed. They do things like put rags soaked in paraffin between each other's toes and then they light them and watch the person hop around with fire between his toes for fun.

But Miss Beatrice floats on, getting lighter and whiter, whiter and thinner, until she's a column of smoke herself. The *volkies* look up from their fires and nod and she smiles at them as if she is the Mother of God. She sees that their houses are made of paper and sheets of corrugated iron and look much worse than the house the three little pigs lived in, the one the wolf blew down. She is almost ready to lead them into the farmhouse, like the Pied Piper, but they're settled in for the night. You can hear the sound of snoring coming through the tin walls, and the occasional cough of a baby.

She glides under the blue gum trees, past the cement dam where the maids wash dishes and clothes. She enters her house through the back door, into the kitchen, up the passage, into her bedroom, where she lies down fully dressed on the empty bed. The voice that was in her before, the frightened voice that was afraid of the dark, that only a day ago spoke to the sleeping man at her side, saying, Henry, I was afraid that you'd leave me alone here in this awful room, I was frightened. The hand that stroked and the voice that whispered, It was so dark here before you came in, I thought I would disappear. That voice is gone, and the body sleeps.

I get like that when I drink but Miss Beatrice was stone-cold sober. They say she drank huge glasses of water, one after the other. She had the thirst that we all have, because of the dry air and dry ground and dry everything. It makes your throat dry and you have to keep wetting it and wetting it. I just add a kick of something, to give the water some taste. Otherwise you're no better than a horse at a trough. I think Miss Beatrice wanted to be like an animal.

She slept in her clothes that night and when she woke up she remembered every single thing although she wasn't sure if it was a dream. But when she saw her feet she knew that she had been walking around barefoot. She got dressed quickly because this was the first day she had ever felt like this and she went into the kitchen. Nomsa was lighting the fire for the stove and September was sitting behind the kitchen-door eating a piece of bread.

Miss Beatrice sat down at the table where the servants eat, and ate *mieliepap* and bread like the *kaffirs*. No knife, no fork, no spoon, just shovelling the *pap* with the bread and swallowing it in big chunks. Nomsa looked at the white woman in her convict's shirt and Henry's pants and those dirty white feet, ugly and scratched. Miss Beatrice began talking about the Future and that's when September came in, to listen. Nomsa and September were careful, the way you are around a dog that's not right. They moved slowly, not showing their fear, as Miss Beatrice talked and talked. Her words darted around the room like flies, dizzy to get out. It was the *volkies'* houses that must be torn down, and the new houses that must go up in their place. She was going to fix the fences and pluck the birds and drive here and there to buy and sell and make Highlands a special place. The *volkies* must grow vegetables and she must grow vegetables, and they must all eat these vegetables along with the *mieliepap* and bread.

Mr. Henry was gone but his clothes were there and Nomsa and September didn't ask, because servants never ask. Did they want to know? I don't think so, because it was better to forget and go on and fix the things that were broken. September knew Mr. Jacobs on the next farm, and Mr. Jacobs would come over and help because September caught some of his ostriches once that had got loose. Mr. Jacobs was a *Boerejood* and he was raising ostriches and buying and selling the way Miss Beatrice wanted to.

A Jew? Miss Beatrice had never seen one, not in England, not here, except for the doctor and his wife who came to the ostrich race but that was different, wasn't it? The doctor you couldn't tell and his wife so faded. How could you know anything about them other than wounds and bandages and stomach troubles? But this man, this Jacobs, he was up and about, with animals in *kraals* and all the farming know-how, specially for this part of the world. Did the Jews run around with the Hottentots and Bushmen, the Xhosas and Zulus? Or did they come here on ships from the East with their spices and wheelbarrows, the way they jammed up the East End, shouting and being poor? But they were not always so poor, sometimes they were very rich and those were the ones to worry about, invisible and clever, always one step ahead. Mr. Jacobs, which Jew was he? Was there garlic in his pockets and a black beard covering his whole face? Or was the Jew part underneath?

Miss Beatrice is angry and cutting her hair because this is not how things are supposed to be. Your neighbours aren't Jews. The Boers are bad enough, and so are the Poor Whites but the Jews. That's asking too much. They belong somewhere else. The night of the walking is spoiled. Ruined by Mr. Jacobs and his tribe on the other side of the fence, being so wrong in this place, so very wrong.

Nomsa is sweeping up hair, long curls of it browning the kitchen floor. She sweeps and sweeps. By the time Mr. Jacobs bends through the back door, the floor is clean and Miss Beatrice is almost bald. But she's not sorry.

Mr. Jacobs is not the invisible Jew or the bearded one and he's not sorry either. He came because of September and the lost ostriches, and his morning is busy and almost over and now this. Not a lady, an English lady, the kind they have in the books, but a stick with a doorknob for a head and eyes like moons. And she's not like his wife, who has patterns and dresses galore. She's dressed like a *klonkie* and what's under there heaven alone knows. Mr. Henry lets her run wild. But wait. He's gone, or in Cape Town, and now she's the farmer, she says, and she wants to know everything and she's staring at him as if he is the last man in the world.

He's ready to put his hat on his head and walk out the door. Let someone else look at those moons. But help, she says, I need some help, and the word is a promise, a promise to his mother never to say no to a woman. So the hat goes down and clenched and they walk out together into the light.

Oh, ostriches. So much to learn. And it was different then, because of the feathers so very valuable in the rest of the world but not so in Oudtshoorn because every *kaffir* had one in his hat. But in Paris, Vienna and so on, it was 1911 and the ladies wore them as if they were gold. Mr. Jacobs is talking and Miss Beatrice listens and she can see the gold in these feathers, as the birds fold them and fluff them. It's different now because the ostriches are like cows. We eat them and make handbags out of them and those feather dusters of course. But then, those birds were money. Big money. Like the duck that lays the golden egg except it wasn't their eggs, it was their feathers. My *oupa* could rattle off all the different kinds. Prime whites, first whites, second whites, tipped whites, best fancy-coloured, second fancy-coloured, spadonas. Then blacks and drabs.

Mr. Jacobs is the Ostrich King. He tells Miss Beatrice because she must know who she is talking to. He started with nothing and now he has the best birds in the world and his children, God willing, will study in England. He loves King Edward. You have to look after the chicks as if they were your own babies, he says. Those first three months the chicks are so frail. There in the pen, she sees them, like porcupines, their feathers so brindle and spiny. Cute with their necks already longer and eyes big and brown. That first year they must be protected from sickness and dogs and jackals. They must eat lots of wheat and *kaffir* corn and when it's raining they must be covered. Green food, cut up, when the veld is dry.

After twelve months, you put them in a big *kraal*, where they eat for themselves. Every day, you pray for rain whether you are a Christian or heathen because of the drought. Drought is your worst nightmare. Lucky you have plenty of *spekboom* and prickly pear on your farm, Mr. Jacobs is telling her, because you can cut them up for feed and the birds will live. When they're sitting on their eggs, don't ever go into the *kraal* because they will kick you to death. Both the males and the females. When you pluck, you keep all the feathers separate. The cocks' wings, the cocks' tails, the hens' wings, the hens' tails, blacks and drabs. Then you put them on tables in a sorting-room. You take the cocks' quill feathers and then separate them into new piles, those prime whites, fancy-coloured and so on. How long, how good, what colour, what part of the bird, then male, female or chick is how you decide.

He doesn't know why he is telling her all this because she's looking at him as if she's standing on top of a mountain and he's at the bottom. Did she hear anything? Miss Beatrice nods so hard it looks like her head is going to come off. Yes, yes, fascinating birds, so lovely, so prized, what could be better in the whole world than to be here right now, in a sea of them. She's happy, she says, have you ever seen so much sun? He hands her his hat and he makes her put it on because the woman is *bossies* or she will be very soon.

And wait, she's thanking him the way you thank your servant and she's walking away, his hat still on her head, her nose tilted back from the top of the mountain. How dare she, he'll show her, he'll watch from his farm as her ostriches shrivel and die. Even better, he'll buy them. Those English, he'll show them. Whatever it takes.

Miss Beatrice is glad to be rid of that man puffing himself up like a pigeon in heat. He's almost as bad as the Boers with that accent so fake as if he went to Eton or Harrow. How dare he. Afrikaans would be better. Afrikaans like plates breaking in your mouth. The men at the station, the Hotel, in the bank, barking Afrikaans. *Ja, nee. Volstruise, gewere, goeie môre* and so on. But this! This insult. As if they were equals. How dare he. He's got to be put in his place, that merchant, that Jew, that seller of feathers.

Then there are the others. Those people that crammed into the house to see Henry's paintings. To stare, and then whisper. Those women, fat with red faces, with their freshly baked *koeksusters* and *melkterts*. The Poor Whites with their smell and brown teeth, at the railways and shops. They won't come to Highlands again. Not one of them. Highlands is heaven and they aren't allowed. Miss Beatrice is running, running and those Russian dogs are behind her.

I think of Skollie and Esther, who walk with me out on the veld every day. Skollie and I have a special friendship because I think he sees Pauline when we are out on the veld together. He lifts his nose as if he can read her smell. He whines a little, and looks at me. I can see myself in his eyes. When I look again she's gone. She must be a ghost by now.

* * *

Jack lies sleeping on his side, his face squashed up against his arm. He could be someone nice but he isn't. Gerda says he's just like Flippie and every man gets cross with you. It's easy for you to say, I tell her. You have four kids.

In the beginning, Jack had more air. He walked with elastic in his feet and I thought he was going to be the manager of a place like Pick 'n Pay. Then we got this kennel job and I do the books and so we stayed. During the day, when the dogs are slow, he tells the Coloured boys to clean the parking lot and he gets the soup machines fixed. But the machines aren't always broken so he comes home and he sleeps. Or he listens to rugby. When I talk to him, he looks very heavy and so I wait till he's asleep. Then I say whatever I want.

Once I was washing my face in the bathroom and he lay there, sleeping I thought, but he had his hands in his pants and you know what he was doing. I didn't know until later. I just heard the bed shaking and I thought he was having a bad dream. I looked in the mirror and waited for it to be over but it went on and on so I thought he must be having an attack. I opened the door so you couldn't tell it was open and then he grunted just like a pig. Next minute Flo is on the bed and she's licking him, there right in his pants, and on his stomach, as if she's having her breakfast. So I closed the door again and sat down on the toilet and I could hear Jack laughing at Flo as if she was his *bokkie*. Then she was at the bathroom door, scratching, and I had to come out as if I knew nothing.

The male ostrich, you know, has it inside, curled up right

inside his bladder. It doesn't stick out. My *oupa* once told me and he showed me how you can tell if a male and female have mated. There by the female's tail, on the left, is a mark. The bigger the mark gets, the more times they've done it.

I wonder if there's a mark inside me.

People say Miss Beatrice was really a man and that Mr. Henry was a woman but nobody really knows the truth. Nomsa, maybe, who dressed him, and lived there in that mad house. Mr. Jacobs was their neighbour but their farms were so big that he'd have to make a special trip to Highlands to look in the window. Nobody knows who was doing what with who. But Nomsa was there, and so was September and sometimes Mr. Jacobs, with Miss Beatrice and those Russian dogs, Leo and Lena. The dogs died the day that Mr. Jacobs told her about the ostriches. She was running and they ran ahead of her and right into one of the breeding *kraals*, chasing the birds like they were guinea fowl. They got a few chicks and were eating them when they fell into the Valley of the Shadow of Death. The ostriches were kicking and splitting them in half before you could say hello. They died with their jaws in a death-growl around the ostriches' necks and they had to bury the whole mess in one big lump. People say that Nomsa took some ostrich toenails and dog hair that day for a special *muti*. Miss Beatrice knew it was all her fault and I hope she never ran like that again.

You can do terrible things when you're happy like a man who choked on a fish-bone at his own wedding. I once nearly choked on some grapes and ended up swallowing them whole. As they went down my throat, I saw myself lying on the kitchen floor, dead.

When you have a farm, my ma says because she grew up on one, everything always goes wrong. If it's not the drought, it's worms. If it's not worms, it's thunder which makes the eggs hatch all wrong and the birds come out like glue. Of course Miss Beatrice never had another dog. When there are dogs, there will always be accidents, like the one with Leo and Lena. Even when the dogs don't chase the birds, even when they grow up with them, the birds *skrik* in the middle of the night from the barking and get themselves killed or hurt. Sometimes monkeys play with the chicks and knock out their eyes. Then the farmers get together and shoot them so that they don't come back. In the olden days, there were wild cats and lynxes and the farmers poisoned them with strychnine. Here there is always something to poison, or shoot, or chase. Sometimes I hear screaming in the night and I don't know where it's coming from, whether it's animal or human, European or non-European. I try to close my ears, or sometimes I take a *dop* for my dry throat and it puts me to sleep.

It's usually gin in the night. Jack and I have beers on the *stoep*, and maybe some brandy and then of course we like Cape wine for picnics and so on. But gin is my special friend and I think of her as a her, someone I would know if I lived somewhere else. She laughs a lot and has a cigarette voice like you hear in the flicks, and she always wears a white blouse with ruffles on the bosom. She looks a bit like Mrs. de Waal only she's fatter. Mrs. de Waal is so quiet but Tannie Gin can talk the hind leg off a donkey.

Miss Beatrice wasn't lonely because she always had Nomsa. My maids never last. They come from all over. Meiringspoort, even Blanco and Pacaltsdorp. There's always something. A man or some babies, or they steal Jack's shirts. Or they drink and the bottles are empty and Jack thinks it's me. There is always a new face in my house but now I don't notice anymore. They all look the same and I call them Lizzie. *Die mies praat jonk,* they always say. The madam talks young.

It's because I began so small. My ma tells everyone I never caught up.

Miss Beatrice was so sad when she lost Leo and Lena. They say that's when Nomsa gave her the *muti* and she got much better. But I think on the inside she went black, like a *kaffir,* and that's when the *volkies* all moved in there and made their fires. She didn't worry anymore about white people, or Mr. Henry, she just made Highlands her country. Of course you can't do that and people like Mr. Jacobs were watching. Somebody has got to watch that woman, they said.

There was no one telling her what to do and so she could have stayed in bed all day long and listened to *Jacaranda Days* on the radio except there was no radio in those days.

She could have taken a long bath or she could have gone to the shops or to the Oudtshoorn Hotel for tea and scones with cream and jam. There were lots of fancy people in Oudtshoorn in those days. She could have visited them in the afternoons bringing a cake or something sweet with her. But she only came into town to buy supplies and she always was with September or Nomsa and people had to look at her twice to see if she was White because by now her skin was very brown. Of course all the mothers were afraid that their daughters would catch what Miss Beatrice had so they pulled them into the Post Office or the General Dealer's when she was there. She must have had that feeling I sometimes get when I am out with the dogs only she had it all the time. You are the wind and no one can catch you.

To make things worse, she wanted to win the feather prize at the agricultural show. There were lots of famous birds who belonged to the Meirings and Watermeyers and P.E. White. Birds like "Karoo Belle" and "Krombek" and "Prince". Miss Beatrice wanted to beat them all. The only time she would go to the Hotel was to try to talk to the other ostrich farmers, in the bar. Now they have a ladies' bar, next to the men's bar, but then there was only one and there were no women in there ever. The men of course were furious because she was trespassing. I don't know if anyone talked to her or if she even got served but she always had some kind of a book with her, like a ledger, where she kept the accounts. I think she sat in there and wrote in her ledger and then the men started talking again and she could listen. It was important because the prices for the birds, for the chicks, for the feathers, were always going up. In those days, a lady went out with an ostrich in her hat, a seal on her back and kids on her hands and feet. They even had pockets in their dresses for little dogs!

First Miss Beatrice found out about fences. My *oupa*, when I was little, almost five feet tall but not yet, would tell me that I was the right height for a fence. The top of my head which was like the top wire would catch the ostrich just where his neck bends so that it would stop him from trying to get out. And then you have to drive long poles into the ground, every four hundred yards or so, to tie the wire around. You can make a fence with bush and so on but it won't last. Miss Beatrice must have ridden all over Highlands for days looking at the fences which were falling down. Of course with the wires it isn't cheap but she wanted everything to be right. Some people near Albertinia have live fences made out of aloe or prickly pear and you can see them from the national road but here wire is better.

She wanted Mr. Jacobs to pay her half for the fence she was fixing since his land was next to hers but they had a big fight over the boundary stones and he said they were all skew. He even said that there were caves on his land, part of the Cango Caves, so some of his land didn't count because it was just air and big holes and animals could fall in it. So he moved the stones forward, and she had to move her fence back and it was a big to-do with the magistrate involved. Then Mr. Jacobs said he didn't like her wire fence, that there were not enough wires, which was a mistake because then the magistrate said he had to build the fence and Miss Beatrice should pay just less than half. Which was good for her because then she could forget about fences and let him do it with his labourers, and not hers. They both had to sign something in the end and Mr. Jacobs was furious. The magistrate was from the Circuit Court and the next week he was in Aliwal North and everyone in Oudtshoorn wanted to kill him for listening to Miss Beatrice but he had already left on the train.

How much money can you make from ostriches? And how do you win the feather prize? Miss Beatrice wanted to know these things so badly because she wasn't just sleeping and eating the way most people do, she was fighting. You can get one pound of feathers from an ostrich, if you pluck it the right way. About fifty quill feathers with four fancy-coloured in each wing. The tails are different. Sometimes you get a hundred feathers. Sometimes just seventy-five. Altogether it works out to five ounces for the quills, five ounces for the tail and six ounces of blacks and drabs. So she knew how much she could get from each bird and then she added up all the expenses of the farm and subtracted them from the price for the feathers, and that would be her profit, if no birds died. If her hen, Molly, or Bliksem, her prize cock, won the feather prize then she could breed them or farm them on the halves with another farmer and make even more money.

I explained this to Jack—how Miss Beatrice could have done it—and he told me it was rubbish because no woman knows how to farm, the way a farmer does. It's not in her blood. He believes that Miss Beatrice never really lived. I say people just don't want to know about her which is why there's that big sandstone wall around her house.

I think she lived and she liked doing the books as much as I do. I always add and subtract here at the kennels. How much dog food, how many boarders, how much to charge per boarder, other expenses and so on. I have an adding machine.

Miss Beatrice was watching Mr. Jacobs, and he was watching her although they were not on speaking terms. She wanted to learn how he had gone from selling feathers to a farm with nearly two hundred birds and he wanted her locked up in a place like Valkenberg. That's what he said, anyway. Some people believe that he was in love with her so badly that he couldn't sleep at night because he was imagining her floating past his window, which could have happened because she really wanted to get inside his skin and find out how he became so rich. Maybe she did go into his house at night and look at his books to see how he had started off selling feathers and taking a percentage, and then using that money to buy a pair of good breeding birds and farm them on the halves. Birds on the halves is when you own a pair of breeding birds and lend them to another farmer who raises them on his land and looks after them. The birds are still yours but you and the other farmer share the money that comes from selling the feathers. Again you have to sign something in case one of the birds dies and you also have to agree what to do about the chicks. Anyway, Mr. Jacobs made so much money from birds on the halves that he could eventually buy land which was not usual for the Jews who did trading, mostly. But that's how he became the Ostrich King.

The wall at Highlands makes me think of the prison and the time my ma caught me running away. I was seven and my sister Gerda was nine and Kloppie, my *boet*, was nearly three. My ma made us all dress up and she told Gerda and Kloppie that they were coming with me to the prison to say goodbye. Gerda was screaming in her deaf voice and Kloppie was crying too, although I don't think he understood what was going on. I didn't have time to take anything I liked, my ma was in such a hurry. Soon we were all walking down the road in our shoes and socks with lace frills, except Kloppie of course, who was in a clean white shirt and shorts. My ma was wearing a pink hat and it was just like we were all going to church. Kloppie was falling because he was so small and I had to carry him. I wasn't sorry because I thought it was the last time. My ma said that I won't be able to run away again because I would be in a prison and the walls were high and there were warders. I didn't cry. I just wondered if there were other children and what they were doing in there. Perhaps they had run away or lied or taken the Lord's name in vain. I saw the prison from far away, a low, yellow building the colour of Miss Beatrice's wall. Gerda was more scared than me because she thought it was all her fault and so she just lay down on the pavement screaming. My ma took my hand and made me step over her and we kept on walking towards the prison. Kloppie was following us like a puppy dog. We stood in front of the prison and my ma told me that was where bad people were and if I ran away again she would take me there. And then we turned around and walked back home.

The first thing you have to learn with ostriches is patience. You can't force them to do anything because they will run away or hurt themselves. Miss Beatrice was in a big rush, though, because she wanted to beat Mr. Jacobs at everything. I'm sure she had September chasing after the ostriches in the beginning, when they ran away. But chasing them doesn't work because the faster your horse goes, the more the bird *skriks*. And then they can run until they drop dead, or kill themselves against fences. Sometimes they just drop down and never stand up again. They live for a few days like this and then they die. If an ostrich runs away, you should get off your horse, and light your pipe, or whistle. The bird will run a short way, and then wait for you.

Miss Beatrice learned the hard way what with the branding and Mr. Henry and then the accident with the Russian dogs. She didn't want to lose any more birds and so she had to be really careful. I think she became an ostrich herself. Her eyes got bigger and her neck got longer, and she got on with the birds so well that people made jokes about plucking her, and selling her feathers. But she didn't give up, the way most people would have. Sticks and stones will break your bones, but names can never hurt you.

Ostrich feathers are so beautiful. I saw a flick at the bioscope and there were can-can dancers in Paris. It looked as if all they were wearing were feathers, prime whites that had been dyed light blue and purple. The feathers were long, the best ones you see at the sorting house or the auctions. Long and full, with that perfect curl backwards. Like palm trees, but only softer. The main dancer had a huge powder blue ostrich feather fan and I was crying because I knew all those feathers came from Oudtshoorn. Every time she fanned herself, the feathers moved like water or singing and the tears just rolled down my cheeks.

Jack, of course, was trying to see if she was naked but then he saw she was wearing a beige bathing costume with sparkles on it. He was disappointed. I told him that the government would never show us a woman in her birthday suit. Doesn't he know that? Of course, but you can always hope, can't you. The people behind us told us to shut up. By then, the can-can dancers were gone. I know they have Busby-Berkeley shows in Cape Town or Johannesburg where you can see dancers like this, but they never come to Oudtshoorn.

Miss Beatrice wanted her birds to have feathers like that. The kind of feathers that take your breath away because they are so big and soft and graceful. You can't pluck the birds too often or else the feathers will get stiff and ugly. My *oupa* said right in the beginning they would just pluck all the feathers off the birds and then slaughter them. But then they learned a system. Pluck the wings and wait. Pluck the tails and wait. Pull out the stumps that have been left behind, just at the right time. In the olden days, the *hotnots* used to pull out the stumps with their teeth. Miss Beatrice probably learned how to do that too, in her convict shirt and *veldskoene*.

Sometimes the chicks had human stepmothers. That was before the incubators. They would wrap some old *hotnot* woman in lots of blankets and stick her on top of the eggs until she had hatched out the last little chick.

Miss Beatrice copied Mr. Jacobs. She wanted an incubator, not some poor old *hotnot*. She wanted to be modern.

The morning after the Russian dogs died, she was a new broom, sweeping clean. Some people say it was the *muti* Nomsa gave her, which was dark brown, like a *kaffir's* skin, and had brown balls floating in it, like *dassie* droppings, not to mention the Russian dogs' fur and the ostrich toe-nails.

I went into a *muti* shop once and there were hundreds of dead animals hanging from the ceiling, some with lots of skin and fur on and others nearly skeletons. The smell nearly made me vomit. The *muti* they gave me for Jack so that he would say nice things to me, smelled like man. I put it in his tea and he didn't even notice that terrible smell, so dirty and unwashed. He just said, Your hair is clean today, and that was it.

Miss Beatrice got herself an incubator so she could hatch out as many chicks as possible. Not all her birds were Guaranteed Breeders because Mr. Henry had bought some breeding pairs that had never produced eggs. It's a shame the way people lie about things like that. There's a lot of cheating when it comes to selling birds because people tell you one story and you spend your money and you get stuck with a bird that doesn't lay eggs, or a bird that's got a tape-worm as long as ten puff-adders. Ostriches die from so many things and all the worms love them, when they're alive and dead. They waltz around when they're happy and then they fall down and break a leg. Nowadays you can fix it but in Miss Beatrice's time you had to shoot the one with the broken leg.

And then they get into fights or run into fences and snap! Another broken leg.

She was lucky, though. Her birds didn't die. Everybody else's birds would get yellow liver or water on the heart but her birds would be fine. The other farmers went mad trying to find out why she never lost a bird after the Russian dogs. She didn't even have the usual trouble with the Natives' dogs who would always come around and scare the birds so that they would run into the fences. When she was alone at Highlands, she was all right. Sometimes I think that's what I need. No Jack, just me and the dogs. I wouldn't even be drinking. I'd be waltzing around like those ostriches, but I'd make sure I didn't fall.

THREE

When Jack woke up, I fell asleep and when I woke up again it was dark and the next night was just beginning.

I go into the kitchen in my nightie with my hair still loose. Jack is having some toast.

Gerda is coming again. Wasn't she here last week? I ask Jack and he says, Connie, you're a *loskop*. Don't you remember?

It's because you *suip*.

I don't care.

Jack is shouting at me and he says that everybody sees what I am and I say no they don't. They can't see anything.

Do you think you're see-through, like a plastic bag? Invisible?

He's taking a bottle of gin out of the cupboard and I think he's coming over to give me a *sluk*. Instead he pours it over my head and I feel like Bridal Veil, the waterfall you see when you're driving in the rain on the old road. The gin is so light and cool and fresh that I want to open all the cupboards and pour everything all over me. Suddenly I think, Oh my God, someone is going to get a match. They're going to punish me. I'm going to burn.

Jack is shouting at the top of his voice, but I can't hear anything except the flames crackling and someone inside my head trying to bang them down with a huge black hammer.

Jack slams the front door so loudly it sounds like the police.

Then he's gone. I sit down. Flo walks over and lies on my feet. All I can think of is Miss Beatrice's farm and how big it was.

Her farm was so big you could get lost on it. Like all the other big farms, each ostrich had his own ten acres and the Guaranteed Breeders, a husband and wife ostrich, had nearly thirty acres. There in the distance, almost a day away, was Mr. Jacobs watching his birds lie down and never get up. He rode out to Highlands and Miss Beatrice was busy with the men building those bungalows and all her ostriches were standing up, as if nothing was wrong. She bent down to knock something into the ground and he could see her breast under the convict shirt and he went blood-red, in front of all those *volkies*. They say he was a religious man and maybe he prayed something to his God, Jehovah.

The dust started to sparkle and pop and he told Miss Beatrice he had to go inside for some water and perhaps the last of the morning coffee. They were walking and their legs were bouncing and light as if the ground was one big trampoline.

Inside the house, Mr. Jacobs thought he was going blind but when his eyes came right, Miss Beatrice's breast was fluttering right by his elbow and it was like someone pushing him overboard. His lips found her hair and he breathed her smell which was like smashed grass. Her eyes lifted, and he nearly drowned all over again. Where were they? Was it the bedroom or behind the door or there on the floor in the living room? Their arms were pulling at each other the way it is when a wave smashes you into the sand and everything goes upside down all at once. For a moment, they looked at each other and remembered that they were in the house in the middle of the day. Miss Beatrice saw where the top of Mr. Jacobs's hair ended and the shape of the curtain behind him and behind that, a tree. But then he moved into her and she heard her first scream and then it was laughing and crying, so loud that she thought Nomsa could hear.

Water on the ostriches' hearts is why he came but that's not what happened. There was water somewhere else only it wasn't water. It was more like fire than anything else. I'm surprised they didn't burn a hole right through the floor. It could have been the *muti* or it could have been the air on the veld early in the morning that touches your skin and makes you want everything. Mr. Jacobs tried to go but that everything pulled him back onto the floor, Miss Beatrice riding him across the Little Karoo as if she was chasing ten thousand lost ostriches. They were chasing and chasing and chasing and finally they found them, high up near the stars, on top of a lost *koppie* that was made out of her rib and his rib woven together. That's when he saw his own God who told him this was not his neighbour's wife, this was an angel, a messenger to tell him that the Messiah was finally coming. He could hear the hoofbeats and her breath and the house swung above him like a lamp and when he woke up she was a fairy, so light and thin and golden and she gave him some pancakes and coffee. He stumbled out of the house and the sun burned. At the end of the day, he was back in his house with his wife and his daughters in their frills and there was more water on the heart. More birds lying down and not getting up.

What he had seen before was feathers, pounds and pounds of prime whites, so full, so perfect that they filled his house with precious things. Now all he could see was Miss Beatrice, those moons of hers staring into him, her hands dry and light and burning all over his body. He blinked and shook his head, and she didn't move or step away. She stood there, like someone on a stamp, and the stamp was stuck to the middle of his forehead and he couldn't get it off. He lay down on the sofa from England and his wife and daughters stared over him but he couldn't see them. The best he could do was cover the stamp with his hand.

While he lay there, some of his birds, the ones who couldn't get up, laid their necks along the ground like the stalks of broken flowers, and died. It rained like mad that night and in the morning they plucked the feathers of the dead birds. They plucked them and then washed them to get the mud off and the feathers were the most beautiful feathers Mr. Jacobs and his family had ever seen. They were so white, so long, so perfectly even on both sides of the shaft. When you picked one up, it moved like the softest of soft winds. Mr. Jacobs got up, and he was the Ostrich King again. The stamp on his forehead with Beatrice on it had fallen into the cracks of the English sofa.

That morning there were bright puddles all over the farms and tiny flowers all over the veld. *Opslag,* my *ouma* used to say. What comes up after rain. You know that there are going to be lots of ostrich eggs, because the ostriches eat the flowers, and waltz from happiness. The Guaranteed Breeders do what they're supposed to do and six weeks later you have a whole crop of little ones.

Were there more eggs at Highlands? Or was the Ostrich King still the king? Nobody counted the eggs but I think Miss Beatrice was winning. Still, the feathers from the birds with water on the heart broke all records at the feather-auction. So Miss Beatrice rode out day after day and counted how many birds she had and it came out to one hundred and fifty-eight.

Was she thinking about Mr. Jacobs while she was counting? Did she see his dark-brown eyes hot as treacle, the treacle burning and pouring into her bones? Somewhere between the seventy-fifth bird and the ninety-third? Or did she see him all the time, sitting inside every ostrich's eye, on his throne, feathers in his crown, Ostrich King of the world?

I think she was laughing and crying, burying Mr. Henry in her heart. At last she believed Mr. Henry was dead and she forgot about wanting him to come back and see everything she had done. For an instant she remembered fighting with him and the broken furniture and the way he fled from her and then it was gone, like someone blowing out a candle. And into that dark, dark room, stepped Mr. Jacobs who was dark himself, not as black as a *kaffir*, but darker than all the men who had kissed her hand and laid their arms around her waist. He was like a bruise inside her, something soft and purple and aching and she wanted him to come back. That wanting made her ride faster and harder, from *kraal* to *kraal*, counting and re-counting bird after bird, getting them mixed up and counting some twice, even three times until her head was aching and she wanted to lie down and never get up.

The twisted trees and the tumbleweeds made her angry and for the first time she wanted green, and the coolness of England. She was hearing old voices, her father and brothers, and what they said about Jews, the men in particular. Something about pointed shoulder-blades and loose, big hands and she was trying to remember if Mr. Jacobs had either. But all she could remember was a black circle, like water going down the drain, except here in South Africa it went the wrong way. Which way was that? She almost spun off the back of her horse just thinking about it.

She remembered her corsets, empty without her, and how they kept and held you and stopped you from flying off things. That's when it came to her, the idea of the day. She would go home and wash up and put on a corset and one of her dresses, the green silk with flowers, and she would get September and the cart and he would take her to Mr. Jacobs' farm but she wouldn't see him, she would visit his wife and his daughters and they would eat finger biscuits. The whirling would go away sitting there in his house, sitting on his English sofa, sitting in her corset and gloves, drinking tea.

Nothing was right, she found out, when she looked into her cupboard. Inside her corset, at the waist part, was a spider's nest the size of a *hotnot's* head except it was white not brown, with sticks in it like the arms and legs of tiny stick people trying to get out of a very thick net. It hung there and didn't move. She tiptoed away and looked for her green dress. When she found it, it looked like slime but she put it on anyway. Something tore at the waist. The dress fitted and didn't fit in very different places because without the corset her body was smaller at the top and bigger in the middle. Nomsa tried to button all the pearl buttons but some popped off and rolled into the cracks between the floorboards. There were tears in the skirt like trap-doors and she remembered that night when she glided in the veld. All those thorn-bushes must have picked at her like nasty little hands.

There were shoes to go with the dress. Moss, she thought, when she looked at them. Stones that don't roll gather moss. When she put her left foot into the dark-green shoe, something crunched at the toe. She shook the shoe and a squashed cockroach, a big one, dropped to the floor.

I would have given up and cried. I would have poured myself a long gin and tonic, especially for the nest. Sometimes those hairy spiders, tarantulas, sit up near the ceiling and Jack has to scoop them down with a broom and I won't be able to go into the room for days without shaking.

Miss Beatrice didn't care. She probably laughed at all the *goggas*. That's who she was. She threw the cockroach out of the window because if you leave them on the floor all the ants come. And then she put on the left shoe. The right one she shook first, before she put it on. Nomsa gave her an orange *doek* from her head which unravelled into a sash to cover the tear around her waist. She didn't look like Miss Beatrice from England, she looked more like a *hotnot*, with that *doek* around her middle. To make things even worse, she had a farmer's tan, with brown forearms and hands, and white, white shoulders, and that head on top, almost bald like an ostrich.

The trip took almost the whole day and by the time she got there she was covered with dust like icing sugar except it was brown. On her head she wore one of Henry's floppy white hats and that was brown too from the dust and her sweat and the sun. They unharnessed the cart and September went to the back of the house, to the kitchen. There were long, thin trees like soldiers and then there was the front door, an oak door from England with a huge brass knocker. Miss Beatrice dropped the metal against metal and after a few minutes the door opened and Mrs. Jacobs was there, staring. She smelled like roses and her hair was wispy and crispy and her eyes were strict like a teacher's. Miss Beatrice heard her father and brothers and out came her goldest voice, the fox-hunting voice, the mistress of manor and servants. It floated like a bell and Mrs. Jacobs just about fell to her knees. What a pleasure, a wonderful pleasure and surprise, not to mention an honour, she was singing.

Miss Beatrice was inside, just where she had planned to be and instead of the whirling there was drumming, something drumming between her legs, because he was there or he had been there and anytime soon he'd be back. Mrs. Jacobs took her hat and the dust fell everywhere like a blessing. Miss Beatrice was gliding and talking and now she was sitting on the English sofa where he'd been lying. She could feel the heat coming up from the chintz-covered pillows. Between the cabbage flowers and the leaves and the baskets there was something simmering. She leaned against the back of the sofa, just where his elbow had grazed the material, when he had covered the stamp, that stamp with her on it.

All the daughters came in. Bertha, the youngest girl with

buck-teeth and *kroes* hair wearing a sailor suit, then Goldie, an odd one with freckles and red hair, dressed to the nines in something very tight at the bust, very purple. The last one was Rachel, who was the most beautiful, except for the fact that she had a long nose. But her hair was right, pitch-black and straight and her skin was pinkish and her eyes kept on shining, not like Miss Beatrice's moons, more like black treacle. Her pa's eyes.

That's when the throbbing moved from Miss Beatrice's legs to her head and her throat dried up and all that fancy talking she was doing came to a dead stop. And Mrs. Jacobs ran out of the room like a mad dog was biting her heels to get Miss Beatrice, to get that English lady, not a lady's lady, but still a lady, something to drink. I would have taken ten whiskeys, thank you very much, and I'm sure I would want some more, even. The maid came back with a tea-tray and Mrs. Jacobs fluttering behind, getting more and more nervous by the minute, especially when she saw Bertha and Goldie and Rachel talking and waving their hands about and laughing as if they had never been happier. Miss Beatrice looked tired, draped against the back of the sofa, the stamp finally come to life but still flat. The girls were talking about patterns and dresses and materials. What did Miss Beatrice like and where did she get that unusual green dress. It was so ... Different. And the moss shoes. Like shoes out of a fairy-tale. And who cut her hair? They were all pulling their hair away from their faces, turning to each other and wondering what they would look like with very short hair. Chatterboxes, Mrs. Jacobs called them, and she sent them to get their father.

They didn't get too far, not even out of the front door, because he was coming home anyway, still dizzy from Miss

Beatrice, ready to take one of those headache powders. Of course when Mr. Jacobs saw her sitting right there on the sofa there was a giant thunderclap but nobody admitted they heard it. Miss Beatrice even raised herself up a little, her hands to her ears and Mr. Jacobs stepped back and touched the wall as if it would help him. The daughters were quiet, being seen and not heard because their pa was there which was a pity because I can tell you Miss Beatrice could have used their words and their giggles to fill up the room. But none of that kind of thing happened. It was Mrs. Jacobs, the hostess, who asked about the drive and the ostriches and Highlands and if there was any news of Mr. Henry. Her voice was crooked-sounding, and then to cover it up, Mr. Jacobs started huffing and puffing about the birds and the plucking and when to pluck and how to pluck and pluck this and pluck that. Which plucking was Miss Beatrice at? The first or the second, the prime whites or the tails? Or the stumps? Because he knew a thing or two about plucking. He could help when it came time. Oh, yes, oh, yes, Mrs. Jacobs chimed in. My husband is the Ostrich King. Isn't that funny?

He looked like the Devil, Miss Beatrice thought, his cheeks red from the sun, his eyes big and dark, that hair as *kroes* as a *hotnot's*. He was walking towards her and she felt herself spinning again, and rolling, just like a tumbleweed. She got up. She had to. She could almost touch his jacket, his sleeve, but she didn't. She looked down by mistake, right there between his legs. It was bulky, like a parcel. Now she was scared and her knees were loose. Mrs. Jacobs was on her left side, and she felt her breath, like roses and tea, and she wanted to be sick.

She knew that he knew, and he changed suddenly, into

gentleness, and told Rachel to take her outside. Miss Beatrice needs some air. She was out on the *stoep* and Rachel had taken her arm and the farm lay in front of them like a village.

The villagers were ostriches and although there was water on the heart most of them looked big and healthy and the fences had six wires and the sneezewood poles stood in the right places, every four hundred yards or so. The land rolled on over low hills and the birds strutted in the distance as if they were on holiday. There was the incubating shed, on the left, and the plucking *kraal* behind it and you could just see the plucking box if you squinted. You could smell soap and the old *hotnot* women were by the stone dam washing the prime whites and fluffing them and they looked like clouds that had fallen out of the sky. This was a kingdom, like the old Zulu kingdoms except there were birds not *kaffirs* in the *kraals*. Miss Beatrice was jealous. Highlands was a funny long farmhouse and her birds were smaller and not so proud and picked in the dirt more like chickens. A cloud went over her heart, like one of those dirty feathers before they were washed. All that seething and longing for more of what she and Mr. Jacobs had chased was now anger, hot as tin roofs. How dare he. A Jew. Not an Englishman, not even a Boer. How could he. Who let him.

Rachel wasn't a farm-girl. She was holding her nose and Miss Beatrice wanted to smack her, but she looked like a clown with those pink cheeks and round eyes. The girl slipped an arm around her waist and Miss Beatrice shook it away. Rachel looked hurt and Miss Beatrice swayed a little, pretending she was sick. Perhaps she could say a tarantula bit her, while she was sitting on the English sofa. It fell on her from the ceiling, big as a mouse and bit her between the legs, right on her shoppie. Shoppie was what my granny called it, the grannie who came on the boat from England, who lived in the streets and was a Cockney girl. The other one was my *ouma*, who wore a *kappie* on her head and made *melktert* and *koeksusters*. In the Boer War they would have killed each other, starting at the top with the eyes.

Should she dance, Miss Beatrice thought? That's what you're supposed to do when the spider bites. So she hopped around a little and shouted tarantula, tarantula, it's so terribly sore. Rachel grabbed her hand and spun her around and suddenly they were dancing like mad in the dust, dancing a hole in the ground. The ostriches stopped looking for things to eat and just stared. Maybe one of them even started waltzing, just to keep Miss Beatrice and Rachel company. At first, the girl and the woman were willow trees in a storm and then they were little fish darting and popping out of the water. Then they were seed-pods and they were hollow and empty inside, with things clattering and clanging right down to their knees. They were shaking and falling, shaking and laughing and suddenly they crashed down into the dust. That spider, Rachel was gasping, it bit me too. It lives in the chandelier.

Wild, wilder than me, Miss Beatrice was thinking as she caught Rachel's eye, blacker than black. She got up and tried to dust herself but bits of her dress came off and you could see her skin underneath. She covered herself with her hands but it didn't help and Rachel ran to the house to get something for her. She came running back with her father's shirt because she had seen Miss Beatrice in town dressed like a barefoot *klonkie*. Miss Beatrice tied it around her waist to cover the holes because she couldn't put it on, no she couldn't. She couldn't be in the place where his arms had been, where his heart was, where his shoulder blades lay. So it sat like a snake around her waist, like the girl's arm, only thicker.

Everything was wrong, and she wanted to go home right away. The way back was long and the sun was sliding already. September was sitting on a stone behind the kitchen, smoking a pipe and talking to the maids, Nonnie and Sarah. They bobbed their heads, and laughed and Miss Beatrice was hot and cold all at once because of the *doek* around her waist and Mr. Jacobs' shirt and the secret that was striped all over her skin. Rachel was still with her but she was busy worrying about the dirt on her skirt and the mess she was in and what her mother would say not to mention her father. She slipped into the house and was gone. September! Miss Beatrice scared herself, her voice was so raw. We have to go. September winked at the sun and tapped his pipe on the stone. He lifted himself up from the shoulders and Miss Beatrice smelled woodsmoke and tobacco and sweat.

Thank you for having me, she was supposed to say to Mrs. Jacobs. Thank you for the tea. When she looked at the house all she saw was Mr. Jacobs' body, the sandstone walls the color of his hands, the roof as black as his hair. No thank you, she whispered, feeling the dust in her mouth. She couldn't walk in that door. It led straight to the engine-room. His heart.

September brought out the horses and they were still tired from before. So they watered them, brushed them, rubbed aloes on their legs. Miss Beatrice was singing, There was a soldier, a Scottish soldier, who wandered far away and soldiered far away . . . and September hummed something very old. By the time they were finished, all harnessed up and ready to go, the sun had melted into a red pool behind the thorn trees.

They climbed into the cart and Miss Beatrice looked back at the house with the lamps all lit and Mrs. Jacobs waving from the window, and she knew that she had burned something down. She was sorry but glad because her old world was gone and the whole animal was finally out. The women had seen her and they wouldn't be quiet and whether they knew or they didn't, she had walked in and walked out of there and nothing was the same anymore. It was the day she broke her sister's arm all over again.

This night was different than the night she had floated. It was moonless and star-pocketed and the lamp on their cart made a circle that jiggled. A lynx stepped into the circle and stared. September clicked and breathed in and the lynx disappeared. Miss Beatrice heard hissing. Snakes? Her word floated like a bubble and September popped it. The sky, he said. The sky is full of hunters and the hissing and chasing is their hunting. Miss Beatrice looked up. Each star was louder than the next. Orion was bellowing and the Lion and the Little Dog up there were panting. The Southern Cross was in a sweat and the chase kept getting louder and louder, hoof-beats coming closer and closer. How do you know? Miss Beatrice asked September. *Ons is die eerste mense,* he said. We are the first people. Ouma Boesman said. She prayed for me. She wanted me to be strong and brave, like a star. She told me why the ostrich doesn't fly. The Mantis stole his fire.

The Hottentot's God, the Praying Mantis. Miss Beatrice saw one, inside the window, poised on the glass. She saw the day, and Highlands, and for a moment the night was gone. But then they were back in the dark and September was there. Tell me the story, September. He said nothing for a long time and Miss Beatrice didn't know if she had spoken or if he didn't hear or if he was not going to say another word until they got back to the farm. You know how that is when you don't remember saying something but you know you wanted to say it, you were dying to say it, to somebody, even a maid or a garden-boy or the neighbour's little girl. I have given up asking Jack because he is like that too. He waits, he doesn't say anything, and then suddenly out of the blue, he screams, SHUT UP!

Here on the veld there was no one to shout like that at Miss Beatrice. September would sulk but not shout. She wasn't sure if he was sulking now. She wasn't sure how old he was either and that suddenly worried her. When the lamp swung to his side, she took a quick look at his face. It was yellow-brown, and cracked like an old apple and he had a peppercorn near his ear. She knew that he must be thinking about his people, about Ouma Boesman, about Nomsa, about the *mielies* he had planted, about the pumpkins on the roof of his *pondokkie*. She asked him, because she was the madam and yes she didn't want to disturb him but why shouldn't he tell her? He had to tell her! September, why doesn't the ostrich fly! Please!

He gave her a sideways look that was sour, but also laughing. *Is die mies nie moeg nie?* Not tired? No, she shook her head like a child. No, no, no. Please, the ostrich.

The Ostrich kept fire under his wing. One day he took the fire and made a big *braaivleis*, cooking something that smelled very good. The Mantis was walking past and smelled the *braaivleis*. He also wanted to have fire so that he could cook just like the Ostrich. So he made a plan to steal the Ostrich's fire. He asked the Ostrich to come with him and they walked up to a big tree full of yellow fruit. The Mantis told the Ostrich how good the fruit was and so the Ostrich started to eat. No, said the Mantis, the best ones are high up. The Ostrich opened his wings to reach up high and the fire fell out. The Mantis grabbed his fire and ran away. Now the Ostrich always keeps his wings close to him in case the fire falls out again. He doesn't flap his wings and fly.

Of all the birds, the ostrich is greatest. That was the last thing September said. That's when the sky really got loud and Miss Beatrice could feel the spears of the hunters, and the coldness of their breath, as they chased the ostrich, the duiker, the springbok across the purple sea above their heads. She and September were driving their cart along the rim of the disappeared moon. Just when she had forgotten everything, the road turned and there was the sign that said, "Highlands." The shape of the house was hard. Miss Beatrice found herself getting stiff and cold and when she lifted herself out of the cart, her feet were alive and hurting. September wasn't smoke anymore. His clothes were old and smelled bad and he shuffled off leading the horses towards the stables.

Is this how life was, Miss Beatrice was thinking. You fly, you swim, you dance, you chase ostriches with Mr. Jacobs, September tells you stories and you fly higher, and then you crash. The crash is how things really are. People aren't nice, and they look at you skew and their breath singes you. The world is full of shops and tight dresses and men jingling coins against their thighs. I wish I could have said to her, Yes, Miss Beatrice, that's when a little *dop* comes in handy. Tannie Gin. She lets you swim and fly all you want, except when you wake up and there's wet moss in your mouth. Nothing a little orange or a *naartjie* won't cure. Or some fish paste on a piece of bread, with a good strong coffee. And then a walk with the dogs. Later, when that sharpness gets to you again, you just visit Tannie Gin again and everything's not so hard anymore.

I don't think Miss Beatrice would have listened to me. She probably would have hated me, the way my mother does and even Gerda and Kloppie. They all think I am a *dronklap* but I don't care. She wasn't like them, though. She wasn't like anybody else.

Miss Beatrice didn't forget about Mr. Jacobs. He used to come to Highlands in the afternoons, when the sun was so hot and so hard it could press you down like a big thumb made of iron. Of course it was nearly a hundred years ago and in those days there were no Safari Suits, nice short-sleeved jackets and shorts in light-blue polyester that you just throw in the washing-machine. Jack wears them, with light-blue socks that fold over under his knee and his comb stuck into his sock, on the right side. His legs aren't so bad. Mr. Jacobs wore long-sleeved shirts and waistcoats and jackets and lace-up boots and a big, felt hat that probably got dark from his sweat. I'm sure he had lots of hankies for rubbing his face, probably red ones.

He would come with advice and some liniment for the ostriches' legs or a new kind of incubating-box. The afternoon when Miss Beatrice came for tea, they pretended to forget. The broken green dress, Rachel and the tarantula, it was as if those things didn't happen. They would start off in their usual way by riding around the farm. At first they would start with the horses and talk about colic and snake-bite and hunting. There was the Queen's birthday springbok hunt and did Miss Beatrice ever see *aasvoëls* who had eaten so much from dead carcasses that they couldn't fly? The hunters liked to catch them with whips around their necks. Miss Beatrice said it was cruel. He had seen a lot of cruel things, he said. How a baboon kills a dog. How someone played a joke on a baboon by putting a dead snake in the shiny paper that goes around sweets. The baboon went mad and tore all the flesh off a baby's arm. He had seen a Boer beat his servant to death. What did she think of the Boers? The women are ugly, Miss Beatrice said. Their coffee tastes good, Mr. Jacobs told her, and they know what to do when a baby is on its way. Miss Beatrice laughed and remembered what her neighbour on the other side, Magda van Wyk, had told her. Use a fowl to clean your chimney. That day it rained on the van Wyk's land and not at Highlands. The Boers are dirty. The Queen's birthday springbok hunt, he brought it up again. He wanted to go but was never invited. It was for the English. Why didn't Miss Beatrice want to go? Maybe, but it's so stuffy. I am too wild now. Look, Mr. Jacobs, I am green like a horse that has never been ridden.

That's when his eyes boiled at her, and he looked like he was about to pull her off the saddle and break her in. But he didn't. He turned his horse around and they rode to one of the ostrich *kraals*. He got back to business, his shoulders square and fierce, his eyes searching for broken fences, sick birds, angry birds that challenge you by sitting, and heaving, their wings black-and-white swells on the yellow sand. A big hare darted in front of Miss Beatrice and she told him what

September had told her about hares. The spirits of your relatives and friends live inside them. I fell into a rose-bush and here, look, there's a star on my knee. Miss Beatrice lifted her leg onto the saddle, rolled up her pants.

Mr. Jacobs was trying to say something about ostriches, about their piss in the spring, when it gets quite red. He was trying, but it was a madhouse inside his head, inside his body and all he wanted to do was go back to the house, and unbutton that convict shirt and look into Miss Beatrice's pants. Miss Beatrice could see his hands, in front of the saddle, hiding and covering. What about horse-sickness? She was teasing now, and it wasn't fair. It comes once in five years, he said stiffly. The horse suddenly breathes heavily, droops its ears, and goes back to its stable. Froth comes out of its nostrils and it dies the next day. They think it's the night air, the wet cobwebs on grass. What about glanders and strangles, she wanted to know. Glanders you have to shoot the horse right away. Strangles a horse only wants to be put in a camp and rested.

Let's go to the willow trees, by the dam. Miss Beatrice leaned forward and bit her horse's ear and suddenly there was dust in Mr. Jacobs' face. Lucky, her horse, was jumping over bushes and tumbleweeds. Mr. Jacobs felt a small stone fly right from Lucky's hooves into his mouth. He pressed his heels into his horse, and he followed her, and the drumming of the hooves was the beating of his heart. They didn't stop at the dam. They didn't stop at the edge of Miss Beatrice's land. They rode to a place that was flat and bare, where the bushes were low and almost black, and there were no more ostriches in sight.

Suddenly a red hanky, flapping from one of the bushes, made Lucky swerve. Mr. Jacobs stopped, got off his horse and so did Miss Beatrice. Mr. Jacobs bent down next to the bush with the hanky, and put his hand on the ground. The earth was dark red and damp. He scooped it up, and it lay in his palms like a small mountain. There is a passage here. I found it one day, he told Miss Beatrice. They knelt down together and started to dig with their hands. Sometimes their fingers would meet underground, and it was more than just fingers. It was frantic and searching, looking for light, looking for dark, looking for some kind of peace.

A foot below the ground, there was a big hole. Miss Beatrice slid her arm into it and the cool air felt like water against her skin. Here, she said, and Mr. Jacobs put his arm next to hers. His fingers—or were they the fingers of some animal, some underground monkey—were talking to her, pressing her palm, her wrist, the spot inside her elbow. The fingers were telling her to follow them, to press the rest of herself into that hole, that moist place that smelled of wax and clay. She pulled herself in, one arm woven around Mr. Jacobs' arm, the other one searching for something to hold. There was nothing but air. Like a diver, she took a deep breath and then she let go of the fingers and the arm. She slid. Little stones fell against her and then it was black. I would have screamed and gone mad but Miss Beatrice just breathed, and kept on breathing. There were more stones falling, and suddenly she could smell Mr. Jacobs right next to her. She reached out and there was his beard and his eyebrows and his hat still on. She lifted off his hat and her hand was in his hair, lost and searching. Suddenly she felt his palm inside her shirt, on her breast. She gulped in air and it shot from her mouth into the hot place between her legs. He tugged at her pants and she pulled at his shirt and soon they were lying in the shell they had made from his clothes and hers. They floated in the darkness and breath, drifting.

She searched into the blackness and when fear rose in her throat, his hand pressed against it, and his mouth opened to hers and she was safe. The cave she was in was him, and she moved in it and it rose up against her. There was a river, an underground river, flowing from her into him, and they swam with it, until it swelled over and flooded them. They were drowning and holding each other, and Miss Beatrice heard words, like rocks, German words. *Geliebte.* There were sparks in front of her eyes and suddenly there was light, yellow flame, and the aching inside her broke loose. It shot up from her legs to her mouth and became mist. The mist fell on them and they bent their heads, their ears cupped against each other. They held each other and rocked. As they rocked, the waters rose a little, then fell, rose, then fell, until the lapping was quiet, but not gone.

Mr. Jacobs shifted away for a moment and Miss Beatrice could feel it like a jab in the stomach. When she looked up, he was holding a candle. Was he an archangel? She had what he'd had the time before when he lay on the English sofa and dreamed. Here it was worse because there was no house, no curtains, no nothing. He stood against the walls of the cave, staring up, the skin tight against his ribs, black hair covering his chest like felt. Above his head was a crown of giant needles, drips of water turned into rock. Cango, he said, this is part of the Cango Caves. The words dropped into Miss Beatrice's lap like pellets. She didn't answer. She didn't want this to be a place where anyone had been. You are the first man, she said. I am the first woman. This is ours. He laughed and said, We're not Bushmen. She was cold, and he knelt and put his shirt around her. I have been to the Cango Caves before, she said sadly. Not this part, nobody has been to this one. Nobody knows about this cave. He said it very strongly, like someone in church.

She told him about going to the main section of the Cango Caves with Mr. Henry, in a wagon along a bumpy road. They said in the *Oudtshoorn Courant* that it was "one of the most romantic and wonderful sights to be found in the colony." Mr. Henry was in a bad mood. They had to camp along the way. There was a big iron gate in the front to stop vandals and you had to pay two shillings. Johnny van Wassenaar, the famous Johnny, was their guide. Everyone had their own candle and you had to hold onto a rope going in. Mr. Henry didn't like it. There was a terrible smell of bat droppings. People were collecting the droppings in two hundred and thirty pound bags. You paid ten shillings for the bags. The candlelight made shadows against the walls and it seemed like the stalactites and stalagmites were alive` and coming to get you. Mr. Henry said he was going to faint. Miss Beatrice wanted to go deeper into the caves with famous Johnnie but Mr. Henry was too bilious. They saw the Monkey Rope which looked like a rope being climbed by a troop of monkeys.

Mr. Henry was sitting there with them in the cave after Miss Beatrice told her story. He was faded but Miss Beatrice could see his face and his floppy white hat. Are you dead? He said nothing and just looked at her. Then she smelled roses and tea, and saw Mrs. Jacobs' hand and her three daughters behind her like big red and black flowers. I took my girls and my wife, Mr. Jacobs said. They held their noses because of the smell. Bertha lost a glove in the Treasure Chamber. They wanted to write their names in candlesmoke but I told them it is not allowed anymore. Mr. Jacobs shook himself and then he started getting dressed. I have to go home, he said. Do you think my husband is dead? Miss Beatrice asked him. Up in the mountains, a man can live for only so long. He's been gone since when? Your last plucking?

Just after the ostrich race. He left in a hurry. He didn't take anything to eat. Mr. Jacobs shrugged and then he sat down on his haunches and buttoned Miss Beatrice's shirt. We have sinned, he said. She took his right hand and put his thumb in her mouth.

His body trembled but he still pulled out his thumb. Don't, Miss Beatrice said. He didn't answer. He stood there while she put on her pants and he stared at her. His eyes were black and scared. Just before they scrambled up through the opening they had tumbled into, she handed him his hat and he jammed it on his head.

When they came out onto the ground, the sun was skew in the sky and the horses' shadows were the size of small houses. Everything looked like it could scratch or sting you. Lucky was lame in one leg and limped all the way home. All the rocks were broken and the air was filled with dust. She didn't even remember when Mr. Jacobs rode off down the road to his farm. She was suddenly alone again, and her bones were sore.

It was the same sore that happened to Marie-Louise Steen-kamp when Pauline disappeared. Your body loses a wing or a shoulder. There's a big piece missing where that other person used to be. Of course with Marie-Louise it was worse because Pauline had been with the Steenkamps since Marie-Louise was a baby.

*   *   *

I never saw Marie-Louise after that day, not in real life. But she came on the TV. She wasn't Marie-Louise anymore, she was Duna. She was all grown-up and had long hair like sand and was on the news because she was a terrorist. I couldn't believe it. Maybe she was someone else but then Jack told me that Marie-Louise had gone to the university and had become a Communist. She got into trouble because she was caught by the police. I didn't ask any more because you don't want to get into trouble yourself. Jack says it's different now because of the new South Africa but I don't care.

Dr. Steenkamp, Marie-Louise's father, used to look after ma and pa. He shouted at them because of the drinking but they didn't listen. I don't go there because I don't like doctors especially after what happened with the baby.

Sometimes I wonder what would happen if I died. I don't know whether Jack would be sad or happy. Most of the time I think he would be happy. He wouldn't have to cut my toenails anymore.

Esther is licking my feet and I can see her tongue coming through between my toes like a red *lappie*. I don't know when Jack is coming back. I never do. The night is in front of me like a long black train with no one else inside. I'm not sure I want to go on it yet.

When is Gerda coming? Did Jack say?

The night is young, just like me. That picture in the bathroom mirror is someone else. They've got it all wrong. I'm still at school, I'm still living with my ma. I need to find something to drink.

I'm not sure if I was in the kitchen before. There's a bottle of methylated spirits by the sink. Ages ago, I used it for the chickens. We got them fresh from the farm. You had to burn off the some of the quills and one or two little feathers that never got plucked off. You poured the meths into a saucer and lit it. Then you held the chicken over the blue flame. That was before Rainbow Chickens.

The meths is still looking at me. The spirits drinkers pour it through a loaf of a white bread to get the blue out. Then they drink it. The meths eats them from the inside out. Faster than *witblits*.

I don't have any bread.

There's a blanket for me in the bedroom. Skollie will fetch it. I'll light a candle and sit up the way they used to in the olden days.

One small sip. I take it into my mouth very carefully. The meths is still blue.

It's cold as dying. The last of my feathers are turning to ash. The mountains are breaking.

FOUR

Miss Beatrice had a vision after she lay down in the cave with Mr. Jacobs. She was going to put a fountain in the middle of the house. She would forget about Mr. Jacobs, she would forget about Mr. Henry.

September made a hole in the floor and put in a round basin about four feet deep. They filled it with water and Miss Beatrice wrote away for some lotus roots. By the time they came, the whole thing was already a flop. A young ostrich had crawled into the basin and drowned, and so had some meerkats. It was like a floating cemetery for the animals and birds that strolled in and out of the house. And then there were the *miggies* that came because of the water and buzzed so loudly that Miss Beatrice couldn't sleep. So she filled up the hole with cement and that was the end of that.

The whole time Miss Beatrice and September were strug-gling with the fountain, Mr. Jacobs was trying to forget that there was a part of the Cango Caves on his land and that he had been there with Miss Beatrice. Every time anyone said anything about the Cango Caves, that their aunt was coming, or that their cousin was in Oudtshoorn and would he and the wife and the girls come along for a picnic first and then a look at the stalactites and stalagmites with Johnny van Wassenaar, Mr. Jacobs would say no. Mrs. Jacobs knew about the wild English girl that had come and had almost fainted but she didn't know about the Caves. Mr. Jacobs struggled so hard because he heard a voice in his ear wondering whether they would name a cave after him if he told them he had found one. Jacobs' Cave? Or something longer like the Cave of Max Jacobs, the Ostrich King? He knew they wouldn't because his name was Jewish and the caves were named after Boers, most of the time. Unless it was the Drum Room or the Monkey Rope.

And then to have people trooping in and out of there with their candles and packets of food would ruin the story he and Miss Beatrice had made, when they lay on their clothes in the pitch-dark. He wondered if they would name the cave Chapman's Cave, after her. But then it would really be Mr. Henry's, not hers. Mr. Henry must be dead somewhere, his bones getting whiter and whiter. That's when he would think about Miss Beatrice again, her pale body gleaming like a knuckle. Could he leave Mrs. Jacobs, Bertha, Rachel and Goldie? Could he leave the house with the big oak door and the English sofa covered with cabbage flowers?

He saw his father, the *smous*, selling buttons and plates from his cart. His father took one of the plates and threw it right at him. The plate broke into a thousand pieces. Would you like the chutney? Mrs. Jacobs was saying and suddenly her mouth moving was the best thing he had seen in a long time. I was thinking, he said, of a long ocean voyage, a trip to the Orient, or perhaps to America.

It hurts when you know someone is lying even though they're looking straight at you. Kloppie, my *boet*, is a big liar. I ask him to come to my house sometimes for a *dop*. He says he's busy or he's in church. You know that's a lie. And he lies to his wife when he says he's going to see a John Wayne flick at the drive-in. Jack says he goes to the *shebeens* and sleeps with Coloured girls. Kloppie used to be a duck-tail. Now his hair is short and he wears a hair-net during the day because of his job cutting meat into blocks at the Pick 'n Pay.

If Ma was alive, he would probably tell her about the meths. That's the kind of person Kloppie is.

Lots of people say Miss Beatrice was a charmer. When she went to the Oudtshoorn Hotel on a Friday afternoon to hear what happened at the ostrich auction, big drafts of charm would come puffing out of the pockets of the billiards table. The men would have to put their billiard sticks down until she had walked out because it was impossible to hit the balls right. I suppose she had the same unpeeled look Kloppie has, which makes you want to button up all the buttons of your cardigan.

Jack is coming in and it must be morning. Have you seen my brother? I ask him while I'm waltzing around pushing bottles into corners, especially the blue one. No, he says, and then he sees it.

Now I'm really going to die. He's going to *donner* me.

But he says nothing and leaves the room. Maybe I should have had the whole thing. Then he would be sorry.

Get dressed, he says. Your sister is here.

When Gerda walks through that front door, I'm shaking. I don't know what it is. I almost want to cry but I don't. You look like a fool when you cry in front of people. Do you remember Mrs. de Waal, the *alkie*, I ask her. Well, the last time I saw her was five years ago, when Ma was still alive. She was sitting in Doctor Steenkamp's waiting room looking at a shape on the carpet that looked like the face of a collie dog stretched very thin. She gave a little jump as if it was going to get up and bite her on the leg. I wanted to say that he doesn't bite. She didn't know that I can see things like that too. Ma, who was waiting to see Doctor Steenkamp, was reading from one of those TV magazines about a little girl who won a modeling competition and went overseas. They took her to parties and made her drink and gave her drugs and her parents didn't know a thing. They were on a farm in the Orange Free State. After a year she came home and told her ma and pa that the drugs made her want to have sex with everyone. She met a *mielie* farmer, got married and had a baby. The baby is only six months old but he looks like a fully grown Italian man.

Doctor Steenkamp gave Ma some blue pills for her nerves. *Hoe gaan dit?* How are you, Gerda?

*   *   *

Gerda is knitting booties for Soekie, one of her grand-children. I'm looking at it and I can't believe it. Now we're sitting in the lounge, on the couch. The room is dark. She probably wants to go for a walk or something.

It's getting hot again and we're walking past the Dutch Reformed Church. It's not Sunday, thank goodness, so everybody isn't there. The steeple looks like a very big witch's hat and I'm afraid it's going to fall off and kill us. Gerda doesn't seem to mind. She has her knitting in her bag. We cross over there by the Museum and I hold her hand like we used to when we were little.

The Museum is closed. Gerda and I try to look through the shutters but you can't see anything. Not even the hem of Miss Beatrice's dress or an old feather fan. We're standing on the grass and we're not supposed to. Let's go have a drink, I say, and she looks at me *skeef* and I wonder if Jack told her about the meths.

But now she's smiling and saying, What is Miss Beatrice up to? It's the first thing she has said since she came and it takes a long time to come out. I'm fine, I say.

An old man opens the door and says the Museum is now open and we can go in. It smells like floor polish inside and they have a picture of C.J. Langenhoven, the father of the Afrikaans language, right there by the front door.

* * *

I wonder if Miss Beatrice ever met C.J. Langenhoven. It makes me laugh just to think about it. She was probably as tall as he was, without the black coat and black hat and glasses. He probably crossed to the other side of the street if she was in town. He probably avoided going into the Hotel.

Every time there was a drought or water on the heart, some of the elders of the Dutch Reformed Church would blame the ostrich feather farmers. God was punishing the vanity. Women were not supposed to decorate themselves like that. They said it was an abomination against the Lord. I don't think Miss Beatrice, Mr. Jacobs or even C.J. Langenhoven listened to them. The town was packed with people who wanted to make lots of money or become famous. It was like Kimberley, with feathers instead of diamonds. I am sorry I was born too late. I wish I could have seen what it was like. The world is so far away now. You can only see it in magazines.

Remember when ma took you, me and and Kloppie to Victoria Bay, I say to Gerda. You snorted like a bull when you saw the water. Kloppie jumped in with his shoes on. I stayed on the edge where the waves looked like giant doilies. I touched the edge of the doilies with my toes and then I looked up to see where the water ended. I want to go to London to meet the Queen, I told Ma. And then I started to cry. You can't go to London so you better stop crying.

Hou op! She pulled my arm and I nearly fell down onto the wet sand.

I love Miss Beatrice because she probably had tea with the Queen all the time when she lived with her mom and dad. It was a King AND a Queen in those days. Remember my scrap-book?

This time there are no *tannies* in the Museum. It's just the old man who let us in. Gerda is looking at some old shoes and programs from America and I say to her, You know who those belong to?

Miss Beatrice was the Queen Bee at Highlands, just the way Mr. Jacobs was the Ostrich King. She had a meerkat called Scorpion, and some fancy Russian dogs that died. I think the meerkat died too, in the fountain.

What is Miss Beatrice up to? I don't know why Gerda's asking again, and maybe she wants me to tell her about the meths and how I'm feeling in the house by myself. I don't know. Miss Beatrice is fine, thank you very much, I say, even though Mr. Jacobs was at home talking about going to America with Mrs. Jacobs and the girls.

At the same time, Miss Beatrice was riding out to the place where they lay down together, inside the earth. She would tie up her horse, Lucky, and sit down on the ground, tapping the soil with her *knobkierie*. She would think about lots of things especially the caveness of the body. Your stomach is a cave and so are your lungs, with millions of tiny live stalactites and stalagmites made out of flesh. She would think about the tunnel Mr. Jacobs was in, when they faced each other, chest to chest.

When she got back to Highlands, the sun was almost gone and there were goosebumps on her arms. September would be putting some of the horses in for the night. Nomsa would be lighting the lamps. September always lifted his hat and looked down and she could see he was full of stories. If he knew about the noise the stars make when they're hunting, he could tell her about her heart and all the secret passageways of the body. Nomsa knew about the juices. She made *muti* and Miss Beatrice had already drunk some of it.

As Miss Beatrice moved around in the house, she could feel that they knew where she had been and what she had done. Even when they looked down, or looked away, Miss Beatrice knew that they knew. They could see Mr. Henry dragging behind her, his hands clasped around her ankles, his feet hooking on the furniture. They saw Mr. Jacobs, more hair than man, fanning out behind her like an Old Testament prophet. The less they said, the more the house rang.

There were still some *volkies* left in one of the back rooms from the time Miss Beatrice built the bungalows. A man from Damaraland, and his pale brown wife. They both had hair the colour of rust. They sat on the floor a lot and smoked clay pipes. *Voertsek!* September said to them one day and it was the loudest thing anyone had said since Mr. Henry was there. They left, the woman carrying a broken suitcase tied with string on her head. The man had empty ostrich shells which he filled with water from the pump. Miss Beatrice lifted her hand to wave to them but September muttered, *Hulle is vuil-goed,* They're rubbish, and so she scratched her arm instead. Then she told him to check the fences.

Gerda is looking at me *skeef* again and is there a bruise by my eye or something? Did the meths eat some of my hair?

We're in that old kitchen again with its empty fireplace and all I can think of is Nomsa and September. They seemed to be together and apart at the same time, their lives starting outside, on the other side of the kitchen-door. Inside the house, they were strangers, and Miss Beatrice began to wonder if she had dreamed that they were man and wife. Was Mr. Henry a dream too? Was Mr. Jacobs a puff of Holy Fire that fell into her lap from some old Bible story? Or was this everyday life not real?

The old man is locking the door behind us and I'm wondering if we were in the *blerrie* Museum at all.

There's an overhead fan in the Ladies' Bar and I'm sitting down at last with a nice gin and there's Gerda, my big sister, with one of her Fantas. She just finished threading a pink ribbon through the top of the first bootie. *Ag, foeitog!* It looks so cute.

* * *

Put down your knitting, and put your hand on my throat, I tell her. I'm getting to the juicy part.

One night Miss Beatrice dreamed that Nomsa had a baby and she was the midwife. In the dream, Nomsa wouldn't open her legs for the baby to come out, so Miss Beatrice had to coax her. She put her hands between Nomsa's legs and pressed them open. Suddenly she was back in the cave again and something dropped and fell inside her so hard that she almost lost her breath. Touching Nomsa made the burning come back a thousand times over. Sweat was running down her neck and she could smell the strong smell of the *muti* except this time it was coming from between Nomsa's legs. September was there and he took her hand and moved it to the dark place where the baby's head was trying to come out. She didn't know if she had to put her hand in there or not. Nomsa was making a noise like the ostriches do when they're trapped in the wires. September leaned forward and licked the sweat off Miss Beatrice's neck. Her knees folded and she fell on top of Nomsa.

Miss Beatrice woke up screaming and knocked a cup off the table next to her bed. She lay in her bed and there was something wet and warm beneath her, as if she had peed. Nobody came in or said anything. She was alone.

She unbuttoned her nightie and dropped it on the floor. Her body was long and thin in the moonlight. She lay there, breathing, looking at the greyness of her skin. She was the wide, open veld, the long earth with its bumps and holes. Her hand passed over her belly like a cloud, then it moved upwards, grazing her nipples. Her back arched suddenly and she could feel her throat closing. Then she was upright and coughing, pulling at the sheet, sucking on the wetness. She fell asleep like that, the top end of the sheet in her mouth, the rest of it wound between her legs.

That's how she was when the sun came up. Her feet were warm and she thought it was a cat. She dressed without feeling the buttons and tried to twist her hair into a knot but there was nothing there. She rubbed the soft, short hairs on top of her head and then she remembered last night and her skin and what it was like to fly over it with her hand. Her throat got dry again. She pulled on those pants of Mr. Henry's, the convict shirt, and the *veldskoene*.

Her body stood outside in the Karoo dawn. At the bottom of the sky were the blue mountains, a long, thick line telling you that you were here, not in England. Miss Beatrice walked across her land to the *pondokkie* where Nomsa and September lived. They didn't want to move to one of the bungalows so they had stayed in the house they had built themselves, of wood and paper and sticks, with pumpkins on the roof and some chickens in the back. Nomsa said the bungalows were going to go away.

Miss Beatrice opened the door without knocking, and it smelled of tar and woodsmoke and wet soil in there. There were garden tools and a cracked mirror and a narrow, sagging bed. Nomsa and September lay on the bed, fully clothed, their backs touching under an old brown blanket that used to be Mr. Henry's.

Miss Beatrice wasn't sure if she was walking in her sleep or not but she found herself kneeling, her face close to Nomsa's, her lips right next to Nomsa's ear. September rolled over and his hand fell over the side of the bed. Miss Beatrice looked at his palm with the dirt etched into the cracks and a thumb-nail like a horn from what happened at the ostrich-branding. She took his hand as if it was a gift and suddenly Nomsa and September were awake. Their eyes looked into Miss Beatrice's eyes. Nomsa wasn't surprised the way September was but they both looked angry, as if Miss Beatrice had taken those pumpkins off the roof.

Miss Beatrice bent her head, her forehead resting against the coarse hair coming out of a hole in the mattress, her knees on the floor which was made of peach pits and dung. I want you to love me, she said. I am sorry. She could hear Nomsa lifting herself and moving around in the musty, dark part of the room behind another curtain. September struck a match and lit his pipe.

And how must we do that? Nomsa said this as she handed Miss Beatrice an old cup filled with tea made from red sticks. The sticks floated on top of the water like tiny logs. You know everything, Miss Beatrice said. You hear what's inside my head. September grunted and spat and looked at her. Then he said, *Die mies is verlief.* In love. Miss Beatrice started to shake and Nomsa threw the old brown blanket over her.

What happened after that is the story you, Gerda, told me a long time ago with your hands and your face and everything else. Ask me nicely, Connie would you like another *dop*? and I'll tell you again. Jack is probably waiting for me to come home to feed the dogs and clean out the kennels. You know I can smell what the inside of Nomsa and September's *pon-dokkie* was like, old fires and sweat and *rooibos* tea, as if it was yesterday? Yes, I'd love a *dop*. Look, the nice barman is fixing me a gin and tonic for the road.

They were under the blanket together, all three of them, and Miss Beatrice was moaning like mad. People say you can still hear that moaning if you go past Highlands when the moon is full. Did Nomsa throw in some *muti* to make Miss Beatrice go mad? So mad her legs were burning in their sockets? Or was there *dagga* in September's pipe that filled the air with that sweet, old smell? Or was it Miss Beatrice who started, who made the blanket into that cave she and Mr. Jacobs were in?

Then they weren't on the bed, they were on the floor, and the door swung shut. The curtain fell down, and so did some spades. September put his hand over Miss Beatrice's mouth, and it tasted like copper. Miss Beatrice felt breasts, and they were Nomsa's and she would have screamed if she could. Then September was behind her, Nomsa in front. The floor made her dirty and there were black streaks all over her face. Dust fell into her hair. *Ai*, Nomsa was singing and suddenly there were birds all over them, feathers and wings and claws.

The pumpkins on the roof started jumping. There was wind inside the house, and more things fell down, like the mirror and cups and some boots. September pushed backwards, and Miss Beatrice went with him. His eyes were shut tight and she could see the stumps of his teeth. Then she saw nothing. Not even black.

Of course what they were doing was so bad it wasn't even a sin anymore. It isn't even in the Bible but if I close my eyes I can see it. September lying down, with Miss Beatrice on top of him and Nomsa behind her. I suppose like a chicken sandwich on two slices of brown bread. Miss Beatrice was there because the dream of the night before made her go and she was the type of person who follows her dreams. She would go up the river right to the source, the place where it dribbles out between the folds of the mountain. You can't find a person like that anymore. A person who gets in his boat and rows up the river and doesn't care what everyone thinks.

I know Jack would say they were *pomping* but I keep thinking it wasn't so bad. September was kind to Miss Beatrice because he was kind like that with the birds and the people, everything that flew, ran and jumped all around the farm. Or maybe he was so scared of Miss Beatrice that his thing went back up inside his body, the way it is with the ostriches. Maybe she scared him so much that it never came down again, even with Nomsa, his wife. Whatever was happening to September, it wasn't happiness. It was more like Pauline and Oom Piet and the Devil, except who was the Devil?

Some light came in, and they all saw each other. Miss Beatrice had her pants down and her bum was white. September's stomach was brown, the colour of dried leaves. Nomsa was standing over them, her long, black breasts swinging. And then Miss Beatrice landed on top of September again, twisting her hips and tightening them like someone wringing out a dishcloth. It was grinding and sad, and someone must have been crying because there was a tear that fell onto the ground, or was it just sweat. Miss Beatrice was pushing herself into September. She wanted him to finish because the darkness of the dream was fading. She could see again and she wanted to go home. September was clenching his teeth and his face was all wrinkled up and Miss Beatrice banged his head with her head and then he came. Miss Beatrice felt *naar* and dizzy from the knock and it went black again except this time it hurt.

When she lifted her head, Nomsa was holding September and he lay in her lap like some old man who has been shot in the stomach. Miss Beatrice got up and left without looking anywhere.

Outside, some of the pumpkins had rolled onto the ground and burst. She was running and tripping, the stones like knuckles under her feet. The ostriches came to the fences and stared, their eyes bulging black lamps. Miss Beatrice ran past the *kraals*, into her house, the screen door slapping behind her. She was in the bedroom pouring water over her head, the dust turning red, making a red puddle on the floor. She could still feel Nomsa's hair, crisp on her back, and September falling backwards, lifting her, his eyes sewn shut with a thousand needles. Water streamed down her legs, through the seat of her pants, and slowly the last of the burning flickered and died.

Gerda takes her hand away. The print of her hand is still warm on my neck.

The barman is sweeping the floor. Jack is probably sitting on the *stoep* having a Castle. Should we go past Highlands just to look at the wall? Or is it too far?

Miss Beatrice didn't stop herself like me. She just went on. She was at the feather auction that same fortnight testing the prime whites and spadonas, running her fingers along the shaft of each feather. She still wanted her feathers to win the first prize at the Agricultural Show. Or perhaps she was afraid of going home, of being in that quiet house, with Nomsa and September. She probably stayed in town till it was dark, having supper, a *bobotie* or pot roast at the Oudtshoorn Hotel. In those days, your horse got some supper too. Good stabling and forage with an attentive groom, is what the old advertisement says. It hangs right here in the Ladies' Bar, in a big, gold frame.

So she sat there, eating at one of those round hotel tables, with hotel silver and thick plates with green lines on the edges. Maybe there was an egg crust on the *bobotie* or mint jelly with the roast. There were feather dealers and feather merchants and ostrich farmers at the other tables, and some visitors from Carnarvon and Calvinia. Miss Beatrice had a dress on over her pants, and one of Mr. Henry's silk scarves around her neck. The waiter had two spoons in one hand to pick up everything, and a white jacket with round buttons. Miss Beatrice looked at his hands, so black against the white of his sleeves, and she remembered.

Did she feel there was something inside her, like an ant or a jewel? Or was it her eye looking back at her from the back of those spoons? Could she walk through the kitchen door ever again?

Around her, the farmers were talking about making dams and someone was shouting about the profits the middlemen were making. Those middlemen who bought feathers from the farmers and sold them to the retail dealers. And who knew what sort of cases the retailers wanted, unless you went to one of those Commercial Sale Rooms in the middle of London? Miss Beatrice had seen those cases, she wanted to say, but she just bent her head. She had gone with Mr. Henry and her father to Mincing Lane, to the broker, and she had seen how the feathers were sorted into different cases for the different markets. The cases were lined with tin or special paper, and then they were sewn up in canvas and shipped. At the Sale Rooms, they were unpacked and laid out on tables with wire in between to separate each lot. And she knew about the demand for thick feathers rather than thin, because it was cheaper to decorate a hat with thick ones.

Highlands was suddenly far away, a toy farm in her head. What happened with Nomsa and September was like lightning or snake-bite. It was over and she was alive and tomorrow September was her foreman. She drank water and whiskey and it burnt. I love hotels with this smell of velvet, Karoo dust and cigar smoke. I would have had a few drinks myself, just to celebrate. Especially if all those merchants and people from Calvinia were staring at me, the way they stared at Miss Beatrice. Some of them greeted her and she was so friendly that it made them smile and forget that she was wearing pants under her dress and big boots.

Once they were outside, under that big Karoo sky, they shook out their gloves in the almost pitch-dark and said *skande, skandaal* and so on. Some of them said that Mr. Henry lay dead in the incubating-house or under the hole for the fountain. A nice lady from Bredasdorp who was visiting her cousin said *Ag, foeitog!* But inside she was thinking of turpentine, flowers, of sulphur and arsenic.

Miss Beatrice wasn't listening to these people. She was staring at the mountains, lying naked in the moonlight. Soon she was back at Highlands and the kitchen door wasn't so frightening. There was a lamp burning low in the kitchen and some *mieliepap* on the stove. She put her finger into the middle of it, lifted a ball onto her tongue. It tasted like paper and ashes. Then she was getting undressed for bed and her room, with its whitewashed walls and small window, was the room of a poor person. A Poor White. Just like me and you and Kloppie and ma and pa. And Jack. There was no fancy oak door or English sofa. There was just the thin bed and the china from her wedding and the old bench near the hole for the fountain. Nothing was fancy. She remembered what she loved to forget, that Mr. Henry had taken everything away, and now even this was small and poor and would never get any better. She would die like some minister's wife, in ugly brown clothes in the middle of nowhere. Mr. Henry had done this, with his horse loving.

She fell crying asleep, dreaming of ostrich feathers, so big and white that each feather was worth a hundred pounds. She was selling them to everyone in the world and with the money she built another house with a Spanish courtyard and five fountains. In the dream, she was wearing a dress made of camel skin and her hair was long again. Then she saw that Nomsa was washing clothes in one of the fountains and September was wading in another one, as if he was looking for crabs. She wanted to tell them to stop, to go back to their *pondokkie* but she couldn't. The words wouldn't come out. September saw her and he waved her to come over, like an old friend. She started walking towards him but it felt like she was walking backwards. Something behind her was falling away and suddenly she was lying in water, in the middle of Nomsa's fountain. The clothes Nomsa was washing were hers and she saw her slime-green dress, floating, and some old corsets and petticoats. She couldn't tell if they were foam or material and she lifted them to her lips and they tasted like that *mieliepap* cooking on the stove.

She looked up and saw that the water was right under Nomsa's breasts and her cotton dress was wet, so wet that Miss Beatrice thought she could see a sea lion under there, or maybe two. Nomsa looked at her, and Miss Beatrice was ashamed suddenly, for falling into the fountain, for eating the *mieliepap*, and for thinking about sea lions.

Her own breasts were hurting and she tried to roll away from them, across the hot sheet, but they followed. Floppy tigers, she called them in the middle of her sleep.

September was outside now, standing naked in front of the house, with a *riempie* around his waist, painting. Attached to the *riempie*, were horns like the gunpowder horns the Voortrekkers had, except September's horns were smaller and filled with different coloured powders, reds, yellows, blacks. He had an extra horn with water in it, for mixing the powders. He painted with his fingers, his tongue and even his eye-lashes and soon the outside wall of Highlands was covered with wild animals. There were giant red wildebeest, black ostriches, duikers and buck drinking from a waterhole. Miss Beatrice even thought she could see a snow goose, flying through everything, completely lost. September was going to paint on the door, when Mr. Henry suddenly appeared and shot him in the back. He fell down and the powders in his horns spilled onto the ground and mixed with his blood. The colours on the wall started to drip and turn red, and soon all the pictures were gone.

Gerda is standing and so is the barman and I'm the only one left. Don't leave me behind. Don't lock me in here!

We're walking home and people are sitting on their *stoeps* and having some drinks. The sun has crashed like some old *dronkie* and nobody seems to mind. I like a summer evening in the Karoo when you hear things calling and whistling.

Jack is making *boerewors* and eggs and we're eating outside on the *stoep* and it's almost a party except he looks cross. I have my bed-jacket on that Ma used to wear and my feet are up and resting on Flo's head. Gerda is knitting a pink bootie, the second one, and it's getting bigger and bigger and I can almost see a pink and gold baby falling out of the sunset into her arms.

I lift my glass, To Miss Beatrice!

Miss Beatrice was in her bedroom one morning, lacing up her *veldskoene* and trying to walk out of the door but her feet were stuck, as if someone had nailed them to the floor. She was bilious and her lips were dry. Moving herself was like moving chains. She could smell the *rooibos* tea and the *mieliepap* and Nomsa from the top of the passage. She rubbed her nose with her sleeve and shook her head to get the *miggies* away. As she walked to the kitchen, the *miggies* buzzed around her like aunties at a christening or funeral.

What about the horns? And the petticoats? And Nomsa's wet dress? Did the spades really fall down?

The kitchen was empty. Miss Beatrice saw a chunk of bread next to her cup and coffee on the stove. The fire was burning and someone had just shuffled the wood because the flames were even and bright. There was a pot with water boiling and an egg jiggling around. She was staring at the egg when Nomsa walked in, with a bundle of sticks on her head. Nomsa bent down, busy with the sticks and the fire. Then Nomsa was wiping her hands on her dress, and Miss Beatrice was dipping the bread in the egg. Glory is sick, Nomsa said. September is with him. Glory! Miss Beatrice felt the word shoot out of her mouth like an arrow. Glory had eaten Mr. Henry's watch a long time ago.

Miss Beatrice walked over to Glory's *kraal* and the *miggies* didn't follow her. Nomsa made them go away. Did she have special *muti* for that? Or did she whisper her secrets into one of those sticks, and wrap some string around it to keep it tight? Miss Beatrice would never ever know. She was glad. Her secret was the cave and everything else was forgotten.

Glory was more than sick. Glory was dead. He had pushed his head through the branches of a tree to eat a quince. The branch was forked and Glory's poor head, with the quince bulging out like a giant Adam's apple, got stuck. He must have pulled and jumped to get free, the way ostriches do when their heads are held. The more he jumped, the more tightly he got stuck. Now his neck was broken, and his head was torn off. Bury him, Miss Beatrice said. With his feathers on? September asked. With his feathers on, Miss Beatrice was going to say, until she heard her own voice saying, Take his feathers. She left September plucking the dead bird.

Did he look up as she walked away? Did he try to see through her shoulder-blades? Could he hear how her blood was ringing? Miss Beatrice didn't ask. Miss Beatrice had seen his finger-nail and she knew what was real. She was swallowing and breathing and suddenly the ground flew up like a magic carpet, and she fell down.

Die mies het geval. She heard September saying this, and then he said, *Staan op.* He didn't come near but she could feel his eyes pulling her up to her feet. She saw him looking at her stomach as if there was a snake there, or a scorpion. There was blood on the front of her shirt but she saw that it came from her hands. You can keep the feathers, she wanted to say, but it stuck in her throat like that big, fat quince Glory ate. Mr. Henry is coming back, September said. Before Christmas. He was looking at the Swartberg Mountains and Miss Beatrice wanted to shake him. He is never coming back, she shouted. Never ever.

The way Miss Beatrice fell down reminds me of the time I fell down and ma took me to the hospital except that Miss Beatrice's ma was in England and the hospital was far away and old-fashioned. I have seen pictures of nurses roaming the wards with lamps and long dresses, and all the people in the beds look very, very sick. All Miss Beatrice had was September telling her to get up, and the ostriches watching her from behind the fence. There was no doctor to say, *God, meisie, jy verwag!* And it wasn't a shotgun the way it was with me, because Miss Beatrice was already married to Mr.

Henry. But there was a gun, and it was in Miss Beatrice's dream, and she wondered if September had dreamed the same dream. He said nothing. He just tied the feathers together with a *riempie* and walked to the sorting-room.

She was right in the beginning of her nine months and she didn't even believe it. The twinkle in her eye was rice, just one tiny grain. Nomsa was the one who washed her clothes. Nomsa was the one who saw how her *broekies* stayed white, even when the moon was full. That's what the morning egg was for. An egg for an egg, although Miss Beatrice didn't even know. Out of the egg comes a fish. Out of the fish comes a person. I am scared of fish, especially crayfish. They look like giant locusts that can swim.

Miss Beatrice thought she was a fairy, but she wasn't. Fairies don't have babies. They just fly around and enjoy themselves. She wasn't flying or floating, or any of those things she used to do. She was sinking, and falling down, just like me. When she went back to the house, she poured water from the water-jug into the basin and let her hands rest there. There were threads of blood in the water from the cuts on her hands. It's only my hands, she thought, and that's when she remembered the blood every month that wasn't there, the high tide that was missing. Her breath stopped. There was shock like what happens on the veld in a thunderstorm and the tree that's left is broken apart and white. A baby. The word was silly as a cake.

And then she forgot. The way you forget your own birthday or the purse inside your drawer. It was easy because there was no one around her to remind her. Nomsa and September would talk sideways, with their eyes up or down or skew, but they wouldn't say what that doctor told me. They had their own babies, who lived with their *ouma* on Mr. de

Koek's farm. They went there on Easter and Christmas and Boxing Day. Miss Beatrice didn't know about that either.

How much can one person forget? Ma told me she forgot when I was born. Was it night or day, I wanted to know. I forget, she said. It could have been either.

You forget the dogs, when you're at the Hotel with your *chommies*. I never forget the dogs. They are with me all the time, each one of them barking in my head. Skollie, the loudest, and Esther, the saddest. Then the boarders, with their desperate barking, wanting to go home with their owners, wanting to leave the Cango Caves. I'll never forget Smiley, the Schipperke, barking for the Steenkamps. Never ever.

FIVE

Across the road, that fat pig, Mrs. van der Westhuizen, is staring at me as if I am Satan. She's feeding her canary. What's wrong with you? Why can't I sleep on my own front *stoep* in the middle of summer? I want to shout but my voice is stuck to my throat. I feel like Gerda with her tongue so twisted up and raw.

I lift my arm as if I'm going to *donner* her but all I can see is the sleeve of Ma's bed-jacket and it makes me sad. Her liver was like a dirty grey sponge at the end, the kind you have to throw away. I had to go to the house by myself afterwards and I was scared. I thought it would be different once she was dead but that same old knot was there, tied around my *derms*.

It was terrible. The smell hit you in the face as if you were lying. She had been wrapping up her own waste matter in neat little newspaper packets and they were all around the room, soldiers marching along the skirting board out of the door all the way to the kitchen. I was the one who had to pick them up and throw them in a big rubbish bag.

When I was cleaning up, I found a baby's blanket, the striped kind you get from the hospital, and I thought it was mine or Gerda's or Kloppie's but then I smelled it and I knew, I just knew, it belonged to my baby.

Gerda got her wedding-band and I got the bed-jacket and a red brooch that looked like a fox's face.

Christmas is coming. Everyone goes to the sea, except me. I'm *poep-scared* of the water because I can't swim.

Where is Gerda? Where is Jack? The front door is locked. They locked me out. They left me here all night long as if I was one of the dogs. The *miggies* have bitten me to pieces. The devils are coming to get me, just like the ghosts of those Russian dogs who went to fetch Mr. Henry.

Some people say that the people of Oudtshoorn sent them. The day that Mr. Jacobs and his family waved goodbye to Table Mountain from their ship on their way to England and America, the ghost dogs went looking for Mr. Henry. Others say that they were chasing a jackal on Mr. Jacobs' farm and they chased him all the way to the top of a small *koppie*. The jackal disappeared behind a rock, into his house. Right near the jackal's house was a tent made out of a man's jacket tied to two thorn trees. Under the tent was Mr. Henry, his face smeared with white clay, like the Xhosa women. The ghost dogs jumped on him and probably licked all that clay off. The *hotnots* who had tied up his cold feet and walked with him were gone. They left him some ostrich shells filled with

water. The dogs drank up all the water and so Mr. Henry
followed them home. They say that he came back to Highlands at sunset, when the sky was burning gold. He walked
between the dogs, his hands holding onto their collars. September was bringing ostriches from one camp to another,
waving a mimosa branch, when he saw Mr. Henry stumbling along, the wrappings on his feet coming undone. He
had his shirt on his head, and his pants wrapped sideways
around his waist. Mr. Henry walked straight into the house,
into the living-room and lay down on the floor where the
hole for the fountain used to be. The ghost dogs had vanished. Scorpion, the meerkat, was standing on Mr. Henry's
chest, his front paws raised, when Miss Beatrice came in. He
jumped onto the windowsill, then onto the sofa, then he ran
out of the door, cackling. There were some meerkat droppings on Mr. Henry's chest, which fell to the ground when
he sat up. Miss Beatrice looked at him and she saw how his
skin was scratched and bitten and burned. His eyelids were
red and his light-brown hair had loops and swirls in it. It's
going to snow, he said.

Miss Beatrice took him by the hand and led him to the
cement dam outside where she scooped water over him, and
made him wash himself. Then she wrapped him in a sheet
and led him back inside. While he stood inside their room,
staring at his shirts and his shoes, Miss Beatrice made ostrich
egg biscuits. The yolk is like twenty-four chickens' eggs. You
can fill two big biscuit tins.

That night they had stew and the sponge finger biscuits for
dessert. Mr. Henry talked about the snow he had tasted and
the stick people who were his friends and his days spent sitting on the *koppie*, looking at birds of prey. He never said a
word about his paintings, or about the fight. He loved the

biscuits and ate two plates full. Miss Beatrice stared at Mr. Henry and tried to whoosh him back to the top of that *koppie* with her eyes. But Mr. Henry sat in his chair and looked around the room and stretched and burped as if he had never left. Then he made a fire in the fireplace even though it was hot and sat on the floor in front of the flames, pulling at his fingers and toes. He even made Miss Beatrice get a tape measure so that he could measure his feet and his hands and write down the measurements on a piece of paper. He put the piece of paper in his top pocket and lay down flat on his back and went to sleep.

Miss Beatrice watched him some more, looking at his hair, almost blonde now that it was clean, and his tight mouth, twisted at the corners. There were flakes of dry, red skin on his cheeks and nose, and his eyelashes were short and white. What she had loved in England was the man in velvet who painted underneath the chairs and on vases and doors. Even the horses she had loved, with their precious legs and thin skins, flying at the finish-line. This man on the floor had nothing, except this poor farm, which her father had found for them, which her father had paid for. And now she knew how to sell her feathers, how to buy a pair of Guaranteed Breeders, breed them and sell them for a profit. Mr. Henry didn't even get the branding right, and then he ran away.

Mr. Henry couldn't fix anything. All he could do was break and break and break. Miss Beatrice nearly jumped on his heart with her boots on. She was the Queen of the Ostriches and he wasn't going to take that away. Then she got dizzy. The blood was rolling and roaring inside her, and she saw a small boat, with a tiny passenger resting on his oars. Wait, she called out. Here's our rope.

She lay down beside Mr. Henry and rolled her face next to

his ear. She burrowed in next to him and he shifted and flung his arm over her, and it fell on her like a log that hurt. But she took his hand and popped his fingers in her mouth and Mr. Henry woke up screaming, my hand, my right hand. I'm cooking it, she said, and put it under her arm and between her legs and around her belly. Mr. Henry was panting and the flakes were coming off his face and Miss Beatrice blew them away like the Southeaster. She put her hands in his pants and his head pressed against her, his nose poking her tigers.

They made something together that was dry and hard. A hot coin fell out from between Miss Beatrice's legs and melted onto the floor. Mr. Henry screamed about the snow coming, as his body twitched and then was still. Miss Beatrice left him there and went to the bedroom, staring into the dark with her eyes wide open. Whose happiness was that? She felt the tiny boatman lifting his oars and she wished him goodnight.

Jack was nice to me, when I was expecting. He made a pot of tea one afternoon and put some rusks his mother had made onto a plate with a doily. I remember tearing the doily and him telling me not to.

Miss Beatrice didn't say anything to Mr. Henry. She couldn't. Did she wrap her stomach with bandages to make it look flat as a pancake? Did she breathe in a lot and talk over her shoulder? The day after the day he came back Miss

Beatrice noticed that Mr. Henry didn't see anything at all, except his hands and his feet. The ostriches could have been big balls of dust, or tumbleweeds with necks and legs. Miss Beatrice didn't have to worry. If her belly was growing out of her shoulder, he would have rubbed his eyes and said something about snow. He believed in snow like it was a religion.

He would talk to September about building snow-sheds and September would rub those peppercorns on his head, trying to see what part of Mr. Henry's head was missing. Maybe Nomsa could make a *muti* for him and they could go back to the time when the farm nearly broke even, and they were selling eggs and feathers and whole birds. You can't twist your feet around, Nomsa said. You can't make anything go backwards. She spat and it landed in front of them, on a spider sunning himself on a rock. The spider ran forwards and tumbled into a hole in the ground.

Those days were long, hot circles. There was no rain and Christmas was just around the corner. I suppose Mr. Henry believed Christmas trees were going to land on the earth, along with the snow. Today you can get them at the OK Bazaars and pick white or light green, or gold, depending on the colour of your balls. Then it was only pictures in books. You couldn't just hop on a plane and fly to the cold. You stayed where you were.

Mr. Henry found a book of the Alps and showed Miss Beatrice and September the sheds that they put the cows in when it was cold. Now you have those mountains on icing sugar boxes in purple and white. Mr. Henry's pictures were black-and-white and the Alps people had feathers in their hats like Heidi's friends. The cows wore bells and looked very old-fashioned. At first, Miss Beatrice thought Mr.

Henry wanted to get bells for the ostriches and she laughed and said, Maybe that's not such a bad idea.

No, he said. We're going to take down those bungalows and build sheds for our birds. Christmas is coming and they need to be snug and tight. That was in the middle of the drought and Miss Beatrice pointed up at the sky which was almost white from dryness. There was nothing tighter than the ground under their feet, she said. Mr. Henry was mad as a snake and shook her so hard that she got a *kriek* in her neck.

Before Miss Beatrice would push back and the furniture would spin around the room the way it did the day Mr. Henry ran away. Now she was scared of him. Mr. Henry had yellow flecks in the whites of his eyes and his arms and legs reminded her of whips. He had been boiled down, and chilled, and boiled again. Like all things that grow in the Karoo, he had thorns, and a poison sac.

My Jack is like that. You have to be careful. I never let him walk behind me. I always turn around. You never know when he might *klap* you on the head. Once he bit me when we were lying down together, and my legs were wide open. He bit the fleshy part really hard, just below the elastic of my panties. I thought a scorpion was stinging me and I almost fainted. He laughed like a drain. I didn't think it was so funny.

After the baby came it hurt down there, not where Jack bit me, but inside. My ma said the doctor had to fix me. I didn't want to think about it or touch it. I pretended it wasn't there. That *blerrie* doctor sewed it close, Jack said to me once. He was lying on top of me and growling in my ear. His breath smelled like those flakes you throw in a fish tank to feed the fish. I felt as if he was squashing me and holding me in one place the way doctors do when they take a picture of your heart and your lungs. One of us is going to pass out, I thought, because there was a big empty bottle of Tassies on the floor. I hope it's me. But it wasn't. Jack pushed himself inside me and I looked into the eyes of the dog. Jack screamed and then he came. It made him dizzy so he vomited on my stomach. The dog licked it up. I lay there staring the way you lie in a hospital bed. Jack was out like a light.

I saw Miss Beatrice then. She came to me like a nurse does, when you push the button next to your bed. It didn't hurt her, the way it hurt me. She was strong as a lion and she was even wilder. You couldn't catch her or squash her like Jack was squashing me. Get him back, I think she said, although I was passing out myself.

I tried. I remembered a game one of my maids told me about. They played it in the location with a piece of paper and some petrol.

Jack was sleeping outside, right here on the *stoep*, listening to the rugby on the radio. He was barefoot. I put the petrol-soaked paper between his toes but he woke up shouting, even before I had a chance to light it. What the *blerrie* hell is going on? He was screaming, and I hadn't even done anything. I told him that my ma said petrol keeps the *miggies* away. I wanted him to have a nice sleep, I said. Western Province is winning! He was still screaming, but now because of the radio. He loves rugby. He remembers when the Springboks used to play teams like the British Lions and the All Blacks from New Zealand, before we stopped playing with the rest of the world.

Mr. Henry took down the bungalows, just as he said he was going to. I am the foreman, he said, and stood there watching as the *volkies* took their houses apart. They weren't big, but they had doors and windows and chimneys which the old ones didn't have. So Nomsa was right when she told September that the bungalows were going to go away. Where are the *volkies* going to sleep? Miss Beatrice was asking. Mr. Henry said, Under the stars. Of course they made new houses for themselves very quickly. *Pondokkies* out of paper and broken wood and anything else they could find. I'm sure they even used broken ostrich feathers in those days, and skin.

The snow-sheds were long and narrow and they had pointy roofs. There were two of them, next to each other. Mr. Henry even wrote away for some trimmings that he could stick on the front so that they looked just like the pictures in the book. But the trimmings never came.

What came in a boat was the giant music cupboard Mr. Jacobs had bought in America, with round metal discs so big you had to hold them with two hands. The discs had holes and ridges, in different places, and you could put them in the cupboard, which was higher and fatter than a grandfather clock. Then you wound up the cupboard with a funny handle and music played. "God Save the Queen" and "Yankee Doodle Dandy." No "My Sarie Marais," or "My Hart Verlang na die Boland." This cupboard stood in the stationmaster's office all wrapped up in planks with rope and big lumps of red sealing wax everywhere. Nobody knew what it was. Some people made bad jokes and said it was Mrs. Jacobs. If Jack was alive back then, he would have laughed.

When Mr. Jacobs came back in 1913, everybody knew, even the ostriches. It wasn't like Mr. Henry coming back six months before, rescued by dogs and almost completely forgotten. First there was the cupboard all by itself which people would come to look at on Sunday afternoons, after church. The station was nice then, with horsehair sofas in the waiting room and no non-European section. On the platform there were geraniums and ferns and it was almost like someone's *stoep*, except that it faced the railway line and the mountains and there were no houses next door. On the train you have to be careful not to get soot in your eye which once happened to me taking the train from George to Knysna. Don't stick your head out of the window otherwise you'll end up wearing an eye-patch for three weeks.

Of course the trains went slower and people took *padkos*—cooked chickens, hard-boiled eggs and lots of *biltong*. It took a few days to come all the way from Cape Town, where the ships were. Goodbye Table Mountain, goodbye Devil's Peak, goodbye Signal Hill. You probably had to go through Bain's Kloof, past Worcester and the Hex River Mountains, past Matjiesfontein, then straight into the Karoo. The vineyards lay behind you. You started to see sheep, and then finally, ostriches. Hops just before Oudtshoorn.

I am sure Mrs. Jacobs was sad to be leaving the ocean behind her. Bertha and Goldie and Rachel were sad too, with mink muffs on their laps that they couldn't use anymore. Later on, one of their pugs had puppies inside Bertha's muff and they had to burn it because of the smell. But Oudtshoorn wasn't so bad in those days. There was the big Christmas Ball and the Queen's Springbok Hunt. Parties galore, my *ouma* would say. Those *Rooinekke* and those *Boerejode* like to dance. Mrs. Jacobs probably had dresses from Paris in long, flat boxes filled with tissue paper and the smell of almonds. Bodices made out of hand-made lace and gloves as thin as spider-webs. Hats like roofs that made your neck hurt if you wore them too long. I've seen the gloves and the hats and the dresses in the Museum. Mrs. Jacobs left them to our town when she died. On a table, the muffs and an umbrella with broken spokes and a big black tassel. Even Goldie must be dead by now.

Did Miss Beatrice leave lots of dresses behind? A brooch or a perfume bottle? Is it really her old green frock in the Museum? Her dance card, her picture album, her pressed *vygies*? Before the wall went up at Highlands, you could see an orange lamp near the window but that was all.

When my *ouma* was a girl, the young men came to court you and you sat in the front room next to a candle. It was usually very quiet. Just you, sitting on a chair, next to a small table with a candle burning down, and the young man on the other side of the table. When the candle went out, the boy went home. If he liked you, he'd come back the next night and you'd sit again. You'd sit and sit, night after night, like those *hotnot* women sitting on the ostrich eggs, until finally he asked you to marry him.

I wonder if that orange lamp at Highlands was for sitting? Waiting? Did Miss Beatrice wait for Mr. Jacobs? They say she was the only person in Oudtshoorn who didn't make a special trip to the railway station to see the cupboard. She was busy, and Mr. Henry gave everyone her regards. My wife is not well, he said, and that made Mrs. Visser and the de Koek sisters look at each other, their eyebrows high, pushing those bonnets back with their hair. Did Nomsa tell anyone about the still-white *broekies*, or did that come later, when you couldn't hide anything anymore? There were no stories on the radio or the TV so people heard everything as if it was written on the walls.

What people remember from that time is the terrible rain that came in the middle of December, on the day that Mr. Jacobs and Mrs. Jacobs and Bertha, Goldie and Rachel came all the way from Cape Town on the train. It swept away half of Laingsburg and nearly drowned all the ostriches in Oudtshoorn. Mr. Jacobs and Mrs. Jacobs and the girls had to wait in the waiting room at the railway station until the rain stopped because you couldn't drive a cart through the mud. Even later, the rain was bad because the cars leaked and you got wet. But with the carts and the horses and all the things Mr. Jacobs had bought in America, it was impossible. Actually, he did have a car in a box, a Ford, but nobody could drive it yet. Some people say that this car was the beginning of the end for the ostrich farmers because you couldn't ride in it without your hat flying off. The next year the ladies wore hats that covered their ears. But I don't think it was the hats. Or cars.

The Jacobs family sat in the waiting room on those prickly sofas. Steam rolled off the roof of the railway station and the windows were all misted up with cigar smoke and breathing. Mrs. Jacobs was wearing a dark velvet dress with long sleeves and a hat, with a velvet bow under the chin. She was dripping with sweat from the crown of her head to her toes, which were wrapped in thick stockings and jammed into long, pointy shoes. The girls were in their sailor suits, even Rachel who was almost a woman. Mr. Jacobs was the hottest, in his thick suit and waist-coat, with one of those bowler hats on his head. He was smoking one cigar after another, taking them out of his breast-pocket which was almost soaked through.

He was thinking about the famous birds that belonged to the Meirings and Watermeyers and P.E. White and his own best birds, and if they were waltzing in the rain and breaking their legs. Or if the nests were getting full of water. Were the dams overflowing and what about the gutters? In his head, there was a big flood and everything he remembered was floating and bobbing in a brown current. Miss Beatrice was hanging onto a thorn tree, the current sweeping against her arms and her breasts. He tried to get her but Mrs. Jacobs was watching so he stopped.

It's almost three o'clock, he said to his wife. The station clock is wrong. Mrs. Jacobs twisted her head to see what he was talking about. She was thinking about the shows she had seen, especially Miss Sarah Bernhardt, and where she had packed the program. She wanted to show Miss Beatrice and the Vissers. The part she remembered especially was the ending, where Miss Sarah fluttered and trembled, lifting herself like a leaf looking for sun. She gave one cry, a long, stabbing breath that made you rise out of your seat, then she died. The audience jumped up and screamed as if she was really lying dead on the stage. Remember the Lady of the Camelias, she said to Mr. Jacobs. He looked at her and almost said, Take off that hat. Instead he lit another cigar, grinding out the old one on the floor.

The program is also at the Museum, laying in the glass case, right next to the umbrella. Mrs. Jacobs didn't throw anything away, especially if it came from overseas. She said they would be collector's items one day and she was right. They weren't stalactites or stalagmites so she wasn't a vandal.

By the time they could leave the station, even the stationmaster was gone for the day. They rode back in the big wagon, and the girls all fell asleep in a big, hot pile. Mrs. Jacobs looked out at the veld and saw how empty it was and it must have made her very sad. Mr. Jacobs was rushing to get back to his birds. He was trying not to think about Miss Beatrice but she was there, leaning against her kitchen door, the sleeves of her convict shirt rolled up. Of course he didn't know about Mr. Henry, and the snow-sheds which ended up saving a lot of ostriches in the big rain. He blinked and Miss Beatrice was still there, in the corner of his eye like a grain of sand. He rubbed his face with his hands and Mrs. Jacobs told him not to rub so hard. Your face isn't a piece of dough. Of course the sunset could make you weep, if you hadn't travelled for days and months to get home. If you weren't hot, and then cold, as the gold and pink light slowly dissolved. You have to love these mountains, Mr. Jacobs said.

Mrs. Jacobs sighed and dabbed a tear which was falling down into her lap. I do, she said. I looked for them in Paris, and all the big cities, Mr. Jacobs said. Behind the buildings, where things ended. But there was nothing. No edge. Here they are again. They look like my hands.

One of the girls stirred a little. Are we home yet? By the time the wagon swung down the long road, it was pitch-dark, with the stars roaring over their heads. The Jacobs farmhouse was just as it was when they left. The big oak door creaking as they walked through it and the English sofa where Mr. Jacobs had lain. They had come back with pictures and programs and new dresses but the house hadn't travelled with them. It looked middle-aged and Mrs. Jacobs wanted to re-cover the sofa and paint the walls blood-red, the way she had seen in some houses.

By the morning, the house had filled out, and it seemed grand again, with its wood panels and taps from overseas and frilly curtains. Mr. Jacobs was talking Afrikaans with the foreman and the girls were getting dressed to go to school. Mrs. Jacobs had lots of lists already and on one list was Miss Beatrice. Tea, with small sandwiches, and biscuits. Maybe some other ladies and their daughters. Mrs. Jacobs was dying to tell Miss Beatrice about England and America because she knew Miss Beatrice would understand these things.

What she didn't know was that Miss Beatrice was at home lying down on her bed, staring at a gecko walking across the ceiling. Was it a baby gecko, or was it a grown-up? For a moment, she wished herself up there, with discs on her fingers and toes, clinging to the ceiling. She imagined looking down and seeing a giant gecko lying in her bed, hands on the covers, small belly under the sheets. Mr. Henry walked in and the gecko raced down the wall and disappeared between the floorboards. Our birds did very well, he said, and she could have sworn his hair was going red. She didn't want to move her head. She didn't want to move anything.

The Israelites have returned from the Promised Land. His voice spun around and around, hitting that spot where the gecko was sitting. You have to go to Jerusalem for tea. But first I want you to read to me, he said. We have to sort some feathers.

She was dressed, stumbling, her eyes squeezed shut in the sun. Under her old skirt, her legs were scratched and blistered. In the sorting-room, she sat on a stool. The dust from the feathers rose in waves. Mr. Henry sat opposite her, with September crouching near a pile of feathers on the floor. You slept through the plucking, my dear, Mr. Henry said. We started after the rain.

September handed him bundles of prime whites, first whites, second whites, tipped whites, best fancy-coloured and second fancy-coloured. Mr. Henry took each heap separately, and sorted each kind into six lengths. He took twenty long quills and made a bunch, then he made a thicker bunch of shorter ones. Miss Beatrice sniffed because of the dust and then she read, Home is the sailor from the sea, The hunter from the hill. And I am the land of their fathers. When she read the part about every fowl of air, Mr. Henry made fake wings from one of the bunches and held it against September's back. Fly away, my birdie, he sang. Miss Beatrice couldn't read any more and she couldn't even look at September. Was Mr. Henry going to hit her in front of September if she stopped reading? You couldn't let him walk behind you anymore. He might just give you a *klap*.

Mr. Henry started sorting the hens' tails into six heaps. He was talking about snow again, and looking at his feet, and Miss Beatrice saw September's eyes move down to her stomach. She put her hand there and it was suddenly much bigger. She almost laughed. September clicked, and Miss Beatrice thought he had a seed pod in his hand but it was his mouth. Was he telling her there was danger? She heard Mr. Henry talking to himself, asking why the hens' feathers were darker. The hens were like the *hotnots*, he was saying to himself. A few light ones, then coloureds, dark-coloureds, short feathers and broken ones. That's how you make the piles. The cocks even have mixed tails! Look at these white tails with black butts! He was showing them to Miss Beatrice and September, very proud of himself.

Miss Beatrice started to read, Oh, to be in England now that April's here, but Mr. Henry wasn't listening anymore. Go to the camp of the Israelites, he was telling her, and spy on their ostriches. Tell me about the nests and the fences. Throw stones at their birds. Make them too excited to sit on their eggs. Drive them off the land! I am just going for tea, Miss Beatrice said. They'll serve you babies' legs on toast so keep your mouth closed. Look under the cup to see if there's any blood, Mr. Henry hissed at her. September carried bundles of feathers out into the sun, and shook them.

I left the baby's blanket right where it was. It gave me the *grils*. They turned the house into a doctor's office. Maybe the doctor gave it to a lady with a baby.

Christmas is just around the corner and I want a real party this time, with Christmas crackers and a nice white tree.

I hear the car in the driveway. The slam of the door. Jack took Gerda to the train station while I was sleeping. He's standing right in front of me and I can't see the sky anymore.

He says I'm living inside someone else's skin. Someone else's dead skin.

So what. My skin is too tight anyway.

SIX

The plain black dress Miss Beatrice wanted to wear to Mr. Jacobs' house was too tight. She had to tear it in the back so that it would fit. Nomsa pinned a lace hanky over the trapdoor. She had a big shawl even though it was hot in case the hanky fell off. She wore lace-up boots, like you see in the Museum. One of the other *klonkies* drove her there because September was busy in the ostrich *kraal*. Miss Beatrice took some ostrich egg finger biscuits that were now rusks. She had a hat on with strings that Nomsa had tied under her chin in a bow.

In those days you had to pray a lot in case you died in childbirth. My *ouma* nearly died five times, she said. I think that Johanna Jacoba on the top of the Swartberg Pass must have died in the back of an ox-wagon, with her baby. I saw her grave with my own two eyes, that day with Jack and the jumping baboons. Was Miss Beatrice afraid of lying down for the very last time, in Karoo clay, with *vygies* and aloes and all those bushes over her head? Of course Mrs. Jacobs thought Miss Beatrice had become a fine lady all of a sudden, coming to visit with biscuits. She didn't know what Miss Beatrice was scared of. It was the same fear my *ouma* had. What about Mrs. Jacobs herself and those three girls? I am sure it wasn't easy. You had to boil everything at home and hope for the best.

Sometimes I wish I had died all those years ago with my cookiebird. I would be the one resting now. I wouldn't have to do anything anymore and Jack could shout and shout all he wanted. I would probably be floating in a giant brandy-cup somewhere, my ears closed up forever. And I would know if it was a boy or a girl floating next to me, like those sad little birds that you can see through.

I must not talk like this because I will fall down and forget to walk Esther and Skollie and whoever else needs to be walked. I have to go before it gets too hot.

You must wait before you have another *dop*. You don't want to pass out where all the dogs are.

Mrs. Jacobs had spent days unpacking everything so that Miss Beatrice could see all the things from America. That music machine was standing up near the front door and Miss Beatrice probably thought it was a grandfather clock without a face, the way everybody else did. Rachel was holding those giant metal records with spikes and holes in them when Miss Beatrice walked in and she asked her what song she wanted to hear before the door even closed. Miss Beatrice had her hand on her back where the hanky was pinned checking to see if it had fallen off. She was trying not to drop the shawl or have the hat fall down over her face. Goldie had got much fatter and her hair was just as *kroes* as it had ever been. Bertha was still upstairs with her mother's toilet water. Luckily Rachel didn't drop that big record on Miss Beatrice's foot and then Mrs. Jacobs was there shouting at the girls for not helping their neighbour with her things. The rusks almost got lost and then Mrs. Jacobs saw them, sticking out from under the shawl. Finally Miss Beatrice was all unwrapped and her hat was gone and you could see how her hair was growing. She smelled cigar smoke but it was from last night. Mr. Jacobs was a dot somewhere, riding near the cave.

Mrs. Jacobs was talking the hind-leg off a donkey and Miss Beatrice followed her into that sitting-room where she had been once before for tea. The room looked exactly the same and Miss Beatrice imagined it would look like this forever, the way the Caves are always the same. What was different was the piles everywhere. Pictures, postcards, programs and souvenirs from overseas. Mrs. Jacobs handed Miss Beatrice a piece of green velvet that looked like a special *lappie* for cleaning very good shoes and said Divine Sarah's dress, my dear. You should have seen her! We waited backstage afterwards and I made Mr. Jacobs buy this. Mrs. Jacobs took the *lappie* back and kissed it. Her eyes rolled as if she was going to faint. You can't understand a word she says but it's pure love, she told Miss Beatrice, saliva pooling at the corners of her mouth.

Miss Beatrice watched the saliva-cups as Mrs. Jacobs went on. Here is the Niagara Falls. She showed Miss Beatrice something that had been melted into the shape of a huge waterfall and was painted blue. Out of a box, she pulled something made of feathers and brightly coloured beads and put it on her head. This is what the Red Indians wear. Goldie has a tomahawk. You should see all the people! More people than you could ever imagine walking down the street together as if it's nothing! And nobody says hello! Nobody knows you! Do you want to look at this? She handed Miss Beatrice the headdress. I think it's made of eagle feathers. It was snowing and we went to the Central Park. We watched the people ice-skating on the pond. We got so wet! The snow melted right down our necks. Afterwards, we went to a huge hall where you could sit in booths under electric lights and drink hot chocolate.

The girls wanted everything. The shops are so big! Almost as big as one of the breeding-camps. Mrs. Jacobs gave Miss Beatrice a lump of tissue paper and ribbon. Open it, she said. Miss Beatrice slowly unwrapped her present. A gold-skinned china doll with a blanket like the *klonkies* have except in different colours and two fat black plaits. On her back, a baby in a long basket tied with tiny leather thongs. That's a papoose, Mrs. Jacobs said.

Miss Beatrice touched the top of the baby's head. There was a patch of hair there that felt more like bristle. I don't think you can take it out, Mrs. Jacobs said. Bertha tried already. It's just the head and some kind of stuffing in there. Miss Beatrice nearly said I'm going to have a baby but she held her tongue. Mrs. Jacobs didn't ask her about Highlands or about Mr. Henry and went on talking about the shows she had seen with Flora Twistington and Maximilian Goetz. They say he is the baritone of the world, she said, and people will stand all night for tickets. Here, look, she almost screamed, unpacking another box. A famous new invention! She gave a stereoscope to Miss Beatrice, on a stand, and even picked some slides of the Pyramids with a Model T standing in front. We didn't go there but isn't this just as good!

We had pudding every night on the boat. They call it junket. Goldie was sea-sick and we bought some cloths in Madeira. The lace is so fine. Rachel was in love with the captain and cried into her cream potato soup because we didn't sit at his table. My girls don't know how lucky they are. I am going to keep everything and eventually it will all be in the Museum.

I thought of you, my dear. I wanted to tell you everything because it was all so unusual and quite, quite brilliant. The actors, the singers, the clever, clever stories! And what amazing new machines they have! To call your waiter, there's a white button built into the wood. Here are all my programs.

Mrs. Jacobs handed Miss Beatrice a pile of stiff pages with a satin ribbon tied around them. Miss Beatrice untied the ribbon and sneezed. My dear! You mustn't wet them! They're all collectors' items! Mrs. Jacobs was quite strict about this and took them back, tying up the ribbon again. Next time I'll show you what you missed. The ladies' dresses and the men in top hats and tails sitting and clapping oh so politely. And we saw ostrich feathers everywhere. Hats overflowing with them. Collar ruffs and sleeves and edges everywhere. It makes one pleased, you know.

Rachel was staring at Miss Beatrice, remembering that mad dance in the sand. How is the spider-bite, she asked. Did it grow or go away? Miss Beatrice looked at the girl with the black hair and rose cheeks and nearly said, It's growing and growing. She wasn't sure if the girl knew or if she was just playing. Women can read secrets, especially here in the Karoo where the air is so dry and there's never any sort of mist to hide behind.

I am fine, Miss Beatrice finally answered. Just a little tired from the last plucking. And then we had to sort and sort. You wouldn't be sorry, Mrs. Jacobs said, If you could see all those hats bobbing along with hundreds of thousands of feathers. And marching too. All the soldiers wear feathers in their helmets. I saw my husband all choked up and ready to cry.

Miss Beatrice bit into one of her rusks when she heard about Mr. Jacobs. The crumbs sprayed onto her lap and she spent some time trying to whisk them onto the floor. Of course Bertha and Goldie and Rachel were watching her. The crumbs lay around her feet like tiny burning coals. Goldie, the pale one with the freckles, was breathing very loudly. Mrs. Jacobs poured more tea and said, We missed Oudtshoorn. Over there, you are smaller than a tadpole. Nobody knew Mr. Jacobs was the Ostrich King. Goldie's breathing turned to snorting and some of the rusk she was eating flew out of her nose. Bertha, the youngest, threw back her head, her buck-teeth raised to the ceiling, laughing like a drain. Rachel shuddered and covered her face. Mrs. Jacobs was looking for a fan or something to slap the silly girls but she couldn't find anything. It was like the last time, except it was laughing not dancing and Rachel wasn't the only one doing it. Miss Beatrice tried not to join in but she couldn't help it. Goldie was so pale and her hair was so shockingly red and then all those freckles were jumping and twitching. Miss Beatrice tried looking at Bertha but that made it even worse. The Cango Caves, Bertha was suddenly screaming, Did you ever see the Caves?

I lost my glove in the Treasure Chamber! We wanted to write our names on the walls! She was slowing down now, panting not laughing, rubbing her cheeks with her wrists. We have caves on our land and we found them. We can show you if you want. We put a red hanky there. Rachel, isn't that true?

That's when Mrs. Jacobs started saying Enough, enough. We have all had enough thank you. Go to your rooms and lie down. They left, Rachel tossing her head, looking like evil because it wasn't her fault. Goldie and Bertha were slow, following their feet, their faces ashamed and red. My dear, said Mrs. Jacobs, You have no idea how wild they are, raised in this place by *kaffirs* and *hotnots*, and then playing with the Afrikaner children who are worse than baboons. I hoped that the trip would civilize them but it didn't. We had a governess from Austria but she left and then they were at the town school which was even worse. They came home braying like donkeys, copying the way the Boer children spoke. The best thing is to send them away to a convent school. They come back ladies. Of course we can't do that. It is not our religion. But you could send your daughter to the nuns to learn manners. I don't see why not.

Having children, Miss Beatrice asked. Do you like it? What a peculiar question, Mrs. Jacobs answered. Of course one likes it. Do you remember when they were born? Was it hot, or windy? Were you shouting a lot? Miss Beatrice asked, sitting forward, her dress pulling around her stomach, her wide eyes staring at Mrs. Jacobs like lights. Mrs. Jacobs put a rusk in her mouth and chewed it slowly. Then she said, These are not things you talk about, my dear. They happen, and then they're over. You forget.

Miss Beatrice asked, blunt as a bullet, Were you afraid of dying? Mrs. Jacobs touched the edge of her mouth carefully and her eyes got very small. I bought a new dinner service overseas. A china pattern you might like. Would you like to see my plates or shall I call your boy to take you home?

Of course Miss Beatrice went home. And she wasn't sorry at all. She took that handkerchief off the back of her dress and let the air blow through, so that her dress filled up like a sail. She didn't care. She saw Mr. Jacobs in the far distance, sitting on his horse and she got up and waved her hat and shouted and she thought she could see him lifting his hat a little but she wasn't sure. She was probably dying for a *dop*, the way I was. I drank brandy sours, so thick they stuck to the bottom of the glass. I made things with syrups, red and very strong, the colour of blood. Jack liked them too, and he made some himself, that came out as purple as a melted crayon. He probably put in a drop of methylated spirits.

I never felt better in my life. I think the dogs all knew I was expecting because they would sniff me up and down, their tails wagging like mad, congratulating me. I wished I could speak to the ones that had puppies. They had all the tricks, like moving the puppies by the scruffs of their necks and licking them clean. My ma was still saying things about the Magdalena Tehuis and how lucky I was that I was with Jack and not on my hands and knees scrubbing the floor of some big old house. I said nothing because children should be seen and not heard but later on Jack and I had a *dop* together and lots of laughs. He was getting pleased, then, and I felt that I had done something right. My ma didn't want the people in town to know so Jack and I were very quiet and at home a lot. We got drunk and put clothes on the dogs.

Back at Highlands, Mr. Henry was there and as soon as she saw him Miss Beatrice wanted to run back to where she had come from. Mrs. Jacobs could move here, to this farm, and watch Mr. Henry measuring his toes, and she could have Mr. Jacobs and the three wild girls. Of course the first thing Mr. Henry said was How big are his birds?

All Miss Beatrice could remember was the girls and not the birds so she said, They seem quite jolly. Mr. Henry was pleased because he saw Mr. Jacobs' birds, big and fat, dancing and tripping, their legs snapping like wishbones. They were standing in the kitchen and Miss Beatrice took her hat off and put it on the table and then she reached up to get the jar of sugar off the shelf. Her dress tore some more and the sound of the ripping made Mr. Henry moan. Miss Beatrice suddenly said, Do you know what it is? He wasn't listening to her so he didn't answer. She nearly said, I have something to tell you but then she saw Mr. Henry's eye twitching, and his mouth moving as if he was praying. We will go back, he was saying. We will leave here and go back to jolly old England.

It was like the snow-shelters only worse. Mr. Henry kept staring at the edge of the mountains the way you play with your wedding-ring. Miss Beatrice sneezed and something wet and warm trickled down her leg into her boot. She wanted to take Mr. Henry and turn him around so that he could see her face and her dress and how she was different but she couldn't do anything except sneeze. We won't stop, he kept on. We'll ride and sail until we get all the way home. Tomorrow and the next day and the next day I'll start making our fortune. Our nest egg. Our prize bird. I'm tired of boiling at Christmas. I'm tired of everything so upside down. Miss Beatrice wasn't, so she just wiped her nose. She knew they could never leave.

Mr. Henry chopped down a thorn tree and put it in the sitting-room where the hole for the fountain used to be. The thorn tree lay back against two chairs like some *dronklap* who had passed out. Miss Beatrice decorated it with buttons and broken ostrich feathers. On Christmas Eve, it was just the two of them in the house with a pot of *bobotie* and rice Mrs. de Koek had made. Nomsa and September had the day off. Mr. Henry spoke about leaving again and Miss Beatrice knew it would go on and on forever. They sang A Partridge in a Pear Tree except there were thorns, not pears on the tree and ostriches instead of partridges. Miss Beatrice's mom had sent a card all the way from England with a picture of snow falling onto Westminster Bridge. Mr. Henry put the card on the mantel and rubbed his eyes as if he was crying.

Miss Beatrice wanted to go swimming in the dam with the *klonkies* but she didn't say so. She didn't miss England like Mr. Henry. She wanted to tell him about the baby after they sang carols but she was too busy in the kitchen with the food. Then she decided she would tell him before the dessert, which was stewed quinces and cream. He had a second helping and then he lay down on the floor and did his measuring. There was some shrinking, he said, but not like

before. He must have been tired from all the adding and sub-
tracting because he fell asleep, the tape measure in his fist.
Miss Beatrice pulled the tape measure out of Mr. Henry's
hand as if it was a long piece of spaghetti. Then she wrapped
it around her stomach. There was something there, like a
very small *koppie* on the veld. One or two inches above sea-
level. Miss Beatrice held it there for a few minutes, staring at
herself, trying to see inside. Then she looked down at Mr.
Henry, lying like a dead person at her feet. Did she think of
stuffing the tape measure down his throat? Or tying it
around his neck and pulling as hard as she could? She just
bent down, and squashed the tape measure into his hand.

He woke up and started talking about England again and
the money that would come from the ostriches. Plucking, he
said, is the trick. Miss Beatrice didn't say anything because
they had just plucked, not all the feathers, but some, and you
had to wait so the birds got strong again. At least seven
months. We will be in England, he said, when it's April
there. We will see buttercups again, and primroses. No more
tumbleweeds and baboons, thank you very much. But it was
Christmas and Miss Beatrice knew that the birds wouldn't
be ready until July and then you had to think about the
prices, and everyone else's crop and what the auctions were
like. You had to worry about water on the heart and all
kinds of worms and whether or not a jackal would come
into the *kraal* at night. And then, of course, there was the
problem with the rain. Too much or too little. Nests in the
mud, feathers ruined, broken legs and so on. And always,
always, the problem of ostriches crashing into the fences. She
thought of Mr. Jacobs and how careful he was, and how he
knew everything and watched everything. He was getting
bigger in her head and her heart and soon his eyes would be

the size of eggs. She wanted to tell Mr. Jacobs about the cave inside her, and what was in there of his. But she couldn't. Could it be Mr. Henry's child? And then she remembered September, Nomsa and the *pondokkie* and what the ground smelled like. She knew there must be a storm inside her, with the little boatman desperately hanging onto his oars.

It wasn't so bad with me because I knew it was Jack. But my ma said it was bad because our wedding came afterwards and everyone in Oudtshoorn knew how to add and subtract. Except Slappie, who walked around with spit dripping off his chin and his hands hanging down by his knees as if he was going to crawl any minute. He frightened the children but my ma said he was all right. He couldn't hurt you because he was skew. Slappie was the only one my ma wasn't worried about. Everyone else, she said, was laughing at her behind her back because of me and Jack. Even though we stayed at home, she said they knew. She said we must keep our curtains closed and not open the door for anyone because it might be one of the van Schalkwyks or the Retiefs or even the Schoenraads asking for butter but really staring at me to see what was going on. Jack said keeping the curtains closed made it worse because then people would think bad things even more, so he kept going around, opening the windows and pulling the curtains back. I got so scared that I went to bed with a nightcap even though it was still morning. You feed the dogs, I said, I have my nerves.

When I went to the doctor my ma made me wear a big bandage around my head as if I had fallen down or something, so that the other people waiting in the waiting-room

wouldn't ask the wrong questions. She also gave me a
knobkierie to walk with so it looked like I'd hurt my leg as
well. There was nothing to see yet but she was still worried. I
wanted to ask her, What are you going to do when it comes
out? Stick fur all over it and pretend it's a dog? But I didn't
say anything because I knew she would shout at me and
when she shouted like that it made me *naar*. Her shouting
was even worse than Jack's because you could see all the
way down her throat.

I'm sure Mr. Henry was like that too only he had an Adam's
apple like a stick and that red-in-the-face look the *Rooinekke* have. I can see Miss Beatrice lying down in the hot
afternoons, closing her eyes and wishing he was on the
moon, a tiny yellow-and-red man screaming his lungs out.
She was falling, falling, like a big stone falling down a cliff
and when she woke up, she was at the bottom of the cliff
and it was dark and she was the one screaming Where am I?
She saw her dress with the trap-door hanging on a hook and
outside the sound of men shouting at each other. At first it
sounded alright, just the busy sound of an afternoon. But it
went on and on, and the voices got raw and Miss Beatrice
looked out of the window to see what was going on. September was there and she thought she saw him push something with his hands. Was it the fence or Mr. Henry or was it
a feather that he was pulling? No, there was something red.
A hanky under the nose? Everything was melting and
shaking in the sun and Mr. Henry was too, his hands
dancing and lunging at September and September ducking
and running away. Running into the veld like a *dassie* or a

meerkat, running and disappearing into the ground. A fist of a cloud moved in front of the sun and the light was dark, almost silver. Miss Beatrice looked at herself in the mirror. Her face was silver too and her eyes were grey and flickering, telling her something she couldn't understand. He who casts the first stone. The words flew into her head and stuck there, like flies on fly-paper.

Nomsa was in the kitchen when Miss Beatrice walked in, and at first she thought it was just like always. Nomsa bending and fire-making, her eyes long and distant, some song inside her from before, when there was a baby in a blanket on her back. But when she stood up, she looked at Miss Beatrice and there was a needle in her look. Suddenly Miss Beatrice was scared of her. Of course nobody said anything because you can't say things like that to your maid. You can't just say what you're worried about. You can't even say What's wrong? You must go on being the madam and asking about supper and what's in the pots. Miss Beatrice didn't even know if there was real blood on the ground when Mr. Henry and September were shouting like that. She was beginning to think it was part of her dream, at the bottom of the cliff and getting dark. It was very bright outside now and that made her even more confused about whether she had seen anything or not. And again, she couldn't ask. So she said something about hearing wild dogs fighting, It must be coming from the neighbour's farm. Nomsa clicked and Miss Beatrice thought she saw a crack of lightning between Nomsa's teeth. That's why people go mad here on the veld. I have seen whole ships coming through my living-room wall, with people drowning and screaming, and it's not funny. Jack says it's Aladdin except he's not in a lamp. He's lying in the bottom of a gin bottle looking for trouble.

I am walking the dogs and there are no bottles to hide or to find out here. I am scared of the ships coming but there are no walls for them to crash through. The sky is my shepherd, I shall not want. The mountains are my walking sticks. Skollie and Esther will guide me through the bushes and over the *koppies*. There are no Valleys of Shadows. It is all light.

SEVEN

When Mr. Henry came back for his lunch, he was ratty and Miss Beatrice didn't ask about September. They had shepherd's pie and milk pudding. Mr. Henry was talking about plucking and it was making him upset. In the olden days, my *oupa* used to say, the farmers plucked every six months, when the fluffy part of the feather was at its longest, and the blood-vein in the feather was dried up as far down as the place where the feather meets the wing. Underneath, the stalk was still alive and growing. But pulling and pulling before this part underneath was ripe made the feathers grow out the next time much shorter. Shorter and shorter every time. By the time the bird was five or six, all you could do with the feathers was make feather dusters. I don't care, Mr. Henry was shouting, not at my *oupa* but at September in his head. In five or six years we'll be hunting quail on the Downs and so what if the ostriches shrivel up and die!

Miss Beatrice said, What about pulling out the stumps the way Mr. Jacobs does? So you cut the white and grey quill feathers after six months, and you leave the stumps in until they are ripe. With the blacks and tails, you wait until the chick is seven months old. Then you cut the quill feathers without letting the stumps bleed. Miss Beatrice was talking very fast, the Ostrich Queen inside her getting big all over again. You pull out two rows of the brown feathers above the quill, also two rows above and below the arm of the wing. But don't leave too much skin exposed and never, never take out the floss feathers which keep the bird warm. Pull out the tail. Two months afterwards pull out the quill stumps. Six months later, do the whole thing all over again, leaving the quill feather stumps in two months each time. So the blacks and drabs protect the quill feathers for the first four months. Make sure to pull the tail every seven months. Be careful with the young birds because the skin is very tender and if you pull out a socket, you will have a blank there forever. You don't ever want to have your birds walking around with blanks in the wing.

Mr. Henry jumped up as if a bee had bitten his foot and clapped his hands on his ears screaming Aaaah! Consorting with the enemy! You talking book! He took his plate of shepherd's pie and threw it on the floor upside down and jumped on it screaming, Rubbish, rubbish rubbish! Miss Beatrice looked at Mr. Henry's boots and how they jammed the mashed potatoes and the minced meat into the floor and she said she was glad they didn't have rugs like Mr. Jacobs. She couldn't stop talking because she had said so little for so long and it all came thundering out like hailstones. About ostriches young and old, the males and the females, the Guaranteed Breeders and the ones that wouldn't, and the chicks that lived and died. The best implements for cutting the feathers are pruning-scissors with two bends. For drawing the stumps, sixpenny pincers or a *hotnot's* teeth are best.

I'll pince you! Mr. Henry shouted and covered Miss Beatrice's mouth the way you cover a big hole in the stomach when the blood is pouring out of it. She bit his hand and he put it in his mouth and almost cried. But he didn't. Instead he swung his arm at her and it got her in the head and she fell off the chair onto the floor. My baby! Miss Beatrice's words flew up and hit the ceiling like a bird trying to fly out of the room. Mr. Henry didn't hear and started going for her again. Stop! She had her arms up now, stiff as thorns. I'm going to have a baby. The words echoed until it seemed as if she had said them yesterday. Mr. Henry just stood there. When you came back, she went on, From the Swartberg. Remember how we lay down together right here on the floor? He looked at her stomach, and then he looked at his hands. Was he counting his fingers or the days?

You could hear something scratching around in the roof and even the back of a clock. It was quiet like it is in school when the teacher says, What are the Seven Wonders of the World?

Then Mr. Henry smiled. He poked her with his finger as if she was a ripe tomato. Boo! He said. Boo to the little one!

Miss Beatrice felt the breath coming back to her and her hand almost touched Mr. Henry's. His mouth got all jumbled and twitchy. Wonders never cease, he said, then he coughed and shook his head, sending away some giant fly.

Mr. Henry didn't say anything about September and the shouting. He was too busy talking about England again and how horrible those Boer children were. He didn't want his boy to grow up in the wilderness running barefoot all day long and playing with beetles. And all those Jewish children with their funny black hair and long noses! There's always boarding-school overseas, Miss Beatrice said, but he didn't listen. He won't put his big toe on any of this muck, Mr. Henry went on. We must pluck.

Miss Beatrice was tired and everything she had said about ostriches was gone, washed away. Mr. Henry patted her hand as if it was a pet. He even was nice to her cheek, leaving a small kiss there that didn't sting. He looked out at the bushes on the veld. We'll have a picnic, he said. At the Cango Caves. Then he walked outside.

Miss Beatrice closed the kitchen-door and made herself a strong cup of tea. In the cup, she saw twirdles, which she remembered from long, long ago. They were there in the tea in England, in the nursery. You had to drink all of it, the skin of the milk, and those lazy twirdles curling in a circle that made Miss Beatrice want to throw the tea on the floor. But you couldn't because of Nanny, who would leave it there on the floor to show Mother. Then you wouldn't get any biscuits. Or no ducks for a week. She looked at the twirdles and they turned into the shape of a baby, the head very big, a small curling circle for the hand. This baby will grow up to be a lion, she was thinking, not an English baby, dressed for the rain every day. We'll chase meerkats and *dassies* and watch the springbok run across the veld. We'll make an egg in a tree, as if we were captured. We'll bring our telescope and check on the ostriches. She put her spoon in the cup and the baby broke up.

Of course Miss Beatrice didn't know what colour it was and whether its hair was *kroes* or straight. She wasn't thinking like that. She was thinking of adventures. I was like that too, when I was expecting, only my dreams had dogs in them. I thought my girl or my boy would love all the dogs and feed them, little balls of dry dog food spilling out of a tiny hand.

I let my hair loose and it feels like yesterday when the baby was inside me. My hair was long like it is now, only then it was thick and honey-coloured. I was the pretty one. Ma made me promise never to cut my hair.

I am walking on the dry earth and I can see everything. The sun is drying up the gin. The child is moving like water in a bucket and I know that it has blue eyes, not washed-out but very bright. Straight from heaven, like my *ouma* used to say. Now the child has an arm around Skollie's neck and that's where I stop thinking because it makes me so happy. You can't cry for nothing, Jack would say if he came here and saw me. You're not a baby, you know. You don't understand, I want to say. There's someone in there.

Miss Beatrice probably didn't talk about it either because it was even worse in those days because everything under your dress from your neck to your ankles was supposed to be dirty and nobody else's business. Today it's just the middle part. Legs and arms and necks are not so bad. Still, your stomach is in the middle and that's where it was happening.

But Jack was happy. I was his fruit tree and he often said there was a big cherry growing there because I had once swallowed a pip. To tell you the truth, it happened outside, under the stars. Tickey, our old dog, was there and we were behind the aerodrome. You could see a small two-seater plane glinting in the distance and the windsock stretched out like an arm with the hand cut off. I remember lying naked on a patch of Cape heather that felt springy and not too scratchy. We were both shivering from the cold, holding each other so tightly that the cold turned into hot. I felt like we belonged to the earth and the fullness thereof, like it says in the Bible. Jack was inside me and I thought I heard someone getting into the plane and starting it. There was a big flame shooting out the back part and it made me scream. Jack had my hair wrapped around his hand like a bandage and a bruised look on his face that said, More, I want more. I licked the soft part just by his collar-bone and he pressed me down against the heather so that I could feel the little stones against my skin. I thought the plane was crashing and I screamed again but it was just us.

When I looked up again the sun was coming up and the plane was still there. The windsock was empty and hanging down and it made us both laugh.

We didn't have to do it outside again because then we were married and we had a bedroom suite and a dressing-table and a nice carpet. Sometimes I buy some Cape heather and stick it in a vase and just look at it. I wonder if that two-seater plane is still standing there.

I am sure Mr. Henry was happy too, like Jack was, when the baby was on its way. That's why he thought of the cave picnic. He wanted to celebrate outside the Caves with a cloth and sandwiches and an umbrella, as if there were oak trees everywhere and lots of shade.

Nobody knew about Cave Number Four then, which is on the farm Nooitgedacht. Ma was dying from her liver. The Nooitgedacht farmer went looking for his cows and fell into a beautiful cave. I told her about it when she was in the hospital. The farmer went back after he had a dream that there was another cave. They had axes and so on and digged and picked their way through all the stones and mud and rubbish. This cave from the dream was even more beautiful than the first.

But there was something terribly sad. I showed Ma in the newspaper. They found old bones, melted candles and bits of cloth. There was also a rock carved with words and pictures. It had the date on it—6.9.1870—and the words, *"Modder het hom toegeval—8 mense"*. That gives me the *gril*s to think that there was a mudfall and eight people were in there. That's who those bones belonged to. They got in but they couldn't get out. The saddest part was a tiny picture on the bottom of the rock of two women with babies in their stomachs.

I had a dream too, except there was no cave. Your ma took the baby, Connie, and she got on the train and went to Ashton. She gave it to Gerda. Gerda sat and watched the baby. She couldn't walk away because she wouldn't have heard it cry. She felt everything with her fingers and her heart. You couldn't have done it, Connie.

I woke up and I looked at Jack sleeping next to me and I didn't say anything. I made coffee and put a little brandy in it to warm me up and burn the dream away.

Mr. Henry and Miss Beatrice didn't know anything about these people who had been sitting there under the ground for about forty-five years by then. It probably would have spoiled their picnic to think about it. It even spoils some of those stalactites and stalagmites for me, because I think of a lot of things like that. Not only the Nooitgedacht ladies with their babies but also Pauline, and even before her. How some people say the Devil's Chimney got its name.

Skollie sees a meerkat and he stops. It's next to a rock and it's looking at us. We're so lucky today. You hardly ever see a meerkat. This one is almost as high as my knee. He's standing up straight like always and he looks like he wants to shake my hand.

They say that there used to be a lake, deep inside the Caves. It has dried up now but they still call that part the Ice Chamber because it's so cool and lovely. I wonder if Miss Beatrice and Mr. Henry went with Johnny van Wassenaar to that part. He was the only tour-guide who went far into the Caves in those days. Of course the Ice Chamber is not far from the Devil's Workshop, which comes just before the Devil's Chimney. Maybe Miss Beatrice was standing there, expecting just like the Nooitgedacht ladies, looking at that fine lake. I wonder if you could go swimming in it. She was the sort of person who liked to do things like that. She probably didn't because of Mr. van Wassenaar and other people in the party.

He was still alive when I was a little girl although he had retired and didn't take people into the Caves anymore. My ma said he liked to talk about the Caves and their secrets but I don't remember if he said anything to me or not. He was a famous person here in the Little Karoo and all the old people loved to talk about how they went into the Caves with him and went down that old iron ladder into Van Zyl's Hall with candles and so on. The ladder was called after Sir George Grey because he gave it to us. I wish I could ask Mr. Johnny van Wassenaar about that day Miss Beatrice and Mr. Henry went to the Caves with him, but I think he's been dead since the metric system came in.

Miss Beatrice was just starting to show, and I don't think she bothered to tie herself up, the way some ladies did in those days to hide their stomachs. She didn't want to remind Mr. Henry that they had been to the Caves before and that it stank like bat droppings and Mr. Henry said he was going to faint. After him going away and coming back there were a lot of things they did over again, as if it was for the first time. They took two horses and a wagon to get them to the Caves.

The road wasn't paved then and I'm sure you got a lot of dust in your mouth. Mr. Henry was wearing one of his floppy white hats and they met Mr. van Wassenaar outside the Caves. It was early in the morning. The cave mouth wasn't the way it is nowadays. They hadn't blown a big hole in it for the dioramas and ropes and lines of tourists. You had to go in carefully, down the Sir George Grey Ladder. But they had to wait outside for a while and someone had some *koeksusters* and fresh bread. Miss Beatrice and Mr. Henry had their picnic but they were saving it for later. The other people were not Oudtshoorn people. They were Meneer and Mevrou van Zyl Smit, visiting relatives here in Oudtshoorn. They probably just thought *Rooinekke* when they saw Mr. Henry and Miss Beatrice and said nothing. I'm sure they hadn't heard about the Swartberg and Mr. Henry and all the stories about Miss Beatrice. They just ate their *koeksusters* and looked old, like the pictures you see in the Museum of the Voortrekkers. Mr. Henry stared at them as if they were giant *goggas* and Miss Beatrice asked for his hat which she used as a fan. Her dress was open in the back and she had something there to cover the hole. I can see her wearing one of her convict shirts like a shawl or tied around her waist.

The people that came late were a schoolteacher and his wife from a farm school in De Rust. Their horse was lame in one leg, they said. The schoolteacher had a pointy beard and a moustache and his eyes were ice-blue and oval. When he tilted his head back, the ovals looked like they were going to loop all the way down his cheeks. He had that Karoo skin, which is almost as brown as a *hotnot's*, except it was drawn tight around the mouth as if he was going to punish you for something. His wife was small and very nervous, and she had her smelling salts ready. Meneer en Mevrou van Huyssteen, the schoolteacher said, his head dipping back and the ovals getting very long. *Aangename kennis.* Pleased to make your acquaintance.

Mr. Johnny van Wassenaar had a small axe tied to his belt, and a lot of rope swung over his shoulder. He acted like a church minister, very strict, although he was a farmer, with a thick greyish beard, and pants made out of hide that were full of smudges. He was medium-size, and getting long in the tooth but he was still fit and his black eyes could pin you to the wall. I saw a picture of him in the Museum once. He was standing on the iron steps leading to Lumbago Walk and he had a candle or a flare of some kind in one hand, and was holding the ladder in the other. He looked fierce, a cave person or cave fox, disturbed in his hole.

With Miss Beatrice and Mr. Henry, it was of course after the Boer War, and Mr. Johnny probably didn't like the English very much. I am not sure if I was Miss Beatrice that I would have gone into the Caves with him that day, especially if I was expecting. They were all talking Afrikaans, or something that was turning into Afrikaans but still sounded quite Dutch. Miss Beatrice and Mr. Henry didn't join in of course because it just sounded like rocks dropping to them. Mr. Henry had his best nose-up look and Miss Beatrice kept fanning and fanning as if she could fan herself up into the air and hover above everybody, still fanning.

They all had candles when they went in, and Mr. Johnny had old-fashioned tools for measuring depth and so on. It wasn't the way it was for Farmer van Zyl, who went in with his slave, Klaas. But there was still no electricity, no generator or anything like that. It was very dark and much bigger than it seems today, with all the tourists and coloured lights. You could see names on the walls like Barend Oppel, 1790, Sir Lowry Cole, 1831, and Sir Henry Barkly, 1874. But you couldn't write your name anymore although I'm sure Mr. Henry wanted to. The smell of bat droppings was there again although this time Miss Beatrice was the one who nearly fainted. Mr. Jacobs came back to her in the dark and she felt his breath all the way down her back. She had to hold on to Mr. Henry's arm. Mr. Henry thought it was because she was pregnant and he patted her on the head.

I stick out my hand and the meerkat comes closer and maybe he will shake my hand after all. I look in his eyes and I see black water and the edge of his heart beating, just like my own. He can hear me blinking. He listens.

Miss Beatrice was feeling all that old warmth rushing through her like a river and she almost lay down right there and asked Mr. Henry to lie down on top of her, so that he could put out the flames with his body. But they were supposed to follow Mr. Johnny, and the van Zyl Smits and the van Huyssteens, and so there was no time for stopping and lying down. Am I glowing in the dark? she wondered and looked at her hand and her arm. And then for the first time, for the very first time, that baby inside her rolled upside down, as if the baby was remembering, and doing happy cartwheels. She started to cry and the tears were hot and landed on Mr. Henry's arm. But he looked up instead of down, and stared at the stalactites pale in the dark like the fingers of ghosts. Miss Beatrice was seeing but not seeing, just dark holes and the water turned to stone, hanging forever like a thousand gravestones. The fire inside her turned to ashes, but then when the baby moved for the second time, it flared up all over again in a burst that made her nearly fall over. Then they were at the underground lake and Miss Beatrice started to take off her clothes because all she wanted was to feel the water around her shoulders, up to her neck. Mr. Henry was hissing in her ear, Don't do that! and the other people were staring, and Mr. Johnny had his axe raised as if he was going to chop off her head. So she stopped, and her elbows stayed bent, and she followed behind like a blind person, still feeling the beard of Mr. Jacobs between her legs and behind her neck and his mouth moving softer than soft.

My wife, Mr. Henry said, *Sy is deurmekaar*. She is confused. He looked straight at Mevrou van Huyssteen as if she was supposed to help. *Sy verwag.* Mevrou van Huyssteen took Miss Beatrice's warm hand. Her own hand was cold and damp and Miss Beatrice knew straight away that the poor woman was *poep-scared*. She was praying in the dark and Miss Beatrice heard the Lord's Prayer, over and over again, in Afrikaans. Miss Beatrice remembered her old self, the tall one, who walked across the veld with a *knobkierie* and she put her arm across Mevrou van Huyssteen's narrow little shoulders and said, It's all right. It's just a cave and there's nothing here except water and stone and this wonderful lake, so delicious, so clean. The schoolteacher's wife couldn't even look at the lake it make her so scared. She was whispering and moaning and suddenly Mr. Johnny growled Sssssh! as if they were in church and they all had to stand there in the dark, *tjoepstil,* staring at the cave the Ice Chamber led into. Rocks lying all over the place as if someone was building something and stopped in the middle. Today that's the Devil's Workshop but then it was the end of the tour and you had to pick up your skirts and turn around. Mevrou van Huyssteen couldn't get going again although everyone else was already walking back on the damp, waxy floor of the cave. She was staring at the rocks on the floor as if they were alive and she said *Bobbejaan* to Miss Beatrice who said, The baboon won't do anything. He's made out of rock. But Mevrou van Huyssteen wouldn't go forwards or backwards. She was stuck there, like Lot's Wife. Her husband the schoolteacher was glaring at her, his ovals pointing to the floor, and he pulled her arm but she didn't budge. She started to shake and her teeth clapped together like shutters, over and over again. Then her eyes rolled back, and the schoolteacher pulled a hanky out of his pocket and said, *Liewe Here*. My wife. She is having an epileptic fit. Does anyone have a spoon? Miss Beatrice remembered the picnic basket and pulled out a butter knife which she gave to Meneer van Huyssteen. He held his wife's head like someone holding a horse or a cow, and put the knife in her mouth so that she wouldn't swallow her tongue. Mr. Henry was catching the fit, because he was rocking and muttering, and you couldn't understand a thing. He was probably back on the top of the Swartberg Pass, even though he was under the ground. He had his hands over his eyes as if there were armies of vultures coming to pick the hair off his head.

So Miss Beatrice and the van Zyl Smits were the ones who had to pick up Mevrou van Huyssteen and carry her the way you carry a big plank. She was stiff from head to toe, even though she was alive as can be. The schoolteacher stayed near her head, making sure she didn't swallow the butter knife instead of her tongue. Mr. Johnny led the way, and he looked grim as the Grim Reaper and it was almost like a funeral, with Mr. Henry at the back, his hands still over his eyes, wailing. Occasionally Mr. Johnny would snap *Links! Regs!* Left! Right! at Mr. Henry, or Miss Beatrice, as if it was all their fault.

Lumbago Walk was hard because the ceiling gets very low and you have to watch out for the smooth little pools on the ground. You have to bend your back which is why they call it Lumbago. I think this is the worst part of the Caves, worse than the Devil's Letterbox or the Chimney because you can't stand up straight for quite some time. And then it's narrow so you have to walk in single file behind some other person who is also dying to walk like a normal person again. Miss Beatrice almost fell onto her face but she grabbed onto the wall and it reminded her of what's inside your lung. Of course Mevrou van Huyssteen nearly fell too and the bigshot, Mr. Johnny, started shouting. This isn't the Army, you know, Miss Beatrice said, but I don't think Mr. Johnny could hear.

Then they came out into a high passageway, and they didn't have to crouch anymore. You could see all those names again, Barend Oppel and so on, and Miss Beatrice wondered how dead those people must be by now. The shoulder of the schoolteacher's wife was sticking into her neck and then the baby rolled again. Suddenly a pain shot down her leg from inside her hip. She kept walking, her ears getting hotter and hotter and she wanted to scream at Mr. Henry to take over carrying poor Mevrou van Huyssteen but he was still coming out of Lumbago Walk, stumbling like a *dronklap*. This wasn't a picnic. This was horrible.

Now they were in the Sand Rooms, which is near Lot's Chamber. It was a long way back to Van Zyl's Hall—past the Drum Room, the Fairy Palace, the Rainbow Chamber, the Bridal Chamber, Botha's Hall. You could only see things in patches, because of the candles—and the patches kept shifting and swerving. Miss Beatrice felt sick to her stomach but she didn't complain. She held on to the schoolteacher's wife like she was supposed to. The schoolteacher gave her a grim little smile when they got to the Rainbow Chamber. Miss Beatrice could feel her legs getting very thick. They only stopped walking when they got to the Leaning Tower of Pisa, which is in Botha's Hall, right next to the Madonna and Child. They laid Mevrou van Huyssteen down. She was starting to come right. Her legs were bending for the first time since the Devil's Workshop. She was saying over and over again, *Ekskuus tog,* I'm sorry, I'm sorry, and searching in her hair for some hairpins.

They were in a group with their candles, helping the schoolteacher's wife to her feet. She was leaning on the schoolteacher's arm and for the first time Miss Beatrice noticed that her shoulder was skew and her hands were puffy. She's not right, Miss Beatrice was thinking.

Mr. Johnny wasn't going to waste any more time and he was showing the others the Madonna and Child stalagmite which looked like a lady with a baby, if you squeezed your eyes almost closed. Miss Beatrice saw it and her hands went up to her stomach, trying to read what was there. She kept staring at the Mother and Child formation, seeing but not seeing, her thoughts lost inside the shape of the stone.

I remember that part. I used to stand naked in our bedroom, in front of the dressing-table which is part of the bedroom set we bought from Jonker's. My legs were the same and so were my arms, but my breasts were getting full as the moon. My stomach rolled forward like a *Boesman* lady's. I would stand there staring until I got goosebumps, then I would get dressed and pour myself a Castle. I would sit outside on the steps at the back of our house, feeling the sun laying itself on my arms like a blessing.

By the time they got through Van Zyl's Hall with its giant organ-pipes and bat droppings, Miss Beatrice just wanted to go home and forget about Mevrou van Huyssteen and her stupid fit and the ugly van Zyl Smits who reminded her of the Voortrekkers except that they didn't have oxen or *kappies*. Every time she looked at the schoolteacher she wanted to shout in his face so loudly that it made his ears curl. Who does he think he is? A Lamb of God? Mr. Johnny was getting on her nerves as well and she imagined pulling him off that ladder he was climbing on and throwing him onto a stalagmite. Last but not least was Mr. Henry, who was already eating a chicken leg, his hand darting in and out of the picnic basket. He had chicken grease on his chin and Miss Beatrice wanted to scratch it off with her nails. So she bumped him on purpose and took the basket away, holding it to her chest as if it was Baby Moses that she had found in the reeds. That's how she climbed up the ladder to get outside, Mevrou van Zyl Smit's fat ankles and hot skirts in her face, the basket hard and scratchy against her chest. The *Boerevrou's* smell was all iron and fish and old cabbage legs and Miss Beatrice wanted to bite and scream and vomit all at once.

They came out of the dampness into the hard, dry light of

a Karoo afternoon. The flickering shapes in the candlelight were all gone although when you looked at Mr. Henry there still seemed to be stalagmites dancing in his eyes. Miss Beatrice looked for a place to spread their tablecloth because she was hungry now, hungrier than ten lions. The van Huyssteens and the van Zyl Smits watched from a big rock they were leaning against. Miss Beatrice found a thorn tree and some small stones and put the tablecloth down, turning her back on all of them. Mr. Henry opened his fly and pissed against the thorn tree and Miss Beatrice didn't even care. She could see Mevrou van Huyssteen putting her hanky over her mouth and closing her eyes and she said, There. She's going to have another fit. Mr. Henry laughed. Then they sat down and had sandwiches and hard-boiled eggs.

Mr. Henry started talking about the ostriches and money and England and Miss Beatrice told him about the baby moving. Really, he said, Poor thing must be seasick. All that underground motion and so on. He looked at Miss Beatrice, his eyes skimming over the top of her head because he was not the kind of man to stare you in the eyes. He looked above, or next to, or behind, his fingers resting lightly on the sandwich.

I must meet the big Jew, he said. He can help us get out of here. We can sell Highlands to him with all the birds on it, plus plus. I am not one for leaving, Miss Beatrice answered. I like the air. There's air in England! Mr. Henry was gritting his teeth. The van Zyl Smits and van Huyssteens were still leaning against the rock and watching and now Mr. Henry turned to them and shouted, Go away! *Gaan weg!* They huffed and puffed and pretended not to hear but when Miss Beatrice turned again they had disappeared.

What is this fever for staying? Mr. Henry jabbed at Miss

Beatrice, his face blotchy with the sun. Look at me. I am being eaten alive. He showed her his foot and she saw freckles on his ankles and a few yellow hairs. Soon it will be a stub. Just some horrible ending at the bottom of my leg. She couldn't say, It's nothing. Your foot is all right. He was seeing with a different eye. And he believed what he saw. This disease was his faith, the rod and the staff that protected him. And Miss Beatrice was afraid. So she said, We'll invite them for dinner. We'll have the mother and daughters as well. I'll make them ostrich egg biscuits. The ones you like.

Poor dear, Mr. Henry said suddenly, just when she was thinking of Mr. Jacob's chest and his beard and all the warmth that was there. You must rest. I'll see him in town. We'll eat stew together at the Oudtshoorn Hotel. I like the way they mash their potatoes. Miss Beatrice said, No! I must have them here! I've drunk from their cups more than once. I've sat on their sofa. I've talked to the girls and looked at their things from America.

EIGHT

The Jacobses came on a Wednesday, late in the afternoon. September was at one of the *kraals*, fixing a fence with some wire and a pole, when he heard a terrible noise, like thunder and gunpowder. He saw a puff of dust on the road, with something black and shiny in the middle of it. Then he saw that the black thing had wheels and was rolling towards him. He lay down his tools and ran back to the house, to call Mr. Henry to get his shotgun. Miss Beatrice was in the kitchen, her hair standing up like wheat, her arms full of flour. Nomsa was there too, and they were cooking ostrich stew and making ostrich egg biscuits. Ostrich Robert, Miss Beatrice said, when Nomsa asked, What are we making, *Mies?* September banged on the back door, and Miss Beatrice opened the top part. His face was streaked with sweat, and the peppercorns on his head seemed to be twitching. *Die geweer, Madam. Waar is*

Baas Henry? He's sleeping, she said, but the look on his face made her run into the living-room and take the rifle out of its case.

She went outside, the rifle heavy on her shoulder, above her the sky burning like the end of the world. By now, the dust-cloud was rolling past the dam and the willow trees, and the incubating-room and the water pump. The black thing wasn't just black, you could see some of the colours of the sky on its shell. There was something inside it. Shapes, like people, but made out of dust. Miss Beatrice had it in the sights of her rifle, when it stopped, unfolding its wings. The dust-people got out and there was a lot of coughing and shaking, and Miss Beatrice heard Bertha and Goldie's wild screams.

Suddenly she laughed and the baby inside her laughed because she loved those funny girls and their *kroes* hair. Now here they were, standing on the ground at Highlands.

Mr. Jacobs had his best beard on. It gleamed even through the dust. Miss Beatrice lurched towards him, as if she was going to kiss him, then she fell back into something that looked like a broken curtsy. She heard Bertha's muffled snort and then the slap of Mr. Henry's hand on Mr. Jacobs' shoulder. What, old man, wet the whistle, soak up some of that soil on your head. When she lifted herself, Mr. Jacobs was staring at her, his eyes cracked open, the brown part so bare it made her insides ache. He was seeing her swollen stomach, the hair longer on her head, her eyes lost and soft. My wife, Mr. Henry was barking, is expecting a bird. Mrs. Jacobs suddenly swept Miss Beatrice into her arms, and Miss Beatrice sank into the smell of toilet water and dust and sweat. *Ach,* Mrs. Jacobs spoke German she was so excited.

Wunderbar! Herzliche Glückwunschen! Sadie! Mr. Jacobs snapped at her.

September was standing next to the car, and looking in. The roof leaks, Mr. Jacobs shouted, Dust and water. In the rain, we sit with umbrellas. Mr. Henry pretended not to see, not to hear. Don't want it. Not here, not now. Just England, and peace. He was thinking, This Jew will help. Come inside, shake yourself, he said aloud. We have a cold collation. And a hot one too!

Miss Beatrice and Mr. Henry led the way to the house, Miss Beatrice with the rifle hanging down, Mr. Henry redder than red. Miss Beatrice would feel Mr. Jacobs' eyes blazing between her shoulder-blades, searching her skeleton for clues. Behind Mr. Jacobs was Mrs. Jacobs and the three girls, and behind them was September, finished with the fence. He was walking to the house, to Nomsa, to the back steps behind the kitchen where he ate his *mieliepap* and drank his coffee.

Miss Beatrice had tossed scarves on the chairs and threaded leaves behind the stale old pictures and mirrors that were there when they came to Highlands. There were purple and yellow *vygies* on the table floating in a tea-cup and the hole where the fountain used to be was covered with pillows and branches. You could smell fruit spiked with cloves, and stew thickening. Mrs. Jacobs settled onto the sofa and the girls flocked around her, admiring and sniffing and not laughing anymore. Bertha was on a footstool, with Goldie next to her mother. Rachel wandered to the window and looked out over the land that was all Highlands. Mr. Henry poured brandies and Nomsa came in with the tea on a tea-tray, with a special tray-cloth Miss Beatrice's ma had made, back in England, before the wedding.

Miss Beatrice was pouring, not thinking, her eyes on the milk, and the tea-leaves, closing her nose to the smell of Mr. Jacobs' cigar. Mr. Henry was leaping—now to the desk to show off an invitation to the King's garden-party, now to the window, scolding the heat in the sky. Miss Beatrice felt herself sinking, and Mrs. Jacobs touched her arm. My dear, why don't you lie down? I'll pour the tea. It's not that, Miss Beatrice said, It's not that at all, her mood hanging on the thinnest of strings. The truth was flaring up inside her, and a flame nearly burst from her chest. She smothered it with her hands while everyone was staring at Scorpion who was tearing one of the pillows to pieces with his paws. Mr. Henry threw milk from the milk jug at him and he jumped onto the window sill and screamed. Mr. Henry shooed him out of the window and came back to Mr. Jacobs, complaining about animals.

Later on Nomsa came with the stew and the oil-lamps were all lit, everyone sitting around the table, not praying, just quiet. Mr. Henry was North and Miss Beatrice was South, Rachel and Mr. Jacobs were East, and the younger girls and their mother were West. They all were still, and it kept the house from flying headlong into the night. They held the roof down with their legs and their elbows. Goldie was the one who broke out, while they were eating, What is this? I love it. And Miss Beatrice said, A special recipe for the Jacobs family. Ostrich Robert. Again, the words of her flight with Mr. Jacobs, that ostrich-chase, and the day in the cave, trembled in her throat, as the baby fluttered and rolled inside her. Mr. Jacobs was on her right side, and with one simple hand, she could touch his cheek, right there where the beard stopped. But she put her side-plate on that hand, just in case, the china cold against her knuckles.

Mr. Henry was banging on the shield of history, raging about ancestors and the misty island that was England. Mrs. Jacobs had her napkin to her lips, and Bertha was staring. Rachel and Goldie were chewing, their heads bent like flowers. Mr. Jacobs said, You wanted to talk about feathers, Mr. Chapman. And the market.

You Jews, Mr. Henry began, and suddenly there were lice falling from the ceiling and making them all itch, You like to get to the point. Mrs. Jacobs stopped breathing, and then started again, taking in a big gust of air. Goldie put her hands to her ears as if "Jews" was still beating against the walls. Mr. Jacobs lifted his knife, then put it down again, and looked at Mr. Henry the way men do in bars, talking about matters commercial and private. He wasn't shifting, or twisting. He stared straight into the center of Mr. Henry's cornflower eyes, and those icy hot eyes rolled up and away, to the spot above the window, to a stain that looked like the head of a spaniel dog. Mr. Henry held his brandy glass as if it was the hand of the dearest lover and lifted it to his lips and drank, like a man praying. He kept staring at the spaniel dog stain, as if he was wishing it would come alive and bite Mr. Jacobs on the leg.

Mrs. Jacobs waded into the silence, lifting a small plate and looking under it, like someone buying crockery. That's the family crest, she said, to no one in particular. Can I see that invitation to the King's garden-party?

Miss Beatrice pulled back her lips in a windy smile, showing all her teeth. Of course, she said, and she got up and fetched it.

Mrs. Jacobs turned the yellowing card in her hands while the room sat still, a boat stuck without wind. They say your mom is a cousin of the King. She turned to Miss Beatrice.

Sadie, Mr. Jacobs growled, Enough is enough. He looked at Miss Beatrice properly for the first time and he saw that the angel was gone. She was brown in the face and her big stomach scraped at the edge of the table. She wasn't light anymore, like the fairy-girl on the stamp.

Miss Beatrice whistled, Yeees, from the back of her throat, staring at Mrs. Jacobs as if she was a shadow on the wall.

I once slept with a Jewess, said Mr. Henry, watching Mr. Jacobs, She was covered with fur like a muskrat.

My daughters, Mr. Jacobs said. Mr. Chapman, my daughters. They were all silent and Rachel was the palest. They were being seen and not heard and they did it so well.

Young virgins, Mr. Henry went on, taking a mouthful of brandy and looking at the tops of their dresses, searching for breasts. I take it your daughters are all virgins, he said, each word so separate, so clean, like those damp serviettes they give you to wipe your hands when you eat crayfish.

Ahh! Mrs. Jacobs dropped a square of Ostrich Robert onto the King's invitation and she jumped up as if she was bitten. I'm sorry, she was saying, and then Miss Beatrice started up, saying I'm sorry, I'm sorry, I'm sorry, as well. I'm not sorry, Mr. Henry started shouting and Nomsa came in with the ostrich egg biscuits saying, *Madam, die baas het geroep?* The *baas* called?

I can add and subtract, Miss Minky Monkey, Mr. Henry said to Miss Beatrice in the clearest of voices, holding up his hands. I still have ten fingers. That stomach you're wearing belongs to our neighbour here. Mr. Ostrich King Jacobs. Have a good night! He left the room, letting the hand with the brandyglass lead, his steps careful and cold. Nomsa screamed Ai! and the ostrich egg biscuits dropped to the floor and she buckled over, as if she was the one having the child.

September was at the window and he was holding something dead. Scorpion, the meerkat, blood covering his jewels. The room was suddenly filled with devils and voices and Miss Beatrice saw the Jacobs family running away, the Israelites running into the desert. The curtains and flowers and all those pillows and cloths were boiling up like the Red Sea, and there was shouting and crying all over the place. Miss Beatrice was standing at the front door, and Mr. Jacobs was pushing his wife and children out into the night. The last look he gave at the house was ruin, and it got Miss Beatrice in the throat, because she pulled at her neck as if the air had turned to ash, and she couldn't breathe.

I know about shame, cookie. The meerkat just looks at me. His whiskers tremble. Then he's gone. *Totsiens,* goodbye, cheerio.

We have to go home, doggies. The sun is cooking my brains. I need a *dop.*

Remember the time I fell out of the car? I was coming back from visiting Ma and I'd had a few drinks. I was getting out of the Volksie—we had a Volksie in those days— and the next minute I was lying down on my bum. Mrs.

van der Westhuizen was feeding her canary and she came running across the street, the box of bird-seed still in her hand. I think I said *Voertsek,* because the next thing I remember is that she slapped me in the face. Shame on you, she said.

I am sorry we walked so far. The stones are burning through my shoes. My bones are old and dry. I can feel my tail-bone, right where I fell out of the car. And then there's my arm, where I fell in the toilet and broke it and my shoulder when one of the dogs pushed me onto the ground. I am not a soldier, but I know how it feels. You have to go around with a body that's broken.

I can see windmills and there's the turn-off for the National Road. It's not the old road. It's not the Montagu Pass anymore. The cars going down had to wait for the cars going up because the road was so narrow. Or was it the other way around?

Why are my hands so old, older than the old road? When did that happen? There's a liver spot that looks like the head of a donkey. I have never seen it before. The dogs are getting *moeg*. Their tongues are flapping like socks on a washing-line. I wish they would carry me home. I wish they were the ghost dogs of Mr. Henry. Esther is lying down. Come on, doggies. We're almost home.

* * *

There's the house and it looks like someone is sitting on the front *stoep*. Is it a policeman?

I go in the gate, and the dogs follow me. I walk up the red steps and yes, it is a policeman. He and Jack are listening to the rugby.

Now they are talking to me and I see black in front of me, with spots that glitter and burst. I walk inside and Jack is behind me and I know the policeman is gone. I *buk* in case he hits me on the head. Where were you? he says and I want to say, I was there by the aerodrome. I was lying down with the garden boy.

I go into the bathroom and lock the door. There's green mouthwash and I drink it and drink it until the plastic curtains are shining and the taps are the softest silver in the world.

When Miss Beatrice heard the sound of that machine Mr. Jacobs and his family had travelled in, it sounded like monsters throwing rocks in the night. It rolled away the way it had come but it wasn't funny anymore. It was like blood leaving the body. Miss Beatrice stood there, by the door, trying to see Mrs. Jacobs' face in the blackness but all she could remember was some screaming that wasn't German and it wasn't Afrikaans. It was Jewish. She couldn't even think about Mr. Jacobs without wanting to die from missing him and now hating him for leaving her and hating her.

Goldie was like a sad clown, and Bertha was plain as the veld in a drought. Rachel was fading, pressed flat like a flower between pages. There were no more laughs. The girls were suddenly old people, and they stared at Miss Beatrice from the dark shapes of the mountains as if she had murdered their mother a hundred times over. How do you go on when bad turns into terrible?

How do you walk into your room when your husband is sleeping in your bed with murder in his heart? How do you walk anywhere? Miss Beatrice didn't know the answer to these things so she just stood there at the front door, like Lot's Wife in the Caves. She was a stalagmite.

In the day, it is hot here but at night it gets very cold. Miss Beatrice didn't notice the cold. She looked at the dark as if there was something there, some animal, some person or even a bird who could tell her that nothing had happened. That the stew was good and the guests left before the dessert. But that didn't explain the faces that hung there like lanterns—Mr. Henry's red blotches, Mr. Jacobs' beard shiny as knives, Mrs. Jacobs' mouth burst open and the girls cracked in the centre like three sad plates.

I have seen baboons wearing *kappies* and spiders as big as your head. But it wasn't the air, it was the bottle. That's my sin. Miss Beatrice, of course, was different. Her sin was adultery, which is written in the Bible. I have never seen anything about drinking there. Or is it one of the seven abominations?

Jack comes in and stands there. I thought the door was locked. I am sitting in the bath but it's empty. He laughs. He's drunk.

* * *

Jack says what Miss Beatrice did was the worst. He says she should have been left at the top of the Swartberg Pass under a pile of stones while she was still alive. Right next to that Voortrekker *vrou*, Johanna Jacoba. I say to him, Jack, We are all sinners, and he laughs and he says, Connie, you are just a *dronklap*. I almost feel like he is glad I am too *deurmekaar* to go out and *vry* someone else's husband.

He gives me the bottle of gin and I'm happy. I have a long *sluk*.

Mr. Henry didn't put Miss Beatrice anywhere. He just went to bed. She was standing all night and looking outside like the nightwatchman. After the bearded bats came the leopards, two of them staring at her with eyes the colour of piss. One of them was carrying Scorpion in his mouth. Miss Beatrice could see the glint of the jewelled collar. The leopards stayed ten feet away, then backed off as if she was giving them the willies. The bitter aloes looked like they were leaning backwards, trying to pull themselves out of the ground and run away to the mountains. The thorn trees and prickly pears didn't budge. They were growing their needles into spears to drive into Miss Beatrice's heart. The *brakbos* which lay on the ground in patches like the wool on a *hotnot's* head, started to wither.

All that food for the ostriches—the *ganna*, the *brakbos*, the *spekbos* and Turkish fig—was starting to die and it was all Miss Beatrice's fault. The air got even colder. Miss Beatrice didn't feel her skin going blue. All she could feel was guilt. The shame burned inside her and didn't go out. Her baby, her softest of friends, was quiet. She wanted to touch her stomach but couldn't. Her hands hung at her sides like old spoons. The moon was a horrible white hole that hung in the sky forever and ever.

By the time the dark faded, and the light seeped in, five hundred years had gone by and Miss Beatrice was still alone, still standing. When Nomsa came walking up the path from her *pondokkie* towards the house to light the fire and cook the *pap* for breakfast, Miss Beatrice just looked at her, and said nothing. Her mouth was too cold to move and her eyes were stuck fast inside her head. Nomsa slipped into the kitchen. Slowly the sun lifted itself and Miss Beatrice felt something light on her arms. There was woodsmoke in the air and the sound of a live person. Nomsa was moving pots and opening windows and humming. The humming came from deep inside her and Miss Beatrice remembered the day of the pumpkins. The terror of Mr. Jacobs and his family got small, and there was a new feeling. Nobody knew how far, just how far, she had flown. She was the Knysna loerie, the bird with the crown and green chest and red underwing. The rarest of Cape birds, hopping from tree branch to tree branch. She would live here, and she would stay.

Nobody knows anything. The words fell out of her mouth like a bit of a song. She lifted one shoe, then the other, and was almost beginning to march. Then something snapped in the lower part of her back, and she was stuck. It was just like Mevrou van Huyssteen in the Caves, except for the epileptic fit. And Miss Beatrice wasn't a plank, she was a claw. That's how Nomsa found her, when she came into the room. Miss Beatrice lifted her head but the pain threw it down again, right towards the floor. September came and he and Nomsa carried Miss Beatrice sideways, across their backs, like a skew child. They took her to her bedroom, which was empty now. Mr. Henry was already gone somewhere, maybe back to the mountains. Who knew anything anymore? Miss Beatrice rolled sideways onto the bed, and Nomsa waved September to go. Nomsa took off Miss Beatrice's shoes and Miss Beatrice slept.

She dreamed of Scorpion covered with blood and when she woke up there he was, wrapped around her feet like some kind of muff. There were dozens of flies in the room and the smell of more animals, all dead. She touched her back and there was something strapped there, a big bundle of fur. And there was more fur stuffed under her dress, right on her stomach. She couldn't tell whether they were *dassies* or meerkats or baboons. She just lay there, and let the smell roll over her like a thick pea-soup fog.

She was too tired to mind. As she got warmer, the baby started to move again. My own private seal, she was thinking, as she drifted back into Dreamland. This time she was in the Cango Caves, and all the stalactites and stalagmites were people, with their feet melted into the ground. As Miss Beatrice walked between them, the way you walk between trees in a forest, she saw Mr. Jacobs and Mrs. Jacobs and Bertha, Goldie and Rachel. They didn't see her, but she could see them. She looked again and noticed that there was more than one of each. She tried to count how many Mr. Jacobs' there were, but she couldn't keep up. There were more coming in all the time and each one got bigger and bigger until the last one was so big that she had to lean back to see his head. She fell over backwards and suddenly she was sinking. It wasn't rock or water, it was sand and it was pouring over her so fast that soon it was pitch-dark and she couldn't breathe or see. Miss Beatrice woke up screaming, her body pressed against the wall, her fingers trying to climb.

Mr. Henry was standing there, still holding the brandy glass as if it was a candle. I hate you, he said, or was Miss Beatrice dreaming? Our guests, are they gone? Miss Beatrice asked. That was yesterday, he said. They left in that horrible machine. They have left us alone. He sat down on the edge of the bed, and took Miss Beatrice's hand. I made them go. I knew what to say. He put his hand on Miss Beatrice's belly. I know who that is. That's a Chapman for sure.

Was he lying? Or mad? Miss Beatrice didn't ask. She just sat on the bed, the animals soft at her back, the baby swaying inside her. Each minute, each breath, was a day for the baby, a bolt of blue sky, a small bit of food. It was all she could think, all she could do. It's just you and me. There's no one else left, Mr. Henry said. Nomsa, she answered. There's Nomsa. She will be there when the baby comes. Rubbish, Mr. Henry said. You will do it yourself. He pulled off the fur from her back and under her dress. Now wash. You smell like a badger. He got up and left. Miss Beatrice looked out of the window and saw September sitting under a tree and smoking a clay pipe, watching the house.

Miss Beatrice went to her wash-stand—the taps hadn't worked since before Mr. Henry's big walk—and poured water from the pitcher all over hands and her arms. She rubbed water on her face and let it drip over her stomach onto the floor, like water sliding over a big rock. She looked in the mirror and behind her face was September, smoke curling from his head. She watched herself watch him, her yellow-white hair still growing like mad, her tortoiseshell eyes wide open, sliding to the left, her nose slightly lifted and pinched from all the smells. The ears were strong and open, and the lips were burst from the cold of the night. This face is the only face in the world, Miss Beatrice was thinking. I am the last one left.

Then September was gone from under the tree. There was an empty place there as if he had been stolen. What Miss Beatrice didn't see was Mr. Henry sitting on an old horse, wearing his white hat, shouting September, September. September walked, and ran sometimes to catch up, while Mr. Henry rode. Together they looked at all the ostriches. And the ostriches looked at them, with those suspicious eyes under long lashes. Mr. Henry wasn't going to wait anymore. He was sick of waiting. He was going to pluck now. It didn't matter that September kept saying, *Baas, hierdie volstruis, hy is te klein.* Or—*Baas, hierdie volstruis, sy vere is nie ryp nie.* Mr. Henry didn't care about how ripe the feathers were or if the ostriches were thin or fat or young. All he could see was the sorting-room, filled to the ceiling with feathers. And the boats going to England were stuffed with feathers, so many feathers that the passengers used them as hankies and threw them into the ocean when they were finished. Mr. Henry was with the Captain, giving him a garland made out of feathers, and the Captain was so surprised that he kissed Mr. Henry on the cheek for thank you.

On top of the profit from the feathers, Mr. Henry believed that he could sell Highlands to Mr. Jacobs, even though Mr. Jacobs was still growling at home, licking the wounds of his wife and daughters. Mr. Jacobs wasn't going to say goodbye to a profit, and if he had double the land and all the ostriches on top of it, he could build a gold house with diamonds and rubies in the chimney. The kind of house that would glitter in the night along with the stars. Mr. Henry thought this was what Mr. Jacobs wanted, because he was a Jew. But he knew that the days of free advice were over. Mr. Jacobs wasn't going to talk about strangles and water on the heart and the best medicine for tapeworm. And he wasn't going to give Mr. Henry any of his good plucking boys, not even for half a day. Mr. Henry had jabbed a hole in his family. Serves him right for basting my wife in those hot eyes, Mr. Henry was thinking. Serves the bugger right.

Mrs. Jacobs believed and she didn't believe. So when she told her friends over tea and scones and cream and jam at the Oudtshoorn Hotel just how drunk and rude Mr. Henry had been, what he said sounded like a big lie with a tiny ship of truth floating inside it, right in the centre. And people always see that ship of truth. It doesn't just float by without anyone noticing. It rolls into a different story, one that has Mr. Jacobs meeting Miss Beatrice in London and them sleeping together at a hotel near that famous feather place. And she takes him to the King's garden party, to show how much she loves him. Ma used to say I like to make stories up but she did it too. I know she was happy when Gerda got married because she thought Gerda liked girls. She never said anything but I know what goes on inside her head. My stories aren't made up. I see who is lying and cheating and sometimes I even think I can see a hole in someone's sock, right inside their shoe.

Jack is lying down on the floor and he's the one passing out, mind you. I'm still clear as a bell. Ting a ling!

NINE

It was a big *skandaal* in Oudtshoorn. Not Jack or me, but Miss Beatrice. In those days, a secret, even if it was the wrong secret, was like wearing a dress made out of rotten eggs. Nobody could stand the smell of you and it was hard just to go around the town and buy your vegetables and flour and rice. People went out of their shops or disappeared behind the counter or around the corner. Of course they would come out again and serve you things because they were so very curious but then they would slap everything down on the counter and maybe even a few things would break but you would still have to pay for them. As if you broke them yourself. Miss Beatrice probably didn't care. She never liked Oudtshoorn people anyway. The only person she liked was Mr. Jacobs. She missed him all the time and wrote a letter every day to him which said how she was not the one who told Mr. Henry about their cave. At the end of the day, she burnt the letter and watched the black bits float to the ground. The smell made her sad and then she would think about the baby and what it would be like when the baby was born. She didn't know if she would live to see the baby's face. Her ma didn't live to see her baby sister. And her grandma died on baby number six. Is that the arm of God? Or is it God just walking away from you because you have sinned?

All this and more, she wanted to ask Mr. Jacobs, or even Mrs. Jacobs, or anyone from that house where things were real, and all the children in place. But Mr. Jacobs would be the best. A man of the world, who made all the engines grunt and click, whose feet were like rocks on the ground. It was sad because she saw what died in his eye that night, the night of the car coming and going. I know because of what happened to Jack. One day, he was strong and rough, and I liked it, and the next day he was just rough. Miss Beatrice was exciting like a bird you catch in your hand, and then she seemed tame. As if the baby held her down.

Some people say you mustn't see anything bad when you are expecting like dying or burning or anything ugly as sin. Then the baby will come out and frighten everybody with a harelip or a foot that's on backwards. That's another reason why I stayed at home so much.

Then there's the baby born with a caul, and the baby that's head is up, looking towards your throat instead of your shoppie. Was Miss Beatrice afraid of these things like I was? Was she afraid of seeing a bad vegetable and the baby getting warts and scars right there inside her? I think she was the kind of person who sailed over stories. She didn't hear the bad things the *kaffirs* were saying like don't let anyone touch the childbirth blood because it is cursed, or the Jews with their old Evil Eye. Was she scared of the germs? Or being alone at Highlands? I think she was afraid of dying, with Mr. Henry gawking at her like she was a fish on a beach and he didn't know whether to throw her back into the water or not.

Of course she wanted to undo that night, that very long night which ended with animals at the waist and foot. Was the baby now growing fur inside her or did that spell fix what was broken? Nomsa was not the kind of person you could ask. She did things, and was silent and she could scare you if she wanted, with her ropes and her bones. Miss Beatrice wanted to go back further, to the beginning, when Mr. Jacobs was sitting there ready to say things about ostrich feathers. She wanted to find him in the world which was getting so much bigger and emptier. Was there a light in his heart somewhere, a picture with Miss Beatrice on it, and maybe even a tiny, tiny baby that had his black hair? She couldn't stop hoping.

She remembered the nice way he took Mrs. Jacobs and Bertha, Goldie and Rachel out of the house, as if he was delivering them from evil, and she wanted to be delivered from evil too. When she went into town, she thought she saw Mr. Jacobs crossing the street, his waist-coat glowing a little, and then she saw him at the Post Office and at the Oudtshoorn Hotel and wait, there he was, waiting for someone, tapping his hat. He was here and there, and every time she saw him he was more handsome. Of course she would get closer and it wasn't Mr. Jacobs, it was another dark-haired man who had bad teeth and wasn't smiling at all.

You could wait and wait for years, like fishing without even a rod. Just standing and waiting and staring, expecting a miracle. I waited myself for someone I never even knew, just someone, anyone who was better than Jack. Miss Beatrice wasn't like me. She got fed up and walked on the ground as if she was killing *goggas* with both boots. And then she decided to go find him.

The bottom of her heart was burning like some rice underneath and the breath in her throat was sharp. You know when someone is hurting you that way, even if they're sitting on some *stoep* in the next town. Miss Beatrice looked at the sky and the mountains around Highlands and Mr. Jacobs wasn't looking for her the way she had hoped. He wasn't spying in the snow-sheds or in her kitchen by accident. So she called September and sent him looking for lost ostriches. She said she had seen them running away towards the Jacobs' place. He must come back and tell her what he saw, even if it was only Mr. Jacobs and some *klonkies* fixing fences. September must tell her where they were standing because then she could go and ask them herself. Excuse me, but did you see my birds running past you? They got such a *skrik* this morning and they have been gone the whole day. It was a male called Blackie with such nice black feathers and his wife, Loskop, who forgot where she had laid her eggs. Poor Blackie had to remind her. They're Guaranteed Breeders, you see.

She didn't tell this part to September because he was just by the *kraal* with Blackie and Loskop in it and he saw Blackie eating some *spekbos* and Loskop sitting on the eggs. The hen sits on the eggs in the daytime because her feathers are brownish and look just like Karoo grass. The cock sits at night because his feathers are black as the sky. September didn't mind going away because going away meant leaving Mr. Henry who liked to talk the hind leg off a donkey while they were supposed to be fixing the pump and so on. Mr. Henry sometimes sketched while he talked and the pictures were like spiders and worms in a nest and the nest was sitting in the middle of a cage. September tried not to see because of the *tokolosh* that hung near Mr. Henry, that sent him running into the mountains like a man who has forgotten his own name.

September took a mule to find the ostriches that were not lost because he knew he mustn't be too fast or too slow. He looked back over his shoulder and there was Miss Beatrice standing watching him and and she was getting round in the middle, so round that anyone could see. Her hand rested there, on her side, as if she was holding the baby in the palm of her hand. Miss Beatrice saw where his eyes were, and she went back into the house.

Did she think of September and the morning in the *pondokkie* where she fell onto the ground with him and Nomsa? It was on the other side of her mind, in the part where the earth is yours and the fullness thereof. Where you can eat from every tree and nothing makes you sick. But that is also the loud side, where underneath the waves are full and you can feel the beginning of a storm that will tear down the sky. She couldn't get there anymore because she had filled up the passageway just like that mud which fell on those Nooitgedacht people and buried them. She could only think of Mr. Jacobs, because he seemed like a house that was safe. He walked through her dreams every night, checking on all the locks and the shutters. He seemed closer than Mr. Henry, who lay there in the bed next to her like some big orange monkey.

She thought of a life with Mr. Jacobs, where he held open her coat, and tied the shoelaces of a little girl that stood between them. Then he tickled the child with prime whites and Miss Beatrice could only laugh at how she reached for the frothy white feathers. She wanted to ask, just once, only once, if that life could be hers. If Mr. Jacobs could remember what they had found in that cave, or on the top of that *koppie*. Could he find what had chased them, what had tied them so closely, the blood beating between them like *kaffir* drums?

Miss Beatrice waited the whole day for September to come back. She looked across the ground but all she could see was the twisted things of the veld. The trees scratching the air with their branches, the stones and *goggas* like moving knots. The birds were quiet, sitting under the roof or near the aloes, their heads pulled down. She wanted to run down the dirt road, waving her arms and screaming, *September, waar is jy? Waar is Meneer Jacobs?* September, where are you? Where is Mr. Jacobs? But the baby was like an anchor, holding her legs still on the wooden floor.

It was almost dark by the time September came back and he had seen only birds—*korhane,* in pairs, walking over the dry ground, weaver birds coming in and out of their weaver hotels in the thorn trees and, of course, ostriches. He had seen one of the weaver birds drink which is bad luck because weaver birds never drink. He looked at her face, stretched at the top from waiting, and he said, *Ek het niks gesien. Meneer Jacobs was nie daar nie.* I saw nothing. Mr. Jacobs wasn't there. September didn't say anything about the birds, especially the bad luck weaver. Mr. Henry came up to Miss Beatrice—she and September were standing by the cement *dammetjie*—and he shouted at September, Where were you?

Miss Beatrice saw Mr. Henry's hand go up and hit September in the face and she screamed, I sent him! I sent him to look for Blackie and Loskop! Mr. Henry stared at her. What's wrong with you, woman? Are you mad?

I saw Blackie go. And Loskop. They ran past my window. She was losing her breath. Mr. Henry waved his hand and nearly spat at September. Get moving! The day after tomorrow we pluck. September turned and walked away, his body disappearing into his clothes, his clothes the colour of the *korhaan*. Miss Beatrice felt the baby roll like a fish diving down to the bottom of the sea. You have lied, she was thinking. The baby knows and is hiding. Poor September. Poor baby and me.

That chap was here, Mr. Henry said. That Jew. I told him I was drunk. Let bygones be bygones. Here? Miss Beatrice remembered cigar smoke. She was sitting on the cabbage roses again and Mr. Jacobs was in the air behind her. He came to one of the *kraals*, Mr. Henry said. I was counting the birds and had to start all over again. He smells money, you see.

He smells me, Miss Beatrice was thinking. Like I smell him. My longing is there in the wind, and it goes to his house as well as mine. It wraps around his neck and against his cheeks, and it goes deep down as well, into the bottom of his pants. Mr. Henry was talking and she was watching his lips move and it was getting very funny. He's coming back tomorrow, Mr. Henry said. We will talk about acres and pence. But look at you! Mr. Henry was shouting now, and Miss Beatrice thought she was going to wee right there, in her panties. The sun is setting on your cheeks, my dear. You are shining like those bright Southern Hemisphere stars. We'll sail home by the light of old Beatrice.

Miss Beatrice looked at her hands and she saw they were swelling. There was something not right but she brushed it away like a *miggie*. I know how you swallow your worst fear. I had mine scrambled on toast and washed it down with some coffee. But it doesn't go away. Your ankles get fat like an old lady's and where are your wrists. I had to take off my watch. Miss Beatrice probably wore hers on her dress. I know she had headaches.

When Mr. Jacobs walked in the door the next day, he was fuzzy like a bad photograph. Miss Beatrice squinted but everything was soft and watery, even the door. Mr. Henry was melting, and so was poor Nomsa, who came with a tea-tray and some rusks. Or bananas? Miss Beatrice was swimming and thrashing, trying to get back to the shore, to a place with edges. And then she started to itch like a million *miggies* had jumped on her bones. Her ears were being eaten and so was her shoppie so all she could do was say hello and goodbye and go to her bed. The voices of Mr. Henry and Mr. Jacobs twisted over her like barbed wire as she itched and scratched, itched and scratched. Thousands of pounds or hundreds? Today or tomorrow or after the plucking? The horses included, along with the birds. Something about the Magistrate's Court and the fences. That's when the head-ache started up like a factory. All Miss Beatrice could hear was booming and steam-pressing and grinding.

She thought she could see Mr. Jacobs standing in the door frame, his beard the colour of crows, his hand lifted to help or to say goodbye. But it was Nomsa, and the hand held some *muti* in a cup which she made Miss Beatrice sit up and drink. This is an old story, Miss Beatrice was saying. I'm collapsing like someone's stupid old tent. You come in and pitch it all over again. Where is Mr. Jacobs? *Hy's weg, mies,* Nomsa replied. He's gone. Miss Beatrice screamed, You bat! and threw the *muti* on the wall. Nomsa scooped up some *muti* off the floor in her hand. She stared into Miss Beatrice's face and said, You will kill us. If that baby dies, all the milk in the world goes sour. Now drink. Miss Beatrice was going to laugh but she didn't. She licked the last of the *muti* from Nomsa's hand, smelling woodsmoke and iron baking in the sun.

Nomsa handed her the chamber pot, the one from England with the roses and thistles on the side, and made her sit. The pee didn't come and then she remembered she had been dry since yesterday, since September coming back and seeing only the birds. Maybe it was the weaver, who never ever drinks, drinking her water. There was something turning inside Miss Beatrice's head. Today was yesterday and the night of Ostrich Robert was now. She wanted to cook and make the house shine but Nomsa made her stay where she was. Then Nomsa was gone and the room was empty and Miss Beatrice threw the chamber pot out of the window.

Sy is deurmekaar. She is mixed up. That's what the doctor said to Jack when I had my headaches. Watch out when she gets like that. Call me at once. I had some brandy when we came home. Jack shouted at me but he was as small as my finger-nail. All I could say was, So what.

I wanted to cook my own kidneys and have them with sauce. I didn't say that to Jack.

Then he started to grow. He got big as a horse. That's when the *tokolosh* dropped in, and scabs fell off the ceiling onto my head. Jack didn't even know. He couldn't see the blood under the bed and all the dead fairies, lying there in a pile.

They didn't come for Miss Beatrice the way they came for me. Jack told me later about the ambulance and Ma there trying to hide me from the neighbours as I twisted and shook. Convulsions, they said, when I woke up in the morning. You had convulsions, my girl. Your blood has some poison. You could have died in your house. The baby, I said, and they looked over my head.

Jack is passed out on the floor and I can't open the door to get out. I must now sit and wait. The gin is gone, and so is that *blerrie* mouthwash. I am looking at Jack's face and there are red veins and his nose has grown fat. His hair, that black hair, is full of stiff grey hairs that look like a bad brush. I remember that horrible dream. Connie, Ma says, I'm giving the baby to Gerda.

Jack's breathing, not talking, and it sounds like an old *chorrie*.

Miss Beatrice wasn't like me. If she'd had what I'd had, she would never have lived. She had the first part, with the blurring and so on. She had the low water and headaches but not the convulsions. She could look out of the window and there was the chamber pot, broken in three pieces. The roses were still fixed so she went outside and cleaned it all up. The piece with the roses she put on a shelf.

The next day, the doctor came to the house. He made her

stand up with her dress hanging all the way to the floor and he knelt down in front of her, on one leg, his arms going up her skirt. He was feeling, not looking, his face turned up to the sky. He was Irish and old, and his eyes were cloudy green bottles in a face full of blotches. Miss Beatrice looked down and saw that his collar was frayed. A mole, like a nipple, stood out on the side of his neck. Not ripe yet, he said, You still have some time. He got up from the floor, his bones cracking. Then he looked at the urine she'd saved in a cup. Not whiskey? he said, with a funny old laugh. And how is the farm?

My husband is plucking. Not today but tomorrow, Miss Beatrice replied. You can see him from here, if you look out of the window. The doctor peered out and there was Mr. Henry, his white hat flopping in the wind, talking to September and three other *volkies*. What a wonderful life, the old doctor said, out here on the farm. And you, my dear madam. The doctor stopped and stared at Miss Beatrice's shoppie, then her titties. Look after yourself as much as you can. Miss Beatrice crossed her arms and then she said, I saw double, even the door was all wrong. The doctor patted her hand, It's your nerves, Mrs. Chapman. Just rest in your bed. The doctor looked at her shoppie again and then he went on, I'll speak to your husband. I'll tell him to get me when the time comes around. And speak to your neighbours, especially the wives. They come in their droves and they know what to do.

Then he was gone in his cart, his leather bag next to his shoes, his dusty black hat holding his head on his shoulders. The smell of his breath still hung in the room like an old meat-pie. There was ash on the floor from his coat and Miss Beatrice swept it away with the sole of her foot. My neighbours, she thought. Ha ha. He doesn't know anything, not even the gossip. She remembered his hands, reaching under her clothes like blind, poky crabs.

The veld yawned in front of her and there weren't any answers. The bush didn't burn, it was only her thighs. His hands were still there and they bumped when she walked. She found Nomsa outside, squatting on the ground. Nomsa beckoned and Miss Beatrice squatted down next to her, half falling, half laughing, her bum in the air. You must learn, Nomsa said, you must dig your own hole.

On the earth there in front of them was a tiny clay ox. Nomsa picked it up and let it stand in the middle of her palm. The children, our children. These are their toys. Then she gave the ox to Miss Beatrice. Our children? Miss Beatrice lurched up again, holding her stomach. The baby was talking, and it wasn't in English. Nomsa stood up next to her. She said something in Xhosa and the baby lay still.

Miss Beatrice walked, ran, stumbled away from Nomsa, as if a bell was ringing behind the willow trees. Was there magic folded inside Nomsa's *doek*? And those beaded bangles with their bright reds and yellows? Were they beacons? Nomsa's eyes followed her, and she could feel them like birds sitting on her shoulders. Here, on the veld, you must learn to see with the skin on the back of your neck. You must wear eyes on your elbows.

Mr. Henry was out the whole day with the *volkies*, gathering the ostriches. He wanted to collect all of them by sunset but it was impossible. The farm was too big. September told him a long time ago that it takes three whole days but Mr. Henry wouldn't listen. Mr. Henry went one way, with September, while the other *volkies* spread out in all directions, each one carrying his own mimosa stick to drive the ostriches back. First they go into one camp, which is large, then they go into the plucking *kraal*, which is smaller, so that they're all squashed together and have no room to kick. But that part comes later. First you have to find them, usually a couple of them every hundred acres, standing there and eating *brakbos* and Turkish fig as if they had all the time in the world. Mr. Henry had a long *sjambok*, not a mimosa stick, and he was waving it around so much that his horse's eyes rolled back and all you could see was milk.

They rode and they rode and all they could find was an antelope lying dead on the veld and *aasvoëls* sitting on it, and gorging, eating first the eyes then everything else. Mr. Henry was staring at these ugly vulture birds with their bald heads and bare necks. They stopped there, while Mr. Henry watched and September went looking for ostriches. Once the *aasvoëls* were finished eating, they waddled around and tried to fly but they were too heavy. They had to run a long way along the ground before they could get up in the air. Mr. Henry was laughing his head off and, as one tried to rise up, he caught it with his *sjambok* around its neck and it came crashing down to the ground. Mr. Henry didn't know about the *goggas* and ticks and lice that live on the *aasvoëls*. They came buzzing in a cloud and he screamed for September. September made a fire and the *goggas* went away.

By the time the goat-suckers came out, at sundown, they had only found four ostriches. They came home in the almost-dark, driving the ostriches in front of them, the goat-suckers flying about in the bushes, calling and weeping, carrying their short, broad heads and wide bills like tragedies. They rode between mimosa bushes and again Mr. Henry had to stop and look at all the small things—the birds, beetles and locusts—stuck on the mimosa thorns. The smell hits you in the face like a smack but Mr. Henry didn't mind. He wanted to watch the butcher-bird flying down with his food in his mouth and sticking it on one of those thorns for a midnight snack. They had to move on so he broke off a thorn with its dead locust as if it was a piece of Vienna sausage stuck on a cocktail stick. He wanted to show Miss Beatrice. He wanted to start a collection.

Puff-adders, *Baas* Henry. *Pas op*. Watch out. September was looking down as they rode, looking for puff-adders lying there on the last of the warmth, their skins the same colour as the ground. Mr. Henry dropped his thorn and the rest of the trip he was quiet, hearing each breath as if it was the last one. Puff-adder in the sand, puff-adder leaping at your horse, at your ostriches, at your very own throat.

I have walked on the veld at dusk, the dogs running in front of me. I know what it's like to imagine those puff-adders, not running away like most snakes, but coming at you backwards, angry for waking them up. I get scared for the dogs. I pray that the Lord will not take one of them away from me and He never has. Me and the dogs walk together through the Valley of the Shadow of Death and it's all right. When the stars come out, just before we get home, I say thank you. Maybe Jack is waiting on the *stoep*, and we'll drown those puff-adders with one sip of gin.

I am sure by the time Mr. Henry got home, he was *poep-scared*. He got off his horse and his feet were numb, hitting the ground like two useless old blocks. September was the one who chased the ostriches into the big *kraal*, who counted fifteen other birds that the other *volkies* had found. Mr. Henry went into the house, which was like a blessing. He left his horse standing outside by the front door. Miss Beatrice saw the old mare there, polite like a visitor, and so she led her away and watered her and gave her some hay.

As she worked with the horse in the dark, she kept talking. Where have you been? What places have you seen? What is the life of the world? Heat rose off the old mare in waves, and, as the waves rolled over Miss Beatrice, she was walking again, across the veld in the night, floating and fearless. She laid her hand on the horse's back, where the hair was pressed flat and dark from the saddle, and she could almost see the mimosa bushes. But she didn't see Mr. Henry catching the *aasvoël* with his *sjambok*, the dead bird lying on the ground next to the antelope bones.

By the time she walked into the sitting-room, Mr. Henry was already *babbelas*, sitting on the floor, next to the hole for the fountain, an empty bottle holding up his hand. He was crying, the tears dropping down onto his thighs. He didn't want to go out again, he said. Not tomorrow, not the next day, not ever. My hand, he sobbed, My right hand. He held it up, as if it was on fire. It's almost all gone.

Miss Beatrice took his hand, and it lay in her palm all folded up like the broken foot of a sparrow. She uncurled the fingers and they lay down for a moment and then they rolled up all over again. Who was the one who could rattle the seeds inside Mr. Henry's head? Who could open the shutters and pull the right levers? She was sorry for him the way you're sorry for someone like Slappie although Mr. Henry came in, and he came out of it, and you could never be sure. When she dropped his hand, he was still crying and suddenly she heard herself say, I'll go out with September tomorrow. I'll catch the ostriches.

That night, she almost forgot the big belly that sat under her dress. She found her old clothes—the convict shirt and Mr. Henry's pants—and opened the seams. She made patches and joins with bits of her old dresses, the green, two reds and a grey, and by the time she was finished she was dressed like a tinker man. She lay down in bed in those clothes, all ready for tomorrow. Her dreams had buck in them, and a hare or two, the hares leaping over her horse like acrobats. The *kaffirs* always say that the spirits of your relatives and friends live in the hares and Miss Beatrice could see the face of her dead *ouma* and her uncle under those stiff brown ears. She wanted to talk to them about living in the veld but then it was morning and Nomsa was there by the bed, with coffee and rusks.

It was so early, there was dew on the fence when she went outside. September had the old mare ready and one of the donkeys and the old mare looked at Miss Beatrice like Smithy, a girl she knew from boarding-school. Smithy had buck-teeth and very few friends. She patted the mare's nose and said Smithy and the mare whinnied a little as if she knew. September was standing there, hanging quietly inside his skin, waiting for Mr. Henry to come. No Mr. Henry, Miss Beatrice said. He's too tired. She looked at his shoes which were not really shoes, just flaps of old *veldskoene* held together with string. She saw his hands, the thumb-nail so stumpy, so hard, as he moved something for his pipe between his fingers. Her heart jagged when she saw that nail.

He held her horse for her and she could see the peppercorns on his head and smell the *pondokkie* all over again. She nearly ran back to the house, to Mr. Henry in bed, ready to shake him and send him out with September. But the sky was blue as a promise and the veld lay in front of them with its stones and its flowers and all the things that crawled and flew that she wanted to see.

They walked, horse-length by horse-length, Miss Beatrice feeling her baby rolling forwards and backwards, banging on her bones. September had to find the ostriches, the way you look for things in a picture when you are small. There's a cat in the leaves of a tree, and another one under the wheelbarrow, and look, there's one sitting inside the wall. The female ostriches you saw when they moved, lifting themselves off the ground in a rush, waving their bush-coloured feathers. The black-and-white males you could see when they were small as a tickey. By the time you rode to them, they were behind your right eye, drifting like clouds. Miss Beatrice pointed, and September went after them, and the hooves they were riding on spun and twirled in the dust. She forgot everything else except the land that was in front of them, with its brown grasses and low, minty bushes, its thorns bleaching in the sun.

She stopped seeing the *korhaans* and yellow canaries and even missed the dead *aasvoël* from yesterday. She was sifting the earth and the sky for ostriches, and each one she saw was a prize. September had four, then five, six, eleven and by the time the sun lay on top of their heads like a burning iron helmet, there were fifteen birds rushing in front of them, September driving them with his mimosa stick, Miss Beatrice trying to head them off in the front. They rode to the big *kraal* and Miss Beatrice held the gate while September drove them in. Some of the birds were getting *bedonnerd*, and they sat down and flapped, and then broomed and broomed like lions, lifting themselves up and running at September, swinging their necks in a fury. Miss Beatrice heard herself screaming and he looked at her, just before escaping through the gate, his eyes meeting hers for the first time that day. They were orange-black like the water in the Kaaimans River, and she got such a *skrik* she nearly fell off her horse. They were close as they'd been that morning on the ground, in the *pondokkie*, only this time there was no shock, only wanting.

TEN

The phone rings and I'm leaving Miss Beatrice burning for September. I'm climbing over Jack and trying to pull the door open. The door bites into him and he rolls and I pull and pull. The phone is still ringing. Maybe it's the hospital and they're calling to tell me my ma is dead but that doesn't work because she's dead already. Jack starts to open his eyes and I end up crawling over him and going out of the door like one of the dogs.

Hello? I am panting and the phone is crackling. It's Gerda and I don't understand anything. Where's Flippie? He always talks. Is he dead? She's shouting like bricks coming in through the window and breaking the glass.

Christmas is back with an empty sleigh and some packets.

There's the tree! There's the tree! That's why Jack was drinking. He put it up when I was gone with the dogs. It has white branches and nice little bells. Jack stuck on some dog bones and dog toys and bright *lappies.*

Hello! Hello! Gerda is gone.

I must get ready. I must cook a nice goose or a ham and some *boerewors.*

The house is hot like an oven and I open the windows. I open and open and open.

My arms don't hurt. My back doesn't hurt. I can't wait to see my big sister.

The dogs are following me. The dogs want to know what happened. I'll tell you, I say, and the meths is staring me in the face. It's under the sink. My hand is on the bottle and then I stop. I can have it later. I can have it with supper.

The next day, Mr. Henry was better and so he went out on the veld, waving his *sjambok*, ready to catch the very last ostrich. Now Miss Beatrice was the one who looked at herself the way you look at a stranger. Her green eyes seemed to be borrowed. She touched her belly and almost forgot what was in there. She wanted to run like the hares and the springboks, losing herself in the holes and the crevices, or just stand in the wind, on top of a *koppie*. Mr. Jacobs was lost, and so was her heart. What was left was the cage of the body, with its secret fires. She looked at Nomsa and what lay in front of them like toast on a tray was the question, What comes when the house is broken in half?

By the time it was dark, the big *kraal* was full. The ostriches stood jammed together, their necks thick as roots, waving in an upside-down sea. It wasn't an easy night, with the clouds rolling above, as if tomorrow was Jericho. Mr. Henry came home, and there was a feather in his hat which seemed more like a knife. They ate in the kitchen, two boiled potatoes and two eggs, while Nomsa sat outside on the step, throwing her bones. Mr. Henry had said a long time ago, Not here. Not near the house.

The plucking would send them all the way back to England, on a boat, with money in bags. She would watch the sun flicker and die, and her child would grow in the damp like a spot of fresh moss. Perhaps she could hide in the Caves with her child, until the train tore its way to Cape Town, with Mr. Henry laughing his head off in the dining car, his fingers and toes almost forgotten.

I have seen those throw-bones the witchdoctors have. They look like the knuckles and ankles of little devil-people. I have been in a *muti* shop with the hanging dead animals, the monkey still screaming, the flesh rotting on his back. He was wearing a big sign that said "No Smoking". I have seen the Indians on stools, grinding the herbs. I went with Gerda and we wanted something for her ears, so that she could hear again but we were too scared to ask. So we left. On the way home, Gerda hit me on the arm so hard it was lame for the rest of the day.

Nomsa got her bones from her *ouma*, who got them from her *ouma*. Miss Beatrice held her breath, inside the house, as Nomsa shook them and rattled them, and spilled them out on the ground. Was she throwing for England? Was she throwing for the baby? Was it September? You can see any shapes you want, Miss Beatrice was thinking. I want the shape of this farm. Nomsa clicked and said *Ai!* and Mr. Henry growled back at her, the way you growl at a dog. There was silence. Then Nomsa slipped into the night like a fish and all that was left was a small dip in the sand.

It was a night of big dreams. Mr. Henry was drowning in money and feathers. He was travelling the world in a fabulous coach. In Russia, he met a man with fire-breathing dragons on his coat. He skated on glaciers and fell in with painters. Miss Beatrice dreamed she gave birth to an ostrich egg and she couldn't get it open. It was hard and closed and it made her very sad. The ostriches in the big *kraal* looked at her and they all wept, tears falling into their prime whites. Miss Beatrice wanted them to stop because Mr. Henry would be furious if their feathers got soaked but they didn't listen. She was trying to stop the crying with cloths and bandages but the tears kept rolling out of their eyes, as big as grapes. The bandages turned pink and Miss Beatrice realized that it was ostrich blood she was mopping up and it was coming down in buckets.

She woke up with the echo of her own scream still plastered on the walls. Mr. Henry lay curled and stiff next to her, like a sea shell. She looked out of the window, the blood banging in her ears, and saw the willows by the dam and the windmill and the incubating-room, the edge of the big *kraal*, the *pondokkies* with their smoke spirals, the stable for the horses, the *koppie* where you could see the world from. She could just see a few ostriches in the big *kraal* if she stretched her neck. Their feathers were clean and there were no ruby-dark puddles at their feet. The world was just as it should be, with guinea fowl running in the dust and a cool breeze touching the trees. The long summer was beginning to fade.

But the dream was still there so she shook Mr. Henry and said, It's not the right time. He stared at her, his eyes runny, his mouth dry and open. The plucking, she said. I think you should wait. It's too cold for the birds.

You can't tell a man what to do, especially in the morning. Miss Beatrice didn't know that, or she forgot. Jack would have *klapped* me or told me to jump in the lake if I said, The dogs are too cold, or, The water is too brackish. Let's give them milk. One morning I gave him a mango for breakfast, instead of the usual *boerewors* and eggs, and he shouted, You call this food? I was going to tell him that a man on the TV said orange-coloured food is good for your bowels but I knew it was the wrong time. It's better to say something like that when you're relaxing and the dogs aren't barking. You just take a big *sluk* of your drink and say, You know, I saw something on the TV once. A man had a mango in his hand.

Miss Beatrice had a big *bek*. A big mouth. She wasn't like me that way. But she was lucky on the morning of the plucking because Mr. Henry was still in his dream, flying around Russia with that dragon-coat man. He looked at her as if she was some girl walking across a farmyard with sticks on her head. He didn't even say Rubbish. He was too busy dressing for Paris, with a floppy black bow tie and one of those soft white hats. He even put on his cream-coloured gloves, with mother-of-pearl buttons. Miss Beatrice never said, Are you going into town? She knew him too well. He loved all those eyes on him, even if they were *kaffirs* and ostriches. She watched him snip the hairs in his nose with a gentleman's instrument. Then he took off his gloves and rubbed his clay-coloured cheeks with some scent on his palms. He turned to Miss Beatrice like a toy soldier, his heels nearly clicking. Goodbye and good luck, he said to himself, after tapping her cheek with his lips. Wish me for England. I'm coming, she told him, and her voice sounded like something blown through a tube.

And she pulled on the convict shirt with all the blue patches. The pants she tied up with string and she jammed on a hat, one of the hats of the *volkies*. What are you doing? You'll get yourself lice! Take off that hat. Mr. Henry sounded *naar* and a little annoyed. I'm not staying behind. Miss Beatrice bit each word. I'm going outside. September! She ran out of the house, shouting, I need my own horse. Mr. Henry was behind her, telling someone, September, Nomsa, Mr. Jacobs or Miss Beatrice's ma, She can't ride anymore. She's all done with the world. She's getting ready to hatch. And then it came out of Miss Beatrice's mouth, the truth under the floorboards, in the dust under the sofa, in the place where the spiders draw their lines in the air, It's my farm, you know. It's mine and not yours. My father's money.

You're my wife, Mr. Henry lunged at her sleeve but he missed. Now take off that hat and go back to your bed! The plucking boys were standing by the big *kraal*, still as the trees, watching but not watching. Mr. Henry pretended to drop something on the ground. He bent down and got up, his hands empty, his eyes trying to point holes in Miss Beatrice's heart, the *sjambok* tucked into his belt like a snake.

The horse was there, the old mare from before, and so was September, holding two others, a gelding and a donkey. Miss Beatrice stepped into September's cupped hands and lifted herself and her stomach onto the saddle. Mr. Henry was growling at her, Don't pluck my prime whites. Don't you dare. Miss Beatrice didn't even bother to say, How can I? She just stared at him as he took the gelding's reins and threw himself over his back, the poor gelding snorting and pawing.

Their horses rubbed flanks and the old mare whinnied, straining to get in front of Mr. Henry's horse as if it was a race. Hold her back, Mr. Henry was shouting. Miss Beatrice held her horse steady and September on the donkey stepped in between them.

The big *kraal* opened in to the plucking *kraal*, which was much smaller. September opened the gate and the plucking-boys with their mimosa sticks drove all the ostriches into the plucking *kraal*. The birds ran with their wings flapping, dust from their feet and their feathers rising into Miss Beatrice's nose and down Mr. Henry's throat. September had a cloth over his mouth and was shouting from under the cloth, *Hierso! Vang hom! Laat hom los!* Here! Catch him! Let him go! Miss Beatrice was staring at the thicket of purple-red ostrich thighs, the long feet with their terrible nails. The thighs pumped forwards not backwards and you could imagine the worst kinds of kicks. The last bird, a thin, spiky brown female, almost ran off into the veld but Miss Beatrice took off her hat and waved it and the ostrich nearly swallowed the whole thing. September was there with his stick, and Mr. Henry pulled his *sjambok* out of his belt and the ostrich ran away from them, straight into the middle of the plucking *kraal*, into the frothing sea of feathers.

It was the same as the branding only there was no fire. There was the sharp smell of ammonia, from the ostriches' piss, and sweat-drops were shining on the plucking boys' faces, even though it was cool. Miss Beatrice felt tight and scared in her chest, as if she was one of the hedgehog-coloured female birds, her wings pinned down by the mass of ostrich bodies and feathers. She was trying to remember birds. Where was Blackie and Loskop? Where was Flatfoot and Silly Girl? But it was just feathers and underground panic, the plucking boys grunting, and Mr. Henry waving his *sjambok* like the wrong kind of cowboy.

Then the ostriches were ready to be driven, one by one, into the plucking-box. They don't go in without fussing and shaking, and some of them have to be dragged, so one plucking boy was waiting at the neck and another one was there to push from the wings. September grunted and the plucking boys shoved and the first bird was suddenly in the plucking-box, the wood bar closing from behind, the bird's round body stuck in the tightest of triangles.

When it came time for the plucking, Miss Beatrice looked up by mistake and got the sun in her eye. So the first bird, a male, had black around the edges of his head and his neck and even his prime whites looked dark. Two of the plucking boys stood on each side of the plucking-box, the ostrich so squashed he couldn't kick or turn around. One boy stood outside the *kraal* to receive the feathers. September put a bag over the ostrich's head with a hole for the beak to stick out of. The ostrich got quiet and serious as if he was the hangman. Then the plucking boys snipped with the pruning-scissors with two bends in them and those heavenly wings were suddenly bare. There was a fight about the stumps. Mr. Henry wanted to pull everything, stumps, tails and even the feathers on the legs and September was saying, *Nee, Hulle sal vrek van die koud. Hulle sal vrek.* Too cold, they will die.

There's no word for *vrek* in the English language. Animals *vrek* and people die in Afrikaans but in English everything just dies. Sometimes I think Gerda will *vrek*, or Jack. It will be dark and horrible and they will be shouting my name, and their shouts will turn into the sound of jackals at night and I will run out of the house to get away from the sight of it.

This wasn't dying, this was plucking. The tail feathers and the black feathers on the body aren't snipped off with the shears like the prime whites. They're pulled out. The plucking boys tugged at the tails with their hands as if they were pulling carrots out of the ground. The feathers came out with a tearing sound that made goose-bumps come out all over Miss Beatrice's arms. Her skin looked bumpy and pinkish as if she was the bird being plucked. She lurched in the saddle and almost fell down but when she heard Mr. Henry hissing under his breath—She wanted to come, Miss Bee, Miss Queen Bee—she sat up again, straight as the head-girl. The tearing was like ripping sheets and it kept on going.

The naked ostrich let out of the other side of the plucking-box looked ugly as death, and just as upset. He was in the bigger *kraal* now, running a little skew across the stones, as if he couldn't balance right. He stopped and shook himself and then stood very still, twisted to the left, like the broken branch of a tree that just hangs and hangs. Miss Beatrice looked into his eye and she saw a milky greenish-grey egg getting *vrot*. Soon there were other ostriches in there with him, some of them raw with patches on their bodies, and blood-spots. They all looked a bit mad.

I have never seen a fresh-plucked ostrich. They never take all the feathers at once. Ostriches with all their feathers on are our trademark but you never see completely naked ones on postcards saying, Come to Oudtshoorn. See our ostrich farms. Even when you're driving along the National Road, you hardly even see the half-plucked ones. Maybe they hide them in sheds so that people don't get bilious along the road when they see all that stretched, horny ostrich skin with bare wings and a few black tail feathers and leg feathers left. What you usually see when you come in the car is the veld and the mountains and as you come closer and closer to the main ostrich district you start to see a black-and-white speck, with a neck, then some more full-feathered birds dotted around and then you know you are home. Gerda used to jump up and down in the back of the car, grunting and laughing when she saw the first ostrich.

I don't know if September was worried about what people would think when they came to visit Oudtshoorn or whether he was just *bedonnerd*. But he kept slamming the yellow wood arms of the plucking-box shut so hard that wood nearly splintered. He was saying something under his breath about the Ostrich with fire under its armpits and how the Ostrich was going to drop that fire and make everything burn down at once. The more cross he got, the more nervous were the plucking boys and the more the ostriches flapped and shook and pissed. When Miss Beatrice looked at the *kraal* with the plucked birds she got all hot and bothered too. It was like all those Evil Eyes staring at you, saying this is very, very bad. After thirteen birds, September threw the bag he had been putting on the ostriches' heads onto the ground. An ostrich stepped on it right away. Pick it up, Mr. Henry was screaming, You black bastard!

September was shaking as he stood there, the whites of his eyes hot as steam. He said nothing to Mr. Henry. All the plucking boys were still, and you could feel a long groan coming up from the ground. They all stood in the middle of the silence, not a church silence, more like the hiss of an afternoon before rain. Miss Beatrice swung herself clumsily off the back of her horse, and went over to the ostrich whose foot was on the plucking bag. She touched his knee. The ostrich moved. She scooped up the bag in her hand, and it was wet and streaked with ostrich droppings. She put it on one of the fence-posts and everyone stared at it, as if it was going to move and start talking.

But the stillness was broken and the plucking started up again, September walking with his face tight as a fist. I'll show him a lesson about birds, Mr. Henry growled at Miss Beatrice, I'll show that *kaffir* what's what. Miss Beatrice hardly heard him. She was staring at the fence-post and what she had done. She had made the plucking go on. The plucking boy taking the feathers was piling them onto a cart, the prime whites and the tails and the female feathers all separate. Miss Beatrice watched the cart getting full and the feathers rippling like wheat in the breeze and there was no going back. All the birds were getting stripped, what Mr. Henry had wanted. It was like fire burning the fields down to the last blade of grass only there was nothing hot like a spark. It was careful and cold. Miss Beatrice tried not to hear that tearing sound of the tail-feathers being pulled but it got closer and closer, as if someone was tearing the ears off her head.

She turned the old mare but Mr. Henry bent over his horse's neck and caught the reins. Oh no, you don't, he said. You wanted to come. You have to stay until the very last ostrich. Isn't that what you wanted? What she really wanted was for him to disappear in front of her but he stayed very distinct, the same hard form she saw in her bed every morning. Where was the man who ran into the mountains, the thin, scared one, not this roughly made monkey, this scar? She felt something wet beneath her and saw that there was some pinkish blood on the saddle. Suddenly the world of feathers and Mr. Henry and September and the plucking boys disappeared and she was inside her body trying to fix the tiny blood vessel that had broken, trying to sew it together again. I have to go home, she said to Mr. Henry, showing him the pink spot on her skirt and the smear on the saddle. He looked away as if she had shown him something festering and rotten.

So Miss Beatrice wasn't there when the sun bled into the sky the way she bled onto the saddle, or when it sank down, exhausted, behind the thorn trees. She wasn't there when Mr. Henry followed September back to the sorting-shed, where the dust rose up from the feathers in big clouds. She never knew if September told Mr. Henry about the dream that wasn't a dream, in the *pondokkie* in the morning. Or was it just about the ostriches, all naked now, and driven together into the snow-sheds.

Whatever it was, they were now alone in the sorting-shed and September was piling up the cocks' wings and the hens' wings and the cocks' tails and the hens' tails and all the blacks and drabs on the shelves. Mr. Henry pulled his *sjambok* out of his pants and he was flicking it across the floor to see if he could pick up feathers that had fallen. He was practising, the way he had practised on the neck of that *aasvoël*. It wasn't long before the *sjambok* curled around September's ankle like a snake, and September fell down. I have to show you a lesson, Mr. Henry was saying, and this time the *sjambok* fell on September's shoulders, splitting the back of his shirt. September found an old branding iron on the ground and when he got up again, there was something in his hand. Mr. Henry was laughing now, and he was back on the *koppie*, his feet wrapped up, his soul flapping in the wind like a torn old blanket. He was dancing in the middle of an ice-cold flame and September was coming right at him, to put that branding iron right on top of his heart. He had to jump like one of those hares who are your very own relatives. He was hopping so much to get out of September's way that he fell against one of the shelves and a pile of tipped whites settled all over him, as if he was the ostrich now, ready to be plucked.

September lunged at him, and more feathers came down, lots of fancy-coloureds and mixed tails. He slipped on the feathers and crashed down and Mr. Henry rolled out of the way, rolling in prime whites and second whites, rolling all over his best feathers. That's when he thought of England and ruin and all the places he wouldn't see if the feathers were spoiled so he leapt to his feet and got to work with the *sjambok*. The *sjambok* twisted the branding iron out of September's hand but September pulled one of the sorting-shelves off the wall and came at Mr. Henry. Mr. Henry remembered the *aasvoël* trying to fly and it was just like September trying to lift the plank into the air and throw it at him. When he wrapped the tail of the *sjambok* around September's neck all he saw was that fat old bird, too heavy to get off the ground. The sound of the neck breaking was just the same.

I don't know why but when I think of Mr. Henry and September, I think of that man in McGregor who was on the TV. He was tired of the *kaffirs*, he said, who had their *pondokkies* right near the white people's backyards. Of course this kind of thing is quite new. They are not in the locations where they are supposed to be. They can come out and put up some corrugated iron and a few bits of wire and suddenly there they are, right by your house. This man on the TV, Gerrit Potgieter was his name, got upset because those *kaffirs* just let their dogs roam all over the place and one day his dog, a big Rhodesian Ridgeback male, went out to the *pondokkies* because one of the *kaffir* dogs was in heat. There was a big dog fight and the Ridgeback came home with a torn ear so Gerrit Potgieter went out to the *pondokkies* to show the *kaffir* whose dog was in heat a big lesson. Something like the lesson Mr. Henry wanted to show September. Gerrit Potgieter later told the policeman that he had warned the *kaffir* before about letting his dogs loose and not keeping them tied up. Anyway, he got to the *pondokkies* and there was the bitch lying in the sun like it was nothing and her owner was sitting on a broken plastic chair behind her, packing tobacco into his pipe. He was a Coloured man, I think. Gerrit Potgieter shouted at him and there was a fight and the next thing that happened was that the Coloured man was lying down on the ground and his head was cracked open where the side of Gerrit's gun had hit him. His wife was crying and screaming. They showed that part on the TV, where she was saying that she didn't know how to feed her children because now her husband was dead and all because of the Ridgeback's ear. Gerrit Potgieter was surprised when they came and arrested him and all he kept saying over and over again was, I told that bloody *kaffir* to keep his dogs tied up. I warned him.

He didn't know you can't do that anymore. He didn't know about the Courts. When Mr. Henry killed September, it was different. Mr. Henry just put the *sjambok* back in his pants and went back to the house and there was no policeman knocking at the door the next morning. That evening he sat down and ate the stew that Nomsa had cut up potatoes and onions for, that Miss Beatrice had cooked in the long afternoon. He didn't change his clothes. There were small broken feathers caught in his shirt and his hair was almost white with feather-dust. There were scratches on his hands from the branding-iron and there was one long brownish-red streak on his neck. He said he was starving and ate everything on his plate. After the meal, Miss Beatrice rang the little silver bell from Sheffield but Nomsa didn't come to the table with the tray.

Miss Beatrice went into the kitchen. The wood fire for

the stove had gone out right when the blood stopped coming. The potato skins were still on the table and the black pots stood all over the place. Miss Beatrice thought she heard moaning but Mr. Henry said she mustn't go outside. She mustn't look for trouble. By the time she had finished in the kitchen, her hands chilled from the cold, brackish water that came from the pump, Mr. Henry had cleaned himself with a damp cloth and gone to bed. It was one of those nights where you imagine a big, hairy spider in every corner of the ceiling, where there's a scorpion hiding in your socks. Miss Beatrice lit all the candles she could find and sat in the living-room, right by the old hole for the fountain. She couldn't help remembering the night Mr. Jacobs had come, with his family, and the red-gold colour of his skin in the candlelight and the soft heat of his eyes falling on the faces of his daughters. Now the room was empty, and the gay pillows seemed tired and useless, and all there was was shadow and places for bad things to hide. But she couldn't go into the bedroom, because Mr. Henry was there, and she knew now that he was the most frightening animal of them all, worse than puff-adders and tarantulas and even a *boomslang*.

There was fire outside. She could see torches and burning sticks when she looked out of the window and it wasn't just the reflection of the candles. Something was big and terrible in the dark, and the *volkies* were moving around. Now and again there was a scream, followed by cries and stamping. Miss Beatrice closed her eyes, lying on the floor against the pillows, and tried to imagine that the sounds outside were just waves, and that the house was a ship. It wasn't like the night where she had stood staring at the veld, watching the night animals. This night you couldn't look because what you saw might turn you into stone forever and forever. Miss Beatrice knew this, she knew she had to sleep and sleep, until the day was there, until something had shifted in the air and some of the poison was gone.

She dreamed she watched September dig a deep hole in the ground. The spade kicked up a pile of red earth and she could see earthworms crawling in it, some of them with their bodies chopped in half from the spade. When the hole was deep enough and wide enough, September lifted her into the air so that she could feel the wind blowing the skirt of her dress over her head. Then he put her in the hole with him and the earth all around them was damp. His lips were on her neck and they were damp too. Miss Beatrice felt the length of her body and she pressed it against September's hard bones. The sides of the hole moved closer and closer together and earth filled her open hands and covered her eyes. She wanted to scream but she couldn't because she was packed with earth and September and there was no space left anywhere, no space even to breathe. She woke up and the baby was turning inside her, pushing on her back, and an overturned candle was lying on the floor drowning in its own wax.

Jack is moving in the house and he sounds like a wolf. I must sit down and be quiet.

You never know what he will do. Gerda is coming, I say, when he crashes into the kitchen.

Merry Christmas.

The baby's ghost lies between us like the ghost of baby

Jesus except Jesus is alive after so many years and our baby is dead.

You don't have to walk the dogs. They're sleeping.

He's raising his hand and it's near my face or is it the meths that he reads in my eyes. The blue meths that he wants, that I want, that's under the sink.

Gerda will save us.

ELEVEN

In the morning you could smell ash in the air and the sky was heavy and grey. Mr. Henry said nothing when Nomsa wasn't there in the kitchen, making *pap* for breakfast. The kitchen was empty, and felt like a ruin or an old cave. Miss Beatrice was the one who fixed the fire for the coffee. All they had to eat that morning was some bread and butter. September's death lay like a skin over the house and the farm. Mr. Henry moved under it, forgetting what he had done, lost inside his shrinking feet and hands, and the song of England that beat inside his head. He started counting the feathers, the ones that were broken, and the ones he could sell. That's when Miss Beatrice remembered the hole in her dream, and the blood on Mr. Henry's neck when he came home, and she wanted to ask, Where's Nomsa? Where's September? What have you done? But the house caught her, with its thick walls and mean little windows, and she was silent. Inside was what she knew, and outside was the truth. She wanted to stay in the house forever, eating the last of the bread and the *biltong* and watching the Karoo winter come and go through the window. But the baby pressed down inside her, burrowing low into her woman's bone and she knew that she had to walk out of that big front door. She had to cross over the river to the other side if she ever wanted to sit on a rock in the sun, running her fingers through the hair of a child.

Mr. Henry wanted to pile all the feathers into a cart and drive the cart to Oudtshoorn. He wanted to go to the feather auction house and get the very best price for what he had done. One of the *volkies* would get the horse ready and some of yesterday's plucking boys could help with loading the feathers. He just had to get up from his chair and tell them to do it. When thoughts of September came into his head, he thought, April. Oh, to be in April. But mixed in with the butterflies and daffodils and fat English cows was yesterday and the mess of the sorting-shed and what was lost, and was still lost. That's when he started counting again, medium blacks and long blacks, chicken feathers and damaged white tails, fringed whites, tipped whites and white tails with black butts.

Still counting, he left the house. Miss Beatrice stared at his back, jealous of those feet that still carried him, that were whole even though he was not. She didn't see how he stopped when he got to the sorting-shed, and couldn't go in. Even if the body was gone, it would always be there. He remembered the long plank and September's black eyes and the peppercorns on his head. Mr. Henry could still hear the sound of his own laugh. Then he thought about the crack as the neck broke and the *aasvoël* lying on the ground getting eaten by *goggas*. He was out on the open veld where the sun bleached and forgave and life lay inside the fat little leaves of succulents.

So he took all that light with him when he stepped into the dark. He was on the *koppie* again, looking down. Everything inside the sorting-shed was the way things are in a doll's house. The feathers suddenly looked very short. Even the plank lying on the floor looked like a small little stick. He looked at the spot where September had crashed down and that was no bigger than a dog's body. But still, it felt as if something had been stolen. As if there was a hole in the air where something used to be. Mr. Henry took a big pile of feathers from one of the shelves and laid them there, to fill up the hole.

When he went outside again, the sky seemed to tilt and suddenly he wanted to vomit. He went behind the shed and dug a hole in the ground with his hands and bent over it, feeling everything that was broken and skew coming up his throat like a dirty old river. When he was finished, he covered up the hole with sand. He stood up, and the sky was pale and there was a chill in the air. That's when he saw the first dead ostrich, lying there in the big *kraal* in front of him, right by the fence. He died on the fences, Mr. Henry was thinking. Stupid old bird, trying to get out. But when he walked closer, he saw that there were dead ones in the middle of the *kraal* as well, their long necks on the ground the masts of boats that had tipped over. The world was still skew, and that river started to heave inside him all over again.

He looked towards the mountains, and saw threads of old fires from last night coming up from the *pondokkies*. There were no *volkies* coming to the farm to work, no plucking boys at the *kraals*. Should he go to the *pondokkies* and see where everyone was? Should he take his shotgun and his *sjambok*? Should he go looking for Nomsa, who used to sit there on the back *stoep* with her medicine bones and give him the *grils*? Instead of going forwards, he went backwards to the house where Miss Beatrice was, to get her to help. She wanted to come to the plucking so now she could help him load up the feathers and put those dead birds away. He hadn't even counted how many. They would drive into Oudtshoorn with their bounty of feathers and sell them. Then they would sell this terrible farm and all those dead birds. Before anyone found out, they would be walking in the Gardens in Cape Town, under the shade of Table Mountain, ready to set sail the next day.

Miss Beatrice was sitting on the floor on some pillows, with her dress lifted, staring at her belly. Next to her, where the hole for the fountain used to be, was a big tin filled with button fasteners. She was going to fix things but then her stomach got in the way and so she was just sitting there and not thinking about anything. She was watching the baby swim inside her. The wave that moved under her skin, across the top part of her belly near her belly-button, made her smile. Suddenly Mr. Henry was there, standing in front of her, his face all white and blotchy and something that smelled bad sticking to the front of his shirt.

Help me, he said, with the feathers. And the ugliness of the night was back with her again, in the fear that tightened his mouth, in the words that came at her like hard little balls. Where is everyone? She wanted to say but couldn't, not wanting the answer, not wanting to know past the walls of her own skin. Again, the question drifted and died between them. She pulled down her dress, left her tin with the button-fasteners on the floor and joined him.

We don't have to do everything, Mr. Henry was saying. Just separate the hens' tails and the cocks' tails and so on. There's a sorting-room in the town where they do the rest. They're expert sorters, those Coloured men. They make such nice and tight little bunches. They do everything, from the scruffy bodies and tails to the prime whites. Chicks, wings, bodies, tails, spadonas, drab-cut bodies, long cuts, flos, broken tails, bloods, female bodies. They know all the names, just like the Jews. We have to find ourself a Jew buyer. If not that Jacobs man, then another one of his tribe. But they say he's the best. He knows what feather will sell, what plume is in fashion. And the man started off selling cooking pots and mouth-organs.

Mr. Henry was talking like this while Miss Beatrice was walking with him, and staring into the *kraals* at the collapsing birds. They were swaying, those lumpy, plucked bodies with their naked wingbones, bloodstains and feather stumps, on top of the stick legs. Look, Miss Beatrice said, pointing at them. They're dancing, Mr. Henry replied. She pointed again, at the birds dead on the ground, some near the fences. Those ones are not dancing, Mr. Henry said, so leave them alone. Miss Beatrice looked around for the *volkies* who weren't there, who knew about ostriches and stop-sickness and water on the heart but the land was quiet and it was just her and Mr. Henry, walking, as the birds fell and died. The sky was white as a chicken's egg and even the thorn bushes and prickly pears looked old and grey. Where is September? She finally said, when each step on the dried-up ground was a step closer to the inside of hell.

September is over and done with, Mr. Henry replied. It's going to be June, or perhaps even April, when our boat docks in England. We'll have two springs and two summers. Your mother will be turning the fat English soil and you'll be sitting with rose petals and a baby on your lap. That's a boat I'm not taking, Miss Beatrice told him, her hands holding the life in her belly. I'm not having my baby at sea. No, I'm not. Oh, rubbish, Mr. Henry snapped back, you'll do as I say. You're my wife. Miss Beatrice felt as top-heavy as the birds and held onto one of the fences. Where is September? She said, all over again. Where is September, the man, and Nomsa, his wife?

There was a thud behind the fence-post she was holding, as another ostrich staggered and fell down on the ground. He's gone, Mr. Henry finally answered, he's taken a holiday. He said he'd be back in four days. But you know how it is with those *hotnots*. They ride off and never come back. She's with him, as far as I know.

Miss Beatrice believed because she couldn't remember the night anymore, with its grieving and fires. She had locked the door on her terror and that dream in the hole. Mr. Henry was swallowing the key, and she let him.

I'm worried about our birds, she said. We must help them. Save the ones that are still standing up. And the chicks. How are they? So they went to the shady spot under the trees, not far from the house, where the *kaffir* boys used to come and look after the smallest of ostriches, where they fed them prickly-pear leaves and other green things cut up small. Of course the *kaffir* boys were all gone. The chicks, who used to hold up their cheeky little heads above those bristly, tortoiseshell bodies, had their beaks drooping forwards and downwards. Their plucked skins were pinkish-grey with a few leftover feathers here and there. Miss Beatrice knew what those dipped heads meant but she sat down on the ground and lifted them into her lap, and tried to feed them some of the prickly-pear leaves. They died in her lap, one by one, and she cried for them, her tears dripping onto the remnants of their rough little feathers. I blame the *kaffir* boys, Mr. Henry was saying, looking across the brown land. I have seen them kicking the chicks in the air, like balls. They fall down and if they don't break their legs, their insides are upset.

How could you? She was thinking, but quiet. How could you pluck them to death? You're making them weak, he said, when she lifted the last little chick onto her lap. It's like babies. They learn discipline when you leave them alone. Don't look at me like that, as if it's my fault. The plucking was nothing. They probably had yellow liver. And the *kaffir* boys finished them off. Let's open one and see if his liver looks like orange peel. No! Miss Beatrice shouted. Don't touch him. Go get a spade.

She sat there under the trees, the dead chicks all around her, like broken-down lamps. She heard a thick flapping of wings above her head as an *aasvoël* sank onto a branch. By the time Mr. Henry came back there were three of them, terrible relatives with meat on their minds. They watched as Mr. Henry dug a shallow grave for the chicks and Miss Beatrice laid them to rest, sprinkling prickly pears and mimosa thorns over their bodies. By the time they got up and went to the *kraal* of the full-grown birds, the baby felt as heavy as a cannonball. Miss Beatrice held her belly as if it was going to drop onto the ground and break open and lie there to get eaten by the *aasvoëls*.

She and Mr. Henry opened the gate to one of the breeding camps and the two living birds stared at them with their milky eyes, their beaks open, their breath coming out in short little pants. In the big *kraal* behind them were the dead ones, their bodies like scratched, sore rocks. There were no droppings on the ground, just ostrich bodies. Stop-sickness, Miss Beatrice said. She remembered what the Ostrich King had told her on the day of their chasing and she went up to one of the sick birds and put her hand up his rectum. Out came one of his droppings, hard as a stone. We must do the female, she called out to Mr. Henry who was in the next *kraal* dragging one of the dead birds by his giant toes. Do it yourself, he said, his voice bitter as aloes. She had heard of giving your birds enemas when the hand doesn't work but it was hard because of their bladders. But she got the lump out of the second bird too and that was that.

She went around like that nurse lady, Florence Nightingale, rescuing quite a few of the birds in this way. Some of the Guaranteed Breeders, the nicest-looking males and prettiest females. She kept thinking, Was it the plucking or some poisonous plant that had given them the stop-sickness? Or was it the *volkies* who had done something terrible because of the trouble with September? Perhaps they had disappeared into the veld, walking around like lots of Paulines. As she unstopped the ostriches, their heads lifted again, and some of them even flapped their wings, so transparent, so useless without even those beautiful plumes decorating them. The wings were skin and hollow bone, like those wing-bones of bird skeletons you see on the floors of the Caves. Their legs were the thick part, all muscle and power. They run with those legs faster than horses and she knew they could *skop* her into the fence before you could say *bokmakierie*.

As the ostriches got better, Miss Beatrice got worse. She saw all those legs coming at her, and that horrible toe-nail tearing her in half. Her face was hot from being outside and she could feel something wet pouring out of her *shoppie*. She looked down and saw that it had filled up her shoe. So she left the *kraal* of the living birds and went where Mr. Henry was, with the dead. He had piled most of them into a corner. Grab one of his feet, he said to Miss Beatrice. And she did. Bending and dragging made her feel like there was someone else driving her body, making her belly hard and numb. I'm sick, she said. Or else it's the beginning. Mr. Henry stared at her, as if she had trampled his mother to death. Go home, he said.

Miss Beatrice walked to the house, not seeing the willow trees or the pump, or the *pondokkies,* or even the sky and the mountains. Her belly was clenching like a giant fist and with it came the factory feeling that used to be in her head. But this time the machine was in her middle and it pressed down and across so hard that she had to stop walking. Sometimes she sat down, and sometimes she went on her hands and knees and pushed herself forwards like a drunk market lady. She didn't see Mr. Henry burning the dead birds but she smelled their skin and their insides and she thought it was herself burning like that. She didn't see Mr. Henry load up the cart with their feathers, not even sorting them, just grabbing fistfuls and armfuls and packing them down. She didn't see him harness the horses and drive away, the giant pile of feathers in the back like a black-and-white haystack. She didn't see him pass the *volkies* on the road, carrying the body of September in a rough coffin covered with aloes and all the bitter things of the veld. She didn't see how some of the feathers floated off the cart onto the coffin and lay there, and how those prime whites were buried in the grave with September. She didn't see how Nomsa looked at Mr. Henry and how her shadow fell across that cart filled with feathers, how it fell across Mr. Henry's face, and the heads of the horses. She didn't see how long that shadow hung over them, and darkened them.

And, after the body of September was in the ground, and all the birds who had died were burned, the *volkies* went back to their *pondokkies*. Miss Beatrice didn't see that either. All she saw was herself, and how she crawled to the house inch by inch until she was sitting in front of the whitewashed wall of her room. She lay herself against the wall because it looked cool, and she let it tear her skin as she rubbed against it. Then she was on the floor on her knees, her forehead pressed to the door, the smell of wood and dust in her nose. She lifted herself and walked around the bed and it seemed like a giant mountain. But the stamping and tearing inside her was even bigger and soon the bed was as small as a thimble.

Jack is holding the bread and I'm pouring the meths through it. It comes out into a cup looking like water.

I pour myself a *dop*. The bread is nice and blue.

I look at Jack, with the glass near my lips.

The only time I have seen you look *poep-scared*, I say, was when the baby was coming and I was crying for my ma.

Mus' I call her, you were asking, and all I could scream was Ma, ma, ma. She was in the garden when you telephoned, watching the convicts move some rocks around for a rock-garden she and my pa wanted to make. They like this plant that looks just like an elephant's foot and she had some aloes and other kinds of succulents. The rock-garden was also supposed to be like a fence because who is going to walk through some prickly pears and lots of other cactus to break into someone's house. Between that and the dogs and Pa's guns you know somebody is going to be looking for trouble when they walk in there by mistake. She was telling you about the convicts and how it was the cheapest way to have a garden, when you said, Ma, Connie is screaming bloody murder. You must come and do something. I think it's the baby. Tell her to have a nice *dop*, she told you. And that is what I did. I had some gin, and then I had myself some nice red wine and by the time Ma came over I was laughing like a drain.

Hou op, meisie, Ma was shouting, and I nearly pissed in my *broekies* from laughing so much. You and her, you held me up and put me in the back of the old *bakkie* with some blankets and a suitcase and I didn't even know what was in the suitcase. I wrapped a blanket over it and that was my pillow. You and Ma sat in the front and I was there in the back with the wind blowing up my dress and the wine and the gin still playing their song in my heart even though the pains were getting worse. I don't remember what happened when we got to the hospital except that the doctor looked like the principal of my Primary School and that's when I did piss in my panties. I thought he was going to hit me but he just put his hand on my arm and it was cold and smelled of something you use to clean mirrors. The bad part didn't happen until later.

While Miss Beatrice was there in the room *stoksielalleen*, Mr. Henry was driving to Oudtshoorn like a blind person, not even seeing the shadow over his head Nomsa had put there. He was going to go to the doctor, the one with ash on his shoe, and he was going to sell all his feathers and he didn't know which one to do first. Then he got all mixed up and was trying to unpack the feathers in the doctor's waiting room and everyone was staring at him and he suddenly realised he should be looking for Mr. Jacobs or going to the sorting-house. The horses had drifted off the road and the whole cart was almost upside down in a ditch. He was sleeping and waking, dreaming and talking, and nothing was straight anymore, not even the road. His hands on the reins looked like hands he had borrowed from a neighbour. He had to stop and write his name on the ground with a stick, and where he was going. Then he was worried about the sea washing it away before he remembered there was no sea. I am in the interior, he said, and his words sounded like words in a classroom on a very slow day. How he got there is a miracle. How he found his way to the sorting-house and then to the place where they have the feather auctions is another big miracle.

Outside the sorting-house, the Coloured men were squatting on the ground. Mr. Henry climbed down from the cart and asked one of the *klonkies*, *Wat gaan hier aan?* What's going on? with his terrible English accent. They didn't answer. Maybe they thought he was speaking English. Inside the sorting-room, in front of all the shelves stacked high with ostrich feathers, a lot of men were losing their tempers at once. Mr. Henry felt *naar*. He remembered that hole that he had vomited into. He remembered burning the ostrich bodies and now this. All this screaming, all these accents. Men from Ireland, from Russia, from Germany, from Poland, from Scotland and France all shouting about prices. The numbers whirled in his head and they made him remember the shrinking. Mr. Jacobs was there, in the middle of a sea of ostrich farmers, and he was holding onto his waist-coat as if someone was trying to tear it off his chest. A Polish man was holding up an old newspaper, with a headline, "London Goes Wild about Ostrich Feathers." And what about Vienna, he was shouting, and the Middle West! Someone else said, Berlin and Paris. We were getting one pound for one white feather! Then a man from Bavaria shouted, Leave him alone. He's a farmer just like you. And a buyer, a buyer, a buyer, a lot of different kinds of voices were saying, Who will buy all our feathers?

Mr. Henry just stood there and watched. He didn't say anything. An Afrikaans man was stamping his foot like Rumpelstilskin and shouting, A thousand pounds a *morgen*, that's what I paid for that *blerrie* farm. Like everybody else, he was shouting at Mr. Jacobs who was now trying to get out of the sorting-room. Mr. Henry heard him say, It's not over. It's just today and tomorrow and last week. Prices go up, prices go down. Then they go up again.

Mr. Henry found himself at the auction house, following the other farmers who were following Mr. Jacobs. The same thing was going on there. Everybody was crowding onto the platform with the auctioneer who looked like he wanted to bang his gavel on some of the farmers' heads, cracking them

open like soft-boiled eggs. An Afrikaner had a magazine
with fashion plates, drawings of ladies holding Pekingese
dogs in their arms, wearing hats so thick with ostrich
feathers you could hardly see underneath. Can't you read,
someone shouted at him, Look at the date! That's last year!
Another man, with glasses and a big moustache, had a picture torn out of a newspaper of a lady in a motor-car and she
was wearing a small hat that curled up around her ears with
roses and a some lace or a veil. No more feathers! The moustache man was shouting. They don't want any more. They're
fickle!

Mr. Henry remembered his own wife, Miss Beatrice, and
the baby, and then he thought of the doctor who had come
and felt under her skirt and looked at the mountains. Was
she lying or was she telling the truth? Was it the baby or was
it something she had done to herself with her wildness and
dreaming and that day on the farm with her hands inside all
those ostriches? Or was it something else that she had done?
He could see her looking at Mr. Jacobs, her body leaning
forwards, her lips parted as if she was going to fall into his
arms. Let her sit there, he said to himself. Let her sit. She can
have her own chickens. She's fickle.

Mr. Jacobs was near him, and Mr. Henry could see where
his beard began on his cheeks. Mr. Henry found himself
talking about Highlands and selling, and Mr. Jacobs was
saying something about selling himself. Another farmer
screamed in his ear, He sold his own place a week ago for
two hundred thousand pounds! Mr. Jacobs or who, Mr.
Henry was asking and the Afrikaner man shouted, That
blerrie Jew! Mr. Jacobs was pressing to get out, but the men
were pulling on him as if he was the oar in the water that
would lift them into the air.

Of course they didn't know how bad it was. They didn't know that Mr. Jacobs' farm, that same two hundred thousand place, would change hands later on for fifteen thousand pounds. Nobody knew that in a few years' time you'd be able to buy an ostrich for seven shillings, that same old bird whose feathers used to cost sixty quid a pound. Mr. Jacobs would survive, because that's how he was, but other farmers would grind their heels in the Karoo dust and curse the first day they ever stuck long knives into prickly pears and held them over fire to burn off the thorns for an ostrich's lunch.

Mr. Henry had forgotten the smell of men's armpits, their breath caked with tobacco and brandy, and the oil of their hair under hats. When he was alone in the mountains, it was the scent of the *aandblommetjie* at night, the little white flower that opens its face to the world at dusk. At Highlands, it was the sharp smell of the birds and the thicker smell of the horses, the *volkies* and their woodsmoke and Miss Beatrice, who smelled like slightly burnt toast. The auction house and all these men was like something greasy and rotten, and all he wanted to do was leave, but where to? The cart was there with all his feathers, the horses standing, one of them with his hoof up on its edge. Mr. Henry found himself standing like that horse, the toe of his shoe pointing into the road, waiting for a plan.

All he could think of was Mr. Jacobs, the Ostrich King, the man who could tell you what kind of feather would be in fashion in six months' time, or even a year. Maybe he should go to his house, to the sofa with the cabbage flowers, and drink tea with the ladies, and Mr. Jacobs would be his kind neighbour all over again. They would talk like old friends about the feather market and its ups and downs, when the next up was coming and who had the finest males in the district. This town business was a nasty mistake.

Then he remembered his dream on the road, unloading the feathers in the doctor's waiting room. He thought he could hear Miss Beatrice moaning, and suddenly he saw her pulling off her clothes. Fickle, he said, but he drove to the doctor's house anyway, with its brass plate on the gate, so shiny and nice, saying Doctor So-and-So. The front door was wide open and Mr. Henry walked into the dark house and found the doctor sitting on his cracked leather chair in his surgery, no patients in sight, just the doctor and a vial in his hand. At first the doctor looked dead, but then Mr. Henry saw that his head with its stray hairs and sprinklings of ash would nod forwards, then jerk up and his green eyes would look so very, very tired, the kind of tired that's like a grey rope holding you between heaven and hell. There was no sleep in it, just this long waking. He spoke to Mr. Henry and it was all about ostriches, and how he had put his nest egg in eggs. And they're not going to hatch, he said with a dreamy smile.

Mr. Henry left without saying anything, and by the time he climbed back on the cart with the feathers, he was thinking about selling again. Miss Beatrice was quiet in his head, and Highlands was far away, almost as far as the mountains. He decided to go to the Oudtshoorn Hotel and look for Mr. Jacobs. They would have some *bobotie* or stew and talk shop, and then he would follow Mr. Jacobs to his farm, where they would rustle papers and sign things and by the morning Highlands and all the birds, dead and alive, and that big load of feathers, would belong to the Jew. But Mr.

Jacobs wasn't there in the Hotel bar that looked like the inside of somebody's heart, so dark-red and soft it was. Mr. Henry thought he could hear it beating or was it his own? He had some drinks, starting with green, then gold, then brownish-black and by the time he walked out of there, he was *lekkerlyf*.

TWELVE

I wake up and I'm not at at home anymore. I thought we were in the kitchen but it looks just like the hospital in here. Where is Gerda? Where is everyone? I'm lying down in a white bed and I'm wearing a hospital nightie and I have a horrible feeling that it's then and not now and the baby just died.

There's an old *tannie* next to me and another old *tannie* next to her. I'm not with the ladies and babies. I look on my hand and there's that old liver spot that looks like a donkey. I'm trying to count my years when one of the *tannies* coughs. I look at her and she looks like the *tannie* from the Museum except the hair-net with the glittering stones is gone. She stares me up and down and then looks away.

What happened? All I can remember is Jack and the meths bottle under the sink. I thought we were going to leave it for later.

The ghost dogs are coming into the room. They're coming to get me. Their fur is all gone and they're ugly as sin.

I'm not Mr. Henry. Go fetch someone else.

They don't listen. They jump on the bed. They have terrible breath.

The doctor comes in and he's old, just like the *tannies*. He says nothing to the dogs.

Alcohol poisoning, he says to me. And delirium tremens.

There's hissing in the air and it comes from the *tannies*. Shame on you.

I want to get up but my legs are *lam*. The dogs are sitting on them. Go away, doggies.

He says I must stay, this doctor who looks like my *oupa*.

That's when Gerda walks in. Now I am really *skaam*. Wait until she opens her mouth. What will the doctor say when the words come out like twisted dragons, when she spits out whole *goggas*.

The doctor checks my blood pressure and everything with his eyes closed as if he is falling asleep. Gerda pushes the ghost dogs away with her hand. I knew they would listen to her.

Where's the baby?

The doctor shakes his head as if I just got all the answers wrong and then he looks at Gerda. As if Gerda can hear.

Now it's just Gerda and me and the *tannies*.

She sits down next to me and looks at me with those hard Gerda eyes that never ever cry.

I need a *dop*. A nice brandy or something. Or a beer. What about some gin?

The *tannies* are listening so hard you can see their ears pointing towards me like flowers.

I need to drink something. I need a *dop*. It's not funny.

Miss Beatrice, Gerda says, and I am so ashamed. The words in her mouth sound so horrible.

She puts her hand on my throat where there's a pipe and a drip or something.

I need a *dop*.

Ssssh. Tell us what happened. The *tannies* want to know.

They're watching me, as if I'm the TV.

Poor Miss Beatrice could have used a *dop* herself, there by herself on the farm, with all the *volkies* back in their *pondokkies*, and some of them coming out to look at the *kraals* and the lucerne fields and the pile of steaming bones left over from the ostrich burning. You could tell from the empty stalls in the stable that Mr. Henry was gone. Nomsa was sitting outside her *pondokkie* in the sun, staring at that *koppie* where they had carried September's coffin, and the place in the earth marked with a thin white cross where he was buried, those white ostrich feathers resting on top of his coffin. Was it the last of his breath that blew them there? The afterbreath that came from his neck after it was broken, that carried him up into the stars where he could hunt wildebeest and giraffe with his ancestors? She was thinking of the hunters roaring at night, racing across the black sky, when one of the plucking boys came up to her. He said he heard something coming from the big house that wasn't a bird or a wild dog, but the sound of a woman so loud that the thorns were falling off the trees.

Nomsa walked down the path with the plucking boy, right by the willow trees, and there was nothing in her arms or on her head. No washing for the *madam*, no sticks for the fire, no bucket of water. She was light because that's how it was without the man who had laid down next to her and eaten her *mieliepap* and her *muti*, with the *baas* gone back into the mountains. When she heard the noise, she told the plucking boy to run away because he mustn't go near what was going to happen. He was almost gone, his bare feet slapping in the dust, when she thought she heard an English word coming from the house. She turned back to look at him and he was staring right at the windows and she screamed, *Voertsek!*

She walked in through the back door of the house, into the kitchen, and it was a place without fire or food. She found some *biltong* hanging from one of the shelves and she cut off a piece of it. Then she started a fire and carried in some water and put it on the stove. When the water was hot, she put the *biltong* in it and some dried leaves she took from a packet between her breasts. This was the special meat water she took to the room that was filled up with the sound of Miss Beatrice and the stranger that was coming to her, that was riding through her body, that was banging its feet and its head against her bones.

Nomsa came into the room and Miss Beatrice was as she remembered her when Mr. Henry was lost on the Swartberg Pass. Her hair was yellow flame and her eyes were light and bright green, like the *opslag* that covers the veld after rain. She was lying on the bed, like a tortoise turned upside down. Nomsa gave her the meat water and Miss Beatrice drank it, swallowing most of it, but spitting out the leaves. Nomsa scraped them off the bed with her fingers and then rubbed them onto Miss Beatrice's forehead and temples. *Staan op,* she said, and Miss Beatrice looked at her as if she had gone mad. But soon she was standing and her knees were bending and Nomsa was holding her and then they were on the floor,

Miss Beatrice on her hands and knees and Nomsa pulling at her hips, singing, making her woman's part swing in a circle, round and round in the same old circle. The big bag inside her that held the baby was peeling back, was opening at the bottom like a giant feed sack slowly spilling out grain.

The world was gone, and the minutes and the hours sat on Miss Beatrice's head and her stomach. The day was crawling away somewhere behind her, and nothing mattered except the engine inside her. She groaned from inside her bones and Nomsa shouted, No! You must save your air. Breathe like a wind that goes in the front door and out by the kitchen. The engine was still and then it started again. Miss Beatrice could see herself going overboard, falling into the cogs and the wheels and the pins and getting all chewed up. She was almost lost, but then she caught the sound of Nomsa's breath in her ear and she copied her, gulping but not sinking, not yet. The break came but it was short, so short and then the engine was grinding again, like some metal monster with five hundred parts. Stop and go, stop and go and Miss Beatrice felt dizzy and *naar* and she vomited and her legs buckled and she screamed and bit Nomsa and the engine raced backwards then it jumped, like a mad old car going up a *koppie* flat out in reverse. Her bowels moved and there was something under her and she was sure it must smell bad if she could smell anything anymore. I'm sorry, she panted, and then the engine went mad again and her legs were loose and flapping and there was more vomit and more shit. Nomsa held her under her arms and Miss Beatrice could see her black skin and that's all she knew until the engine spun itself loose so hard that there was no more spinning left.

Then it was quiet for a moment and Miss Beatrice looked up, and there was a black hole in the roof of the room,

round like the feed sack, round like her *shoppie*, round like
the head of the stranger who was coming to her, now
rushing, now waiting. Through the hole, she saw stars and
that's how she learned that the day had fallen to the earth
and it was now night. Nomsa was singing to her about the
sky, and telling her to count stars with her pain, to count all
the hunters and the wildebeest and birds. Miss Beatrice knew
that September was there, and that he was watching them,
and that he had died because of her husband. She said,
Sorry, and Nomsa slapped her and said, Look! Then she was
sitting on her feet, and her *shoppie* was burning but Nomsa
was holding her legs apart and she looked down at what was
growing between her legs, and she saw a small brown patch.
Ai! She heard Nomsa clicking and the sound was like a key
turning in a lock and opening the door.

Dunsa! Nomsa was shouting at her and she felt the
pushing start, and it was hard but it had a shape and a place
to go and it wasn't like the mad part, with her legs flapping
and everything going forwards and backwards all at once.
She pressed her head against the bed and it felt like she was
pushing a big old lorry up a hill. The pain was there but it
was more like a stretching and pressing now, and she knew
she could do it, she knew she could.

She rocked back, and counted more stars and Nomsa gave
her the meat water again. Nomsa flicked at her nostrils and
she breathed in deeply through her nose, and then Nomsa
tapped on her jawbone and she let the air rush into her,
through her mouth. Then the engine inside her driving her
into the earth started up again and she was on her hands and
knees and Nomsa was shouting like a thunder clap, *Dunsa,
Mama! Dunsa!* She felt her forehead pressing against
Nomsa's head, bone against bone, the baby inching out of

her, her shoppie suddenly burning like mad, right down the middle. Then it stopped again, and she lay back and she breathed and she thought, I could die, but I won't. Then it started and she was up, her knees burning somehow, like her shoppie, her wrists white. She heard in the back of her head the sound of something tearing. Oh, the birds! The poor birds! She lost that one, and it was almost overboard, the grinding inside big as a monster.

It wasn't the birds. It was Nomsa taking the sheet off the bed and tearing off a strip that she rolled into a long rope and tied around her own waist. She stood against the wall and Miss Beatrice crawled to her and took the ends of the sheet and pulled, and every time she pulled she could feel her woman's part stretch, and as it stretched, her mouth stretched open so wide that the corners cracked and bled. Then Nomsa sank down onto the floor and grabbed her arms so that they faced each other and squatted, like old *kaffirs* sharing a pipe. They were stuck together in a dance and the humming came out of Miss Beatrice into Nomsa, out of Nomsa back into Miss Beatrice.

Ma would have shouted and said something about frogs and vermin but I wish when my baby was coming that someone had taken me off that bed where I was lying, the same place I'm lying in now, this hospital so white that your eyeballs ache just looking at the wall. Miss Beatrice was there on the veld where I would like to have been, right there with the *dassies* and the *goggas*. She could hear everything screaming and whistling in the night, and one of the sounds she heard was her own. She remembered September telling her how the stars kept roaring and she roared with them, as she counted each little pinprick, each stabbing hole in the black sky.

Where I was, was alone. The doctor had come into the room, just like now, except he gave me something in my arm that was hanging there, next to a plastic bag. He said it would make the whole thing go faster and I thought I saw a golf ball lying in his pocket, his fingers curled around it, or maybe it was a giant pill. Jack was there in the waiting room with Ma and they were smoking her Westminster 30s. I lay there by myself in the snow-white room and the pain sat on top of my belly like some horrible old devil and all I wanted to do was get up and press myself against something or someone. All I could think of was my dogs and who was going to go on the veld with them and scratch that skinny little fur under their stomachs. The only time I laughed was remembering the water rushing down onto the floor, all that water that came from the baby, and the dogs standing in a circle licking like mad, my toes and the inside of my knees and my ankles. Flo, my basset, got the tips of her ears all wet with that juice and Jack kept saying, *Sies!* and kicking her away. But I didn't mind.

Every time the pain came, I tried to put Skollie, my Alsatian, and old Esther in nurses' uniforms there by the end of the bed. I made special holes in the nurses' caps for their ears. Maybe that was like seeing a ship sinking and everyone drowning right there in the middle of your room, when the drink sits in your head making terrible pictures. I couldn't tell whether the dog nurses were from the gin or the pains. They were nice in the beginning, but when they started to bark and curl up their lips so that you could see the beginning and the end of their teeth, I got scared. Did the barking start after the injection the real doctor gave me, or before?

Are my ghost dogs their cousins?

There on the farm, Nomsa was telling Miss Beatrice about the bird in the net bag that was clawing its way into the light. Miss Beatrice was lying back against the wall, her legs stretched out, sweat dripping off her chin onto her open stomach. Where is Henry? she asked Nomsa, as she saw the sky getting pale, and the day coming back to the world. Mr. Henry, he took the horses and the feathers. One of the *klonkies* saw him on the road, going to *Baas* Jacobs. Then Miss Beatrice crawled on her hands and knees again as if she was on the road to Mr. Jacobs, but she wasn't. She was pushing down but she was getting tired and all she wanted was to stop working so hard, like some slave man in the bottom of a ship. I want to go home, she started to cry, and that's when Nomsa puffed herself up like a *tokolosh* and bared her teeth and screamed, *DUNSA!* so loud that all the fence-birds got embarrassed and flew away.

Nomsa sat down next to her and pressed the heel of her hand against the crown of Miss Beatrice's head. Miss Beatrice felt the bones of Nomsa's hands and her arms on her head, as the baby pressed against her woman's bone. She pushed and she pushed and the baby moved down. When the pain stopped, and she rested, the baby went back up again. She could feel it going backwards and she cried.

* * *

Mr. Henry was sitting on the *stoep* at Mr. Jacobs' house. The house was empty and dark inside and no one was there. He was drinking from a bottle in his hand and waiting. Mr. Jacobs finally came, and Mr. Henry knew it was bad because his wife and his daughters must be somewhere else. Mr. Jacobs opened the door and he remembered the part where he went inside and watched Mr. Jacobs light the lamps. The sofa with the cabbage flowers was drooping and the room looked sad and beige. Mr. Henry heard himself talking and laughing but he wasn't sure what was funny. Who will buy my prime whites? My spadonas, and beautiful drabs? Not to mention all those chicken feathers? Maybe it was the dust on the feathers tickling his nose, or maybe it was the names but Mr. Henry was giggling and hiccupping as if Rachel and Bertha and Goldie were sitting in his head and pulling faces. Mr. Jacobs said something about family in Calvinia and Mr. Henry burped like a fish. That's when he picked up an ostrich egg shell that had holes at both ends and a painting wrapped around the middle of Mr. Jacobs' farm at sunset. He looked in the holes and the yolk that was missing made him think of Miss Beatrice's ostrich egg biscuits. I think my wife's having a baby, he said, and the laughing came back, so hard this time that it shook him from head to toe and he dropped the painted egg on the floor.

He was picking up pieces before you could say *Swakopmund*, trying to find the oak door and the trees and bits of the sky. There was a tiny ostrich head, and a piece with its full black body, and all he had to find was some white wings. When he looked up, Mr. Jacobs was staring at him, his beard thick and heavy like a curse. He made Mr. Henry

think of the giant in Jack and the Beanstalk, the story his
mother, sweet mother, had read to him in the nursery in that
damp house on that damp English soil he missed so much.
Where is the Beanstalk? he wanted to ask but the words
were broken in pieces like the egg and what came out was
Beans. Go home to your wife, Mr. Jacobs said, and it didn't
sound kind. Wife was like knife and home was a fat, burning
coal and Mr. Henry didn't want either.

He went outside because Mr. Jacobs put him out. Everything was a puzzle and all Mr. Henry knew was that there
were fixed eggs at Highlands and he was going to get one
and give it to Mr. Jacobs all painted and nice. He saw himself out in the sun with his paints and his hat, painting Mr.
Jacobs' farm on the egg and having a jolly good time. It
would look even better than the old egg and Mr. Jacobs
would be happy this time, not angry. He would sell him the
farm and the feathers and the birds just as he'd hoped.

He was falling into the darkness with Mr. Jacobs standing
behind him, but he had an idea and a plan and just had to
remember which one was which. Then he was back with his
horses, and they were following the moon which hung over
Highlands. That's where he was going, and the animals
knew and everything wasn't so bad. He still had something
in his bottle to keep him company, something that was sharp
and strong. The song in my heart was in his throat and he
was remembering that soldier, that Scottish solder who wandered far away and soldiered far away. The *jakkals* and the
bobbejaan and all the night animals heard him singing,
There was none bolder, with good broad shoulder. They
must have laughed their heads off because they knew he was
going to get caught, like those people in the Devil's Chimney
who get stuck half in and half out.

The splitting-in-half-with-a-burning-axe pain was what Miss
Beatrice had, but now it was different. She sweated and her
eyes burned and her vomit lay on the floor like a country.
Why? She suddenly asked Nomsa and it was Why are you
helping me? but the rest of the words didn't come out.
Nomsa said *Kyk die hare!* Look at the hair! and Miss Beatrice knew whose baby it was and that the river of Fate was
funny and crooked. She cried for all that was lost and gone
and suddenly she wanted to leave everything behind—
Nomsa, the baby, the hole in the roof and that pale end of a
moon that hung over their heads like a bilious old lady. But
then there was joy that stormed into her body, catching her
heart and her eyes and pushing that black wisp of hair into
the world. It got bigger, then smaller, and Miss Beatrice was
suddenly afraid it would disappear back inside and never
come out. Then the pressing came back, with Nomsa's hands
on her legs and this time she felt strength like God's right
arm pushing through her. Her shoppie was burning hot and
stretched wide and she didn't know whether that head
would split her in half down the middle like the axe from
before. She put her hands on her legs and she felt Nomsa's
hands and they were both shouting and fighting. The sun
shot through the roof onto her head and her shoulders
through that hole Nomsa had made. She lifted her face to the
light and the smell of the veld fell upon her. She felt bigger
than all the trees on all the *koppies*, bigger than the mountains in the distance, bigger than the Kamanassie Dam. Her
mouth was rounder than a hundred pumpkins fallen off the
pondokkie's roof and her arms were long enough to pull
down those faded old stars and make them count their own

pain. In that moment of light and fury, the baby's head shot through her shoppie and then came the shoulders and brown little body covered with the softest of cheeses. Miss Beatrice lay back on her elbows or was she now on the bed? And the baby lay on her heart. It was the Karoo after rain and the *opslag* was everywhere, precious green shoots all over the ground, and all the ostriches alive again and waltzing. She and the baby were swimming in pools, and the water was both red and white. It streamed over them like a thousand blessings and they lay in it together and cried, the baby without tears and Miss Beatrice with so much water pouring out of her eyes that she saw a rainbow reaching from the tip of her nose to the baby's chin. A girl, she heard a trumpet, as she looked down. It's a girl. And she was the angel and trumpet, holding that girl.

THIRTEEN

Mr. Henry had the last *sluk* from his bottle and he threw it behind him the way people throw a horseshoe over their shoulder for good luck. The light was hurting his eyes. Go away sun, he was saying. Go away. The horses' heads were drooping as they shuffled along the dirt road, puffs of dust coming up from their hooves. The road rose up and then it sank down and that's when they saw Highlands and the ostrich *kraals* and the willow trees and the stables. They lifted their eyes and their feet and soon the cart was bouncing along over the stones, Mr. Henry holding his head and the reins, shouting Whoa! and Slow! But the horses were just like the sun and they didn't listen. Mr. Henry didn't know which tree was which, the blue gums at the gate or the willows by the dam. Everything flew past his face in a blur and the mountains were almost upside down.

Sailors at sea who haven't seen land aren't even so bad.
The horses were going faster and faster and bits of the cart
were coming off onto the road not to mention the feathers.
The horses got to their stables and Mr. Henry was mad as a
snake but his head was too hot and too hard for shouting.
He just left them standing there by the stalls for the *klonkies*
to fix up. All he wanted was that egg for Mr. Jacobs so he
went straight to the ostrich *kraal* with the Guaranteed
Breeders, the live ones left over from that terrible plucking.
The first husband he saw was just getting off the eggs
because it was light and now it was time for the wife. He saw
the three eggs lying there in the hole September had dug for
them. It was two yards wide and eighteen inches deep and
filled in with sand in case of the rain. He remembered September telling him that you make the hole so wide to stop
the birds throwing up dirt against the sand with their bills.
Some farmers build little huts or weather-screens over the
nests but September said the plain sand nests were better.

Hearing September's voice buzzing in his ears was even
worse than the headache which was hanging onto his side
whiskers and shaking his head like a rattle. He was even
remembering the part about the sitting and which couples
keep the eggs hot from the first to the last day, and the lazy
ones who leave the eggs alone for up to an hour at a time,
but still bring out nearly every egg. The less they are visited
the better, September said. People make them *skaam*.

I'm visiting them now, he told the voice of the dead man,
and no one will stop me. Of course these birds were still
plucked except for some black tail feathers left on this male
and the female with a spray of soft brown feathers on her
back. The female was settling down on the eggs and she was

looking for feathers to cover them completely but her feathers were mostly gone. She rattled her empty wings, opening and folding them like a broken old fan. Mr. Henry opened the gate and walked into the *kraal* and the ostriches didn't seem to mind. He scooped up some cut-up prickly pears in his hand and held it out in front of him. What he didn't hear, what he couldn't hear, was the squeak in the shell that came up from the baby ostrich inside the shell ready to hatch. The hen felt it in her middle like a piercing and she broomed at the cock to listen. They heard it again and suddenly she was on her feet and she and her mate were flying at Mr. Henry, their naked wings stretched wide, their bills wide open. Mr. Henry was up against the fence when the first long toe-nail caught him on the lip and pulled down, like someone opening a can of sardines. Mr. Henry lifted his arm over his face but that was a bad idea because it was just another place for a toenail to go in and tear.

He fell down and they kicked him and split him lengthwise and sideways. It was worse than a lion who does your throat and then you are dead and ready to be eaten. This furious splitting and kicking is why ostriches don't need to fly. It's fight not flight and Mr. Henry didn't know until the end but by then it was too late. If he'd carried a good bush instead of the cut-up prickly pears or if the squeaking from inside the shell hadn't happened but it did. So he was lying there in his own blood and he felt with the hand that could move the buttons on his shirt and it was not his shirt which was unbuttoned but his whole chest. The longest tear was right down the middle and he tried to close it up with his hand because he knew the insides mustn't come out. Not now, and not yet. He was packing something that felt like worms back into his stomach when black rolled in front of him. It cleared for a moment and he saw the hen's wild eye, staring at him and he knew she was the one who had done that tear down the middle. Or was it the cock? The cock's leg was coming at him again, and this time he rolled onto his stomach. The toenail tore him open from his neck to his bottom and that's when the ostriches stopped.

He never got to the nest to pick the egg that he wanted to paint so that he could give it to Mr. Jacobs in place of the one that he'd broken. He didn't even die with the egg in his hands. He just lay against the fence, cut up like fruit salad and the birds stood over him, staring and waiting. It wasn't like the snapping of a neck. There was dripping and seeping into the ground and perhaps that blood mixed with water made some fancy pink stalactites and stalagmites underground. Of course the sun was beating on the eggs while the ostriches were watching Mr. Henry. The hen looked back and the cock saw her and he backed away a little, and she went to the eggs and sat down. Now they had two things to do and it made them unhappy. The male paced around, twisting his head between the nest and Mr. Henry. The hen sat high on the eggs and her bill kept opening and closing as if she wanted to speak.

One of the plucking boys saw the horses and the cart and went to the big house to tell Nomsa and Miss Beatrice that Mr. Henry was back. He knocked on the kitchen-door and when he heard silence he shouted, *Die baas is terug!* The *baas* is back! and ran back to the stables. Miss Beatrice pushed again and the afterbirth came out with a sigh and a soft plop. It lay there in front of Miss Beatrice and Nomsa like a glossy wet cushion made out of red-purple velvet.

Then Nomsa's head was down and she was chewing on something and biting and it was the cord, thick as your thumb. Miss Beatrice saw that Nomsa was naked or was she dreaming? Then the walls of the room were completely gone. There were empty horns and nails on the ground and the sky was the colour of a bruise. Miss Beatrice caught the flash of her own face inside Nomsa's eye and she could have sworn it was the face of a small Cape fox. She heard the slap-slap of Nomsa licking the baby and Miss Beatrice growled. Nomsa stared at her and that's when Miss Beatrice bit her. Nomsa twitched, and ran into the veld.

Miss Beatrice held the baby to one breast while she scratched for food. Her fingers broke easily into the earth and she found grizzled bulbs and roots knotted like hair. She ate, and some of it was wet, but not wet enough, and she knew she had to go deeper. Her arm was inside the earth when the sky above her head cracked open. The wind was coming up like a thousand running soldiers. Miss Beatrice breathed it in and it told her everything in the world all at once. There was the breath of the newborn child like mint and the dark, stringy smell of Mr. Henry. Nomsa came to her on the wind, smoky and sharp but sweet all the same, and she knew the *kaffir* woman was near her and wanted her child.

There were long scarves of dust in the air and they curled around Miss Beatrice and the baby and Miss Beatrice clung to her, murmuring, Precious, Precious, Precious. You are Precious. The wind tossed the words around and around till they sounded like waves coming in, and hitting the sand. Miss Beatrice's mouth was on the baby's eyelid, her nose and the top of her head and the ssh, sssh of her voice was the water noise and the wind and the child's breath all mixed up together.

Precious opened her mouth and began to cry, the saddest of birds, and Miss Beatrice felt as if someone had *skopped* her in the stomach and then in the head. The crying was long and thin and it was like wire cutting cheese and the cheese was poor Miss Beatrice's heart. She held Precious' head with one hand and her breast with the other and she tried to put the two together but Precious arched her back and screamed.

Then the needles of rain came down and they lifted the sand up and the sticks started to jump and dance. Miss Beatrice felt her breasts swell and harden as the rain poured down on them. Her milk came spraying out and you couldn't tell which was milk and which was rain. Miss Beatrice lay down like my doggies and covered her baby and poor little Precious cried and cried until she found the nipple and closed her mouth around it.

They lay there like that until the rain stopped. Then it got cold, the way it gets in the Karoo in the middle of the night, and you have to get that blanket out of the cupboard and your old shortie pajamas aren't enough.

Miss Beatrice looked at her arm and the hairs were all up and her skin was rough. She didn't know what she was anymore. She got up, Precious still sucking her tittie, and she looked behind her almost expecting to see the wheat and brown tail of the Cape fox sticking out of her bum. All there was, was a dent in the sand and something white. She pulled the white thing out of the ground and it was a beautiful ostrich feather. A prime white, *nogal*. She pulled some more and there were more feathers, all big and fluffy, probably left over from some ostrich that danced around like a *dronkie* and passed out. Miss Beatrice took the feathers and wrapped them around Precious and she looked like those can-can dancers except she was so tiny and grey. She held her and held her and rocked and sang and whistled to get those arms and legs warm but nothing stopped that bitter Karoo wind.

Gerda is up and walking in the hospital room and you'd think she was the one having the baby. Her face is red and she looks like she's ready to burst.

Must I go on? Is it so bad?

The next minute she has me out of the bed and the ladies are staring their eyes out and she's putting my slippers on my feet and looking for my clothes. She has my skirt around my neck and she's rushing like mad. I can't stop, I won't stop. The words are falling through my zip and into her hands.

When my baby was born, there were no feathers. Everything, as well as the baby, was white. They told me that the baby came out smelling like Cape wine and I didn't know whether it was a joke or not. I saw it in the doctor's hands and my heart burst like those Chinese lanterns on the klapperbos tree but it was gone in another room, in another place, and I was fast asleep. When I woke up, I was alone, and no one came for a long time. I felt my stomach and it was sewn up and empty, and outside I thought I saw the purple flowers of a jacaranda tree. They were falling, and drifting, and I must have slept again because when I woke up

there was Ma and there was Jack. Jack didn't have any car-
nations with him, or even some chocolates or a bottle to
celebrate. That's when my breasts started to hurt and I
looked at them and there was something wet coming
through that hospital dress. Ma put a *lappie* over me before
she even said hello.

We're taking the lift and my clothes are on backwards but I
don't care anymore because I'm going home to my dogs. I'm
going home.

Miss Beatrice was all alone on the veld in the wind with her
baby and nothing to cover them except those prime whites.
There at the edge of the world was the red hanky, like a
tongue torn out and flapping. What it said to her, in the
wind, was Come. It pulled her legs. So she walked towards
it, with the baby in her arms and the last of the afterbirth
blood dripping onto the ground. The mountains were like
big stepping stones. She was lifting her legs over them, one
by one. There was the ship mountain, with its big sail, and
on the other side of it was the frosty bonnet, someone
whose head had frozen up in a storm. When she got to the
back of the bonnet, there was just one more, the honeycomb. Jack says that's on the other side but I think he's the
one who can't see the shapes properly. He didn't grow up
here like I did. He didn't see how they led water onto the
lucerne.

Miss Beatrice needed those big boots for stepping across
the world but she had nothing except Precious crying against

her, driving her to walk and walk and find that small red flag. When she got there, she scratched the wet, cold ground, like a *bakoorjakkals* or that same old Cape fox looking for a house. The hole was there and she went into it as if it had a door and a welcome mat.

There in the cave, it was like that night after Mr. Jacobs left Highlands with his wife and his girls, making another black spot in that very black sky. The night of the staring night-animals except this time Miss Beatrice was not looking over the fence. This time she was one of the night-animals herself, the yellow fur on her head up and stiff and her nose sniffing the dark cave air for stories of strangers. The first scent she smelled was a man in some *veldskoene* with brandy on his tongue and a broken down pipe in his back pocket. She was pacing and growling because this wasn't the place where she and Mr. Jacobs lay down together anymore. She looked through the dark with her fox's eyes and saw the name Frikkie like a bunch of sticks scribbled on the wall. Suddenly this place was a common place, with other peoples' loud voices spoiling it all. They were gone but they would be back and Frikkie would lead them around telling them that he had found this cave when he was chasing a rabbit with his Ridgeback.

You can't tell a bitch where to put her puppies. You can't chase her out from under the bed or make a nice box for her in the kitchen. She goes where she pleases and that's how it was with Miss Beatrice. She scratched and clawed and bit the air and hissed at those *blerrie Boere*. After she spat and spat until there was no more spit left, she sat down under the name of Frikkie and left him with a pile of fox droppings.

If it was me there in the dark, I would be too *poep-scared* to move. I would be stuck like those fat people in the Devil's Chimney. The dark makes me think of the end of the world and the Valley of the Shadow of Death.

Miss Beatrice didn't worry. She slipped from the light dark into the deeper dark, with her soft baby sleeping against her heart. *Ag,* no man, I would be thinking, please let me out. I don't want to meet those Nooitgedacht ladies down there, dying in the mud with their babies still in their stomachs.

Did she ask herself there in the dark, Is my Precious black like the cave or white like the feathers? Or is she the colour of *rooibos* tea? She should have looked at her outside in the sun, in the wind, in the world lying there like a rusty big ship high above her head. You could stare and stare in that cave and see nothing, like those blind people who sit and make tray cloths.

Miss Beatrice searched with her fingers and feet and she found a place that held her and poor Precious like a big hand. Was it the hand of God just resting there for them? Or was it the inside of some big dead animal?

They sat there, in the cave inside a cave, and Precious drank from Miss Beatrice. All there was, was the baby's mouth on Miss Beatrice's tittie. The rest of the world was gone, like a train gone out of the station a long time ago. And it was quiet. So quiet, Miss Beatrice could hear the blood singing through Precious' body, the tiny sound of a very new life.

This is the Peace that passeth understanding, this is the milk of human kindness.

For me it was another story.

* * *

Gerda is pushing me, holding me, carrying me, out of the lift, and no one notices. We're outside and the holiness of the world is upon us.

Everything was light, and the baby was gone and they came and pumped out my breasts and gave me some pills. I could see everything and it was ugly and sharp and it hurt my eyes and I would rather have been down there in the dark with little Precious, little lamb of God.

Even though I am so scared of the dark.

All the stalactites and the stalagmites and the curly ones called helictites were covered by the black like some lady's grand piano covered with a black velvet cloth. Crystal Palace, Fairyland, Drum Room, Coffin, the Tunnel of Love, Ice Chamber, Throne Room, Van Zyl's Hall, Madonna and Child, Peach Brandy Bottle, Lot's Chamber. All the formations sat there in the dark, showgrounds closed for the winter.

Miss Beatrice felt breath on her shoulder and it could have been little Precious or a *dassie* or some ghosts. Or was it herself, breathing? Now what was that again? A stick or a stalagmite, sticking out of the ground like some damp finger?

And then it happened like they say it happened to Pauline except this was bliss and not fire. Those soft rocks went inside her, and she moaned and she cried and she rocked.

She was on the edge of something yawning and open and impossible and then it burst and she tremored and fell through to the other side. Then it happened all over again and the stalactites and stalagmites picked her up and poked her and entered her this way and that. She shook and twitched so much that she didn't know if she'd ever come right again. The cave itself was singing and moaning with all the voices of the Boesman painters and the Nooitgedacht ladies who were dancing together between the Organ Pipes and Cleopatra's Needle.

Nothing was still anymore, not even the water, which came up and licked at Miss Beatrice. It touched her bum and her shoppie and now the trembling inside her was so strong that she burst all over again, this time with lights and a fairy band and all the hundreds of thousands of ghosts clapping like mad.

She fell down and lay there and didn't get up. The water went back to its place and so did the Boesman painters. The Nooitgedacht ladies disappeared and the stalagmites and the stalactites grew still again.

Miss Beatrice sat up, in the pitch-dark, and she felt for her child. Precious was gone. She looked with her fox eyes and saw nothing. She felt with her fingers and her legs and even the hairs on her arms but nothing was there. The small soft mouth had fallen off. The little arms and rolled-up legs weren't lying beside her anymore.

Nothing moved. Then the same old Devil who had sucked up the baby in the dark came to Miss Beatrice and put his hand into her chest. He squeezed her heart and her lungs and everything in between. He twisted her throat into a knot so tight she could hardly breathe. She sat there like someone who is deaf and dumb and paralysed.

A *miggie* buzzed near her ear. Or was it the baby? Precious! Her heart flamed up and she started to crawl and run and breathe, searching like mad in that horrible, horrible place for her child.

Those stalactites and stalagmites were like teeth and Miss Beatrice hit them in the the dark, to make them let go. She hit and she smacked and the crying grew louder and louder.

She ran amok in there, worse than all the vandals put together. She smashed droplets and icelets that had taken millions of years to grow less than the tip of your fingernail. She was shouting and crying and suddenly the cave was full of a million Miss Beatrices all screaming, Precious, oh my Precious!

And there, out of the fluttering dark, came a light of one candle. Miss Beatrice fell silent. She smelled wood smoke and *muti* and *mieliepap* and suddenly she was back counting the stars again. She was pushing her baby into the world and Nomsa was there by her side. Nomsa! she called.

The light stopped and then it disappeared behind the Lost Wing of an Angel. Then Precious cried, and Miss Beatrice went away from the light towards the sound of her child. Was she here by the Pulpit or the big Throne? The cry came back right next to her. She grabbed into the air and all she got in her arms was a big empty echo.

The light was now in a different place. *Yiza!* Nomsa was talking and clicking and the clicks were like little stones falling into the cave from the sky. Miss Beatrice didn't know whether it was *iqanda* or *uxolo* or *ixesha*. The words clattered back and forth, between the cave walls and floor. They bounced between the formations.

Nomsa was the bat. She was clicking her way to the child,

following the map of her echoes. Miss Beatrice was the *jakkals*. She scratched and whined, and ran this way and that, but it didn't help. The light went out and she suddenly felt Nomsa brush past her, the *kaffir* woman's breath on her neck, her *kroes* hair tingling as it touched Miss Beatrice's forehead.

Miss Beatrice grabbed her arm and she twisted, but Nomsa wasn't her sister. She had arms stronger than trees, arms that could carry a dead man. She gave Miss Beatrice a *klap* and the next thing she knew she was lying on her bum. Miss Beatrice got up on her knees and there was Nomsa's ankle, fat and black and right there by her teeth. She was going to bite but then Precious made a noise, so soft and sweet, as if she was puffing a tiny pillow in her cheeks. It made the milk come again, running hot down her chest, and instead of going for Nomsa's ankle, she went straight for her heart.

You see those *dronkies* in the location on a Saturday morning outside the bottle store fighting over a man who is lying passed out in the gutter. You see their bright *doeks* and their broken teeth and you wonder which one is going to win and which one is going to the hospital.

But this wasn't a man they were fighting for. It wasn't September, or Mr. Henry or even Mr. Jacobs. It was Precious. Miss Beatrice used her father's fists and the teeth of her grandfather and every lamp and mirror and candlestick she had ever touched. Nomsa spat and it was the poison of all the worst animals that landed all over Miss Beatrice and made her scream.

Have you ever looked in the eye of a woman and seen how she wants you dead?

I see that in my sister's eye and I always thought it was because she was deaf. But she wants to see me gone. Pouf! Like a rabbit that disappears out of a hat.

I am rolling down the street like a tumbleweed.

Miss Beatrice was beating and beating with all the life in her arms and legs but it wasn't enough. Nomsa was bigger and the anger inside her wasn't just Precious. It was all her children who she had left and lost, and all the white noses and bums she had wiped, long lines of them, so many that they were like guavas in a tree going *vrot*. She was shaking that tree at Miss Beatrice and smacking her with it, over and over again in the stomach, right in that empty soft place where Precious used to live.

Miss Beatrice had Nomsa's head and neck in her hands and she tried to twist it and snap it off but Nomsa curled around her like some monster with a fat black tail and picked her up in the air and threw her down on a bed of stalagmites that bumped and banged all Miss Beatrice's bones. Like a miracle, Miss Beatrice got up but Nomsa spat again, this time right in Miss Beatrice's eyes. The poison made her see Nomsa taking Precious away, leaving her with her breasts wet and her heart empty. Stop! Please!

She was screaming even though all she could see was purple ropes. She reached in the dark and her nails were out and pointed but all the fox tricks in the world were not enough.

Nomsa! This time it came out of the past, out of the kitchen at Highlands, an old order from before. Nomsa was touching Precious. Miss Beatrice knew it, she could smell it, but she couldn't find them in the dark. She couldn't see what was shadow, or skin or cave. Nomsa was lifting little Precious from her shelf, there by the Devil's Letterbox, still wrapped in her prime whites. NOMSA! It was worse than a thousand ostriches brooming at once. It stopped her own heart when she heard it.

It didn't stop Nomsa. She took Precious and ran.

The light twinkled on again, and Miss Beatrice was reaching for it, and trying to catch it, but it danced up and away, and she wasn't quite sure where it went. Was Nomsa running like mad through Botha's Hall and Van Zyl's Hall, right out of that big hole at the front of the Caves, where they now sell chicken pies and cooldrinks out of a machine? Or was it somewhere else, some other part of the Caves where nobody had ever been before?

Miss Beatrice dragged herself up and tried to chase after her but she kept running into the stalactites and the stalagmites. She cut her head open and blood ran into her eye. She could still hear Precious' crying and the sound of it made her breasts swell and get hard like rocks. They ached and throbbed and the pain of it went up her shoulders into her head and all she wanted to do was grab that little girl and let her suck and suck until the milk was all gone. Until it had moved out of her titties into that little mouth, down the mouth into the stomach and into those thin little legs.

Was Nomsa still in the Caves? Or was she out there on the veld, looking for shade? Miss Beatrice didn't know. She couldn't see properly anymore and now she wasn't sure if she was hearing right. All there was, was the drum beat of her own heart. She wished she could tear it out of her body and leave it there on the cave floor. But it kept beating, steady as an old dog.

It was the heart, they said to me when I asked in the hospital. The baby had a hole in its heart, and it was leaking. So I know how Miss Beatrice felt and how horrible it sounds when you hear the sound of your own stupid blood thumping around in your neck and the other one, the baby, is gone.

We're walking under the shadow of the Dutch Reformed Church and Gerda covers her face and I don't know if she's lip reading or cloud reading or going mad. She can't see my mouth, no yes, she can. She's carrying me.

I wanted to tell Jack about the hole but he said, No, I don't want to know. He was looking at me *skeef* and I know he thought it was all my fault, as if I was the one who poked the hole. Ma I could hardly see because I was crying so much and she looked like a person standing behind a waterfall. Her voice was the same, and she was saying, *Ag, foeitog,* but it sounded as if the hiding part was over. Is it a boy or a girl, I asked her, and she said, We don't know. The doctors said nothing when I asked them. They just gave me an injection and the next thing I knew it was the next day, and some Maltabella for breakfast that had lumps in it. Then it was too late to keep asking and asking. What you don't know can't hurt you, Jack said, and he told me that he had buried it under the lemon tree with Lady and Dandy.

When I get gas in my stomach it makes me remember how it feels when the baby moves inside you like a bird in a bag. For a while, all I wanted was to have that feeling back but then they told me I couldn't because of my blood pressure. And there was Jack who was always drinking in the bar of the Oudtshoorn Hotel with his friends. The only males are the dogs and that's how it still is. When the lemons are ripe, I get really sad and once I was back in the hospital and they had to pump all the Tassies and gin out of my stomach just like now. But most of the time, it's not so bad and I manage all right. You can't complain when you have a job with the South African Tourist Board, especially these days.

Mrs. van der Westhuizen is staring at us. So what if Gerda is walking on her own two legs and I'm not. Walking is for the birds.

I'm surprised people don't blame Miss Beatrice for what's happening in this country now but maybe they have forgotten. Lots of things happened on the day she lost Precious in the Cango Caves, screaming in the middle of all those ostrich feathers, and everybody said at the time that she was the one whose fault it was. Not just the child, but Oudtshoorn and Mr. Henry and the whole feather business. *Daardie vrou,* they said. *Sy is 'n heks.* That woman is a witch. They never knew about Nomsa.

FOURTEEN

It's the house without Jack. He's walking the dogs, Gerda says. I see him on the veld, stumbling, the meths still burning inside him and I worry. Gerda is banging around the house while I sit on a chair in the kitchen like somebody's maid. I look down. My legs are filling up with water. My ankles look like two plastic bags full of water and ready to burst.

The water is already up to my head. It's spilling out of my eyes.

Gerda comes in with a pile of old newspapers and she's tearing them up and shouting. I want to finish my story. I want to have a drink but she's pulling at me and showing me this thing called the Truth Commission and it's about these policemen who did torture on some Coloureds, and they left them standing there with bags on their heads while they had a nice *braaivleis*.

The bags remind me of the ostriches.

Now she's going through the rubbish and she has the empty meths bottle and she's showing me and growling and I don't know what it has to do with the newspapers. Is she going to burn something in a dish?

I'm in the room with a lion or leopard except it's my sister. I wish I had one of those sticks the circus people have and I could get her up on a chair with her paws in the air, begging.

She's talking to me. Ma, she says, and my insides freeze. Ma.

Again, she has the newspaper and she points to the word, Truth. I want to tell the truth, she says, and it sounds like the worst thing I have ever heard. *Ag* no, man, I say, let bygones be bygones. *Moenie ou koeie uit die sloot grawe.* Don't dig old cows out of the grave.

She's got a pencil and she's drawing on the wall next to the fridge like a Bushman. She's gone *bossies*.

There's a stick-lady, with a baby, and then she draws a bigger stick-lady and rubs out the first baby. She gives a baby to the big stick-lady and then she draws a third stick-person. The third one has no ears. My heart freezes all over again.

I know what she's going to do. I can finish the drawing myself. The big stick-lady gives the baby to the one without ears. I take the pencil myself and draw ears that look like hooks. The ears equal the baby.

The big stick-lady feels better now. The other two have both lost something. They're equal.

I'm the smallest stick-lady and I'm not surprised. It probably wasn't so bad. I was so young and Ma was worried and so she took the baby, my baby, and gave her to my sister. The baby died anyway. I didn't have to see anyone dying.

How Miss Beatrice got out of the Caves nobody knows. Everything inside her was broken. She couldn't even see the blue sky anymore. All she could hear was Precious crying and that's what got her back to the farm. She followed the thin, tearing sound of her baby's voice and it took her past the honeycomb and the frosty bonnet. The rusty Karoo bushes stabbed at her boots and her arms but she couldn't feel anything. She was black inside, blacker than the Caves.

When she got back to Highlands she was so *deurmekaar* that she almost fell over Mr. Henry, lying there just outside the *kraal* with an egg finally in his hands. One of the *volkies* must have put it there. But he was already dead. Or was he? Some people say he spoke to her before he died and that was the curse. But how could he have known about Precious unless it was the *volkie* who put the egg in his hands and told him? I think if he said anything it would have been England and how his blood was dripping into the wrong earth and couldn't she help him to get back there, where his real house was. His voice was the only thing that was whole and even that was starting to bubble bright red. She looked into his chest because she heard the crying where it was all open. Precious was screaming again but this time her cries came out of the torn parts of Mr. Henry's body. Miss Beatrice reached down and put her hands in there to get her out but she couldn't.

One of the plucking boys saw her kneeling on the ground with her hands stuck inside Mr. Henry's chest and he went to get Nomsa. But Nomsa wasn't in the kitchen and all the plucking boy could smell was ash and old *rooibos* tea that had been cooking for days. He went to the *pondokkies* and called for her and everybody said she was out on the veld digging up roots for her *muti*. They had seen her carrying ostrich shells filled with water around her waist and an ostrich skin bag with sticks in it. She was walking with the sun on her left shoulder and one of the *volkies* said he saw her standing on the top of a *koppie*, looking across the veld for baboons. He thought she was going to cut off their tails.

What you couldn't see was the tiny red flag in Nomsa's eye, when she was standing there watching Miss Beatrice scrambling over the bushes and stones. You couldn't tell whether she saw Miss Beatrice falling into the ground, dropping down with her baby into the Banqueting Hall. Nomsa was drinking from the ostrich shell and it covered half her face. Was it really water or *kaffir* beer she was drinking and did it make her *dronk* so all she really saw was a baboon by the red flag? Was it a day or a month that she stood there, and was it really a *koppie* and not the black rocks of the Swartberg Pass?

But she didn't come back and that was enough. She didn't make *mieliepap* or coffee and she didn't sweep out the back *stoep*. She left without telling Miss Beatrice and that's what maids like to do. Sometimes they say they're going to visit their child or their sick auntie for four days and you think they'll come back but they don't. They go off with a small handkerchief-bundle and you're never quite sure if there's a spoon in the middle of it or a bottle of salad oil. They like to rub the oil all over their faces and hands until their *kroes* hair is dripping and their faces are shiny like mirrors.

Of course Miss Beatrice was not the kind of madam to count the spoons or watch out for the salad oil. She let all the *volkies* do what they wanted. People say that you could smell Highlands from miles away because of all the strange things the *hotnots* and *kaffirs* burned. You couldn't tell if it was *muti* or *dagga* or rotten ostrich egg or all three mixed up together. They say it began the day Mr. Henry was *skopped* by the Guaranteed Breeders and Miss Beatrice sat on the ground with her hands getting cold behind his heart. By the time she got up, it was nearly dark, and her fingers were stiff. The fires had started the way they started when September died but it wasn't the smoke that lifted her up from the ground, it was the smell. Part of the smell seemed to come from the ostrich egg lying there next to Mr. Henry's body. The other part was the smell of a dead person. If it wasn't for that smell she would probably have stayed there, sitting on the ground till the next morning's frost. But she breathed it in and it made her look down and see what was really there. Even still, she didn't jump or scream the way most people would. She lifted her hands out of Mr. Henry's body the way you take your hands out of the bowl when you've been mixing up some mince meat with onions and salt for meatballs. She wiped her hands and went back to the house. Precious' crying had faded and faded until all that was left was a twitch in Miss Beatrice's right eye. Did she think of Precious at all? Could she see the pitch-dark cave with Precious lying on top of the prime whites? I would have worried about the bats. They fly out of the Caves at night to feed and in the mornings they come back. They make droppings which they used to sell in bags. Did Miss Beatrice imagine all the droppings falling over poor Precious and burying her alive?

I sit on the *stoep* waiting for Jack. I said to Gerda I never want to see you again or your husband or your kids. Go back to Ashton. Go back to your furniture shop with all those old kettles and *riempie* chairs.

I am watching the cars go past. How do you forget when something terrible happens like my baby with a leaking heart? I drink and it goes away but the next morning it's all back, and I have to start all over again. And each forgetting with the bottle is different. Sometimes the door that closes is made of iron, and sometimes it's thick and padded like a velvet cushion. Once the door that closed was a beaded curtain except there was broken glass where the beads are supposed to be and you couldn't go in or out without getting cut.

What Miss Beatrice didn't know was that a plucking boy had come to the house when Precious was being born and that Nomsa chased him away. He was of the Bapedi tribe, and so were his elders who had lived in three *pondokkies* right next to each other. She didn't know how the *kaffirs* talk and talk, how they see everything you do. They sit in your house in the middle of their blackness and they watch. They see my bottles and that's why they leave me. I never told Jack but I know it's true. Sometimes they steal a bottle or two, usually the ones I put behind the Bendix or in a bag of dog food. I know it's them because they take off the pictures. They like coloured pictures of grapes and ladies holding baskets and the mountains of the Boland.

The Bapedi must have talked and smoked and said to themselves, This child we have not seen. I know that the *kaffirs* are really scared of a miscarriage or a still-born, because after my baby was gone, no one would come into my house to make the bed, or wash the dishes or clean anything. Jack did everything and it was terrible to see him like that.

All the *volkies* were scared of me. Where was the child? Where was it hiding? Where was the blood? I used to think it was all in the hospital and under the lemon tree but I don't know anymore. The *volkies* probably thought I was going to kill everybody, starting with Jack and Ma.

At Highlands it was the other *volkies*, who were not Bapedi but *hotnots*, who had seen Miss Beatrice walking with Precious. But it was the Bapedi who believed that when a woman gives birth and the outcome is bad and she hides the child, it causes hot winds to blow, and the whole country dries up and dies. The rain is too afraid to fall near the place where the blood of the child is lying. The woman has hidden blood which was not ready, which was not thick enough to make itself into a man.

While the Bapedi elders were talking, Miss Beatrice was trying to come right. She was trying to see properly because she knew she needed her eyes to find her child. She needed her eyes and her feet and her hands and her titties. Nothing was working except her titties which kept spraying milk. The milk soaked through her convict shirt and dripped onto the floor. Her hands were numb and her feet were hot and red as a bush fire. And they hurt. Every step she took was terrible. Even the milk dripping on them didn't cool them off. The world she saw out of her eyes was dark and the people she saw in it were stick-people like the ones children draw. The only thing she could hear was the lost echo of poor Precious, still crying in the dark, making those feathers swirl around and around. She had to get back to the Caves. She had to get back. She had to start all over again and follow that cry right from the beginning.

The Bapedi spoke until late in the night and they decided they would fix what was broken, using the old ways. They would ask Miss Beatrice where the blood of the baby was hidden. Then they would dig into the ground and sprinkle the hole with two kinds of roots prepared in the special way. This earth they would throw into the dam, and then they would take the water from the dam and sprinkle it where the blood had been shed. The Bapedi women would take the blood and the earth and make it into a ball and then turn that ball into powder. They would fill the horns of oxen with that powder and give it to the little girls. The girls would go to all the edges of the land and make holes and then sprinkle the powder into these holes and say, Rain, rain! That's when this terrible thing would be taken off the roads and the rain would be able to come back.

The Bapedi came to the back door of the house when it was almost light. One of the men used his *knobkierie* to bang on the door. Miss Beatrice heard the sound and for a moment she thought it was Nomsa coming back with her child. A tiny star bust right between her two top ribs. But she opened the door and there were the Bapedi, three men and two women. She didn't know if they had come from the North in the olden days or whether they were from the Fish River or Natal. She didn't even know that they were the Bapedi who lived in the *pondokkies* with the other *volkies*. One of the men stepped forward. He was very thin and his dark skin lay in pockets on his shoulder blades. His teeth were big and broken and his eyes were hidden in wrinkles.

All Miss Beatrice saw was a string-man, with a cork for his head and corks for his hands and feet. She blinked and he turned from a cork- and string-man into a Bapedi and then back into cork and string. He went back and forwards like that while he talked and Miss Beatrice had to keep blinking to get him right in her eyes. Where is the child? he was asking, and suddenly Precious' screaming came back and the prime whites were blowing like mad. Nomsa was running and she was taking the baby and these stick- and string-people knew where she was. Miss Beatrice was the one shouting, Precious is gone and you took her. She picked up stones and started throwing them at the Bapedi and she didn't even see that some of them were carrying *knobkieries*. *Gaan weg! Voertsek!* Go away! she shouted just like a *Boerevrou*.

That's the blood of the child, one of the women screamed, in Bapedi, pointing a stripe left over from Mr. Henry on Miss Beatrice's arm. She started to wail and cover her eyes. The other women joined in the wailing and then they all started to wave their arms as if the Devil himself was standing in front of them. The Bapedi man who stepped forwards bent down in front of Miss Beatrice and picked up a handful of earth. Miss Beatrice saw him bending and she thought he was going to hit her back with a handful of stones like it says in the Bible so she slammed the door shut in the Bapedis' faces.

The Bapedi didn't go away. They squatted on the ground and the women moaned about the drought that was going to come and burn up the land. Miss Beatrice looked out of a window and saw them standing there shaking those heads that were cork. When her eyes saw real arms and legs again, it looked as if they were going to bash down the front door with their *knobkieries*. Then the main one spoke, and it was in the Bapedi language. We must find the woman Nomsa, he said. She will help us. Then they got up slowly, and left.

Were they coming back with fire? Did they have knives and buckets filled up with stones? That's what I would have worried about. But Miss Beatrice didn't care. All she could think of was her child, and whether Precious had turned into one of the Bapedi, with a cork for a head and arms and legs made out of string.

Miss Beatrice stood there and watched until they passed between the thorn trees and you almost couldn't see them anymore, just the occasional bright twist of the women's *doeks*. After they were gone, she looked at her own feet just to make sure they were still feet and not corks. She got such a *skrik*. They were now so red that they looked like the comb on my *ouma's* prize bantam. Drip, drip, went the milk from her titties, down her legs onto those poor feet but nothing could put out that fire.

She touched her bosom and it was hard like *spanspek* and she knew she must find that baby. The wanting grew and grew, until it burst in her ears and drove her outside, back to the veld she had walked across just yesterday. Now of course it was worse with her feet so red and her eyes seeing wrong but she couldn't stay, no she couldn't. She didn't even see Mr. Henry lying there in the sun, the *aasvoëls* whirling over him, landing with a thud in the dust next to his broken head. He was dead but she was alive and so was poor Precious, if only she could get there fast enough. She needed her child to take all that milk before it turned into cheese and then into rocks.

That's what they didn't tell me about at the hospital, or anywhere else. They didn't tell me the part about your breasts getting so full and heavy. You want your baby so much to take all that fullness away from you and I didn't even know how to find mine. At least Miss Beatrice knew where to go, even though it was a mistake. I lay in the hospital, and then I lay at home and Ma came over and gave me some hot *lappies* to put there and slowly it got better. She was telling me how she gave me a bottle and that only the *kaffirs* feed their babies from their titties but I could hardly listen to her. All I wanted was that baby in my arms and I knew I could never have him or her. That's when I cried and asked Jack again, Was it a boy or a girl? He wouldn't tell me. He just wouldn't because he didn't want to get sad himself.

This time Miss Beatrice saddled up one of the horses, a sulky old mare, and rode where she had walked the day before. She lay with her back on the horse's back as if she was lying down in bed. Every so often they would stop and she would hold the reins with one hand and her aching breasts with the other and tell that old mare where to go. She passed the frosty bonnet and the ship. She didn't see the Bapedi who were on the other side of the *koppies*, looking for Nomsa. They were on Mr. Jacobs' farm and they were talking to the *volkies* there, and asking them if they had seen the woman with her ostrich shells and her skins. The *volkies* pointed and it was somewhere between the foot of the mountains and where the red flag was, near the Nooitgedacht place where the ladies with their bellies were drawn onto the rock. When the Bapedi stopped under a tree and the women prepared the horns to fix the curse, they saw Nomsa walking, but she was coming the other way, and her ostrich shells and her skins were gone. She was like Hagar in the desert without her boy, her arms hanging at her sides, the palms turning towards the Bapedis' faces. They could see that she was walking like a person who has given something up because the Bapedi can see things like that whether it's the toffee that's hidden in your fist or a *tickey* in your shoe.

They greeted her and she greeted them and the man who had stepped forwards in front of Miss Beatrice's house said to the others, We must take her and hold her until she tells us where the child is. She looked at them and she asked them, What are you afraid of? and so they told her about the curse on the country. That's when Nomsa knew she must lead them to the place where the falling began, where Miss Beatrice made her nest after the rain. There was something for them there but it wasn't everything. She couldn't say that because they had made up their minds.

Where she had been and what she had done only the *korhane* knew.

Of course Miss Beatrice was riding, still lying down but now with her left hand holding her right breast. She tried squeezing it to make the milk come but it was so sore that she cried out loud and the wind blew sand down her throat. When she got to the red flag on the stick she saw that some animal had chewed it and it was almost gone. The horse dropped her head right away and started nibbling on the greenest shoots she could find, nuzzling the dusty ground with her nose. Miss Beatrice almost fell off the horse and when her hand touched the saddle, it was wet with the afterbirth blood that still flowed. This time she dropped into the ground, heavy with terror. The sound of Precious was gone and Miss Beatrice stumbled into the darkness searching for even the tiniest echo of her cry. She had a stump of a candle in her pocket, which she took out and lit. Again she saw the name Frikkie on the wall and it gave her the *grils*. She followed the shapes she remembered to the place which is now the Letterbox and Banqueting Hall but the names of course were different then. That's when she started looking on the crevices and in all the places with bits of rock like shelves for that spot where the baby was lying. She searched the wet stone and the floor that smelled of wax and clay with her hands like a blind person gone mad trying to read the whole Bible in braille all at once. But there wasn't even the slightest drift of a feather, or the touch of something soft and alive. Her hands kept scrambling all over the place, two fleshy spiders going up and down, sideways and around. The blue swirls of the ceiling and the pink streaks on the wall all turned pale. It wasn't like the time before when all the stalactites and stalagmites were moving this way and that. This time it was more like a graveyard and each spike of water turned into rock was the spine of some dead person or animal frozen underground forever.

She stood there waiting for something to move, for a voice or a feather or a breeze, but it was quiet. After a while, she thought she heard a soft drip, a thump, but it could have been the water slowly dripping into stone, or her heart. Then she heard footsteps and rock being scratched and men's voices talking in Afrikaans almost like that tape you hear nowadays when you come to the Caves and they switch off the lights and you can hear Oubaas van Zyl shouting at his slave-boy, Klaas. Except this wasn't van Zyl or even Johnny van Wassenaar. It was Frikkie and some friends. Miss Beatrice crawled into the part they now call the Chimney which is just like a woman's shoppie, if you ask me. She waited there, not stuck but still quite tight. She couldn't see but she could hear and they were talking about *Duitsland* and a big war and not fighting for the *blerrie* English, no matter what happens to the feathers. Frikkie was the loudest and probably the fattest. Then there were more footsteps and there were people with bare feet, skin slapping against rock, and some sticks tapping here and there. Miss Beatrice knew they were not friends of Frikkie's because they were clicking like *kaffirs* and almost singing with their breath. *Ai!* was one sound and then there were trills of *Ais!* and suddenly Miss Beatrice heard Nomsa. She shifted so that she could almost see out of the end of the Chimney and what she saw was Nomsa scratching on the ground and picking something up and giving it to the Bapedis. They all looked at it, and it was black and shrivelled and suddenly Miss Beatrice heard herself shout, It's mine! and the Bapedi froze with the dried-out stump of her baby's cord passing between their hands. That's when Frikkie and his friends turned around and walked into this part of the cave, at the very end of the Banqueting Hall. Of course they all had guns and they were going to shoot the Bapedi just like the farmers shoot the Bushmen when they come onto their land. Never mind the Battle of Blood River. But then Miss Beatrice started to scream and laugh all at once and was telling them about bullets in caves bouncing around and hitting you in the stomach because you're such a fool and her voice seemed to come from nowhere but it echoed and trembled and everybody got very scared. *Duiwelsvrou, duiwelskind,* Devil woman, Devil's child, the *Boere* were shouting and scrambling all over themselves to get out and maybe they understood what she was saying and maybe they didn't. The Bapedi were wailing again, and they said in their language that this was the voice of the child whose blood was not ready and the end of the world was just beginning. Only Nomsa knew the inside of Miss Beatrice's scream from the time of Precious being born. She stood while everybody else flew out of the cave like those bats. Then she looked at the crevice which was really the Letterbox where Miss Beatrice was, and she put the stump, which had fallen, into a small hole. Miss Beatrice was going to grab her like the time before but her feet were too hot to move. All she could do was shout, Nomsa, and it came out like Om. Nothing more than the breath banging inside her own head. The rest of her voice was gone. *Moenie worry nie.* Don't worry. Was that what Nomsa said? It was too late to ask because she was already gone.

Miss Beatrice was alone again. She came out of the Chimney and picked up the stump and this is when she cried and cried, the way I cried after my baby died.

She cried all the way past the colours and the name of Frikkie on the wall and the opening back onto the veld where the sun was rolling like a *dronklap* behind the clouds. Miss Beatrice cried past the frosty bonnet and all the same old mountains that would never be alive or dead, just there.

It was the same with me except I never saw my baby alive, like Miss Beatrice did. I never knew what was gone from me. I never said hello or goodbye, or Look at that funny face! I used to tell this to Jack when the lemons were ripe and I would think of what was under that tree, and whether it was a heaven or a hell down there for the little one and what was left of the old dogs. Jack would go away when I talked like this and I sat and I drank all by myself and tried very much to forget what I didn't see, why I didn't know. But it was hard and the hospital would come back to me and the jacaranda trees all lost and blue out of the window and I cried like Miss Beatrice did all over the horse's neck and shoulders, only it was usually one of the dogs who got wet. Sometimes I was sorry for her because it's worse to know what you've lost, like having a dress made out of gold thread and violets and then suddenly one day it's gone out of your cupboard. Other times I was jealous and spiteful because she lost her baby as if she was a sock or a hanky and then she went back and got the stump. I didn't even have a stump or a minute with the baby which they say is like being anointed with oil the way the people get in the Bible when things are going well.

I am waiting for Jack to come home. I have never waited so hard in my life. I can't lift my feet anymore.

FIFTEEN

That day coming back on the mare Miss Beatrice cried for everything. She cried for September who would never see Precious and she saw the peppercorns on his head and the way he fell back onto the floor in the *pondokkie*. She cried for his neck that was broken. She even cried for Mr. Henry when he poked her belly and she remembered the way he was when they married and he had white smocks and big hats and an easel that he liked to set up on a country lane with cows in the background and bluebells and other flowers you will never ever see in the Karoo. Of course it was England. She cried for her mother who was sad when she married Mr. Henry because he liked horse racing and cards and his special friends and her father who smoked and tapped his pipe and fixed everything by sending them to Highlands when Mr. Henry's debts were higher than any of those low

English mountains. Here we have the Drakensberg and many others and of course Table Mountain.

She cried for the ostrich that died trying to eat a quince and she cried for the ones that danced too much and broke their legs. Then she cried for the Russian dogs and everything else she had known that had died.

When something dies there is a hole, like a shadow, that stays behind. That's what Miss Beatrice was crying for as she rode. All the gaps and holes where people or *goggas* or ostriches used to be. You can't fill them in. They're just gone forever and ever, no matter what the ministers say. I always cry at the bioscope especially when they show films like "Waterloo Bridge" about the lady who walked along the bridge. She stepped into the road on purpose into some lorries and then they drove right over her. She was beautiful and missing and then dead. That man who she loved came and he had a charm in his hand that she had given him but it was too late.

But sometimes in real life the ending is different but that part only comes later, when you least expect it.

I see Jack in the distance, an old *oom* coming home. The dogs are running ahead.

Esther has her head in my lap and I'm crying so hard my ankles are getting thin again.

I want to say, Did you know? but the words get stuck in my throat like fish bones.

Jack says why didn't Miss Beatrice call the police and I say, *Ag* no, man, how could she? How could she say what happened in that cave even before Nomsa came? How could she say I forgot where I put her?

Miss Beatrice didn't know what Nomsa did with her child, I tell Jack.

She didn't even know anymore if it was Nomsa that took her. Sometimes she remembered rolling and rolling and maybe she rolled on top of her baby and squashed her. Maybe Precious fell on the ground right in the beginning, when they climbed into the cave. Ma knew a lady who was sick and the doctor told her not to kiss her little girl or her boy but she didn't listen and so they both got sick and died from her kissing. Miss Beatrice could have hurt poor Precious by mistake and then woken up and she was gone and it was dark and there was nothing to remember.

I don't know what she would have done if she had known all the places Nomsa went that day. I don't know whether she would have laughed or cried. As it was, she was crying and that didn't stop for days and days and it went on at Mr. Henry's funeral. It was hard getting him into the Karoo ground which is baked hard like very stale bread. It was even harder with him because people said he didn't want to be buried there and his soul was making the spades buckle and the *volkies* who were digging the grave fall down. Miss Beatrice even cried about that. How sad it was that he was going into this earth, in the wrong place, under the wrong stars, without seeing Precious.

The only thing she didn't cry about was the thing everybody else was crying about which was the end of the feather market or so everyone said. There were some people who could look into the future and see that there was a living in the ostriches but they were a few. Mr. Jacobs was one of them but he had sold his farm at the height so no one was sorry for him at all. *Blerrie* Jew, they said, as they packed. Or maybe they said it in Russian or French or with one of those Scotch accents. All those fancy farmers and feather buyers who used to go to London and Paris and Vienna to see their feathers being sold and marketed, who came home with Irish linen and flowered plates, and gilt mirrors for their wives and their daughters, were leaving Oudtshoorn. They were selling their ostriches for shillings, those same birds whose feathers used to sell for forty and fifty and sixty pounds. The auction house was all closed up, and so were the ladies' shops and the General Dealer. It was like the plague only there were no bodies lying in the street. People who went to the Post Office and the Railway Station rushed in and out and then they went home. At home, the women counted sheets and fixed blankets, and saw what could stay and what must go, while the men smoked and pulled their eyebrows together, and made the children scared. Yes, there was crying, and it went on behind those thick curtains, in the houses with their gold taps and their tiled floors. And there was also talking because Frikkie had come back from the Caves with a story that everybody must hear, and the Bapedi told the other *volkies* who told the maids and the garden boys, and the children were standing right there in the kitchen, and the children went to tell their mas and their pas, and their *oumas* and *oupas*.

The story had many arms and legs, just like a tarantula, and it hung in everybody's house, on the ceiling. It was the reason for everything that was bad in Oudtshoorn. It was the Bapedi curse on the country except it was a curse on the feather market as well. Everybody was bitten, but in a different way. Of course the Bapedi believed that the baby came out dead and was hidden and that was the terrible part. The white people believed it was Miss Beatrice who killed the child and now that child was a Devil, living in the Chimney, and speaking in her voice. That's when they began calling that part of the Caves the Devil's Chimney and people wanted to go there and climb in and see for themselves. There was still enough oxygen in those days.

So they went and nothing happened but they still got scared. The white people blamed Miss Beatrice for the feather collapse and some of the *volkies* thought it was Nomsa and her *muti* who had killed the child of her husband out of spite. Nobody wanted to see them again. Soon it was 1915 and a wall sprang up in front of the house at Highlands after the New Year. Who put it up nobody knew.

Nomsa came back and she had nothing and Miss Beatrice had nothing. They had both lost all the love in their hearts and with Miss Beatrice they say it was most of her mind as well. People saw her in and out of those Caves, looking and looking, the way I used to look for chameleons on the bushes in the afternoons, when I came home from school. It looks like a stick or a leaf but then you go closer and you see those eyes rolling up and around and those fingers and toes divided in the middle. Miss Beatrice looked but that never happened.

Nomsa and Miss Beatrice lived at Highlands together and some people said they slept in the same bed and that's what killed September, Mr. Henry and Precious in the first place. All of these stories you could hear like dreams in the bar of the Oudtshoorn Hotel before closing or early in the morning with coffee.

And then there's the part about Pauline.

Nomsa didn't leave with the salad oil that day and she didn't forget the ostrich shells and the ostrich skin bag under a tree. She went to the red flag and felt her way into the earth with her hands and her feet, like a *dassie* going into his hole. She followed the sound of Miss Beatrice bursting and moaning and being twisted this way and that. The whole of the Cango Caves was like a giant aching shoppie, and Nomsa was right in it, looking for Precious.

There by the place where Frikkie had burnt his name on the wall, Nomsa lit a candle. She saw Bushman paintings of ostriches and buck and stick-men underneath Frikkie's name and they seemed to be racing and racing to get to Miss Beatrice and jump right on top of her. She followed them as they ran deeper and deeper into the Caves, to the place where Miss Beatrice was lying and twisting.

The stick-men and the orange buck and the smoky black wildebeest went for Miss Beatrice, as she moaned and groaned and hung onto all those shimmering stalactites and stalagmites.

All that time, Nomsa was searching for Precious. She was looking for the child of her husband behind every formation. Behind the Japanese tree, and the Fairy Bed and the Wing of a Lost Angel. It was hard because of the noise from Miss

Beatrice and the Nooitgedacht ladies not to mention all those stick-men and the Bushmen painters.

When it was finally quiet, and the wildebeest and the golden buck and everyone else had gone back to their places, Nomsa saw Miss Beatrice lying there on the ground, like a dead person, her titties glowing white in the dark. Precious cried and it was like the sound of a tiny mouse in your kitchen and Nomsa and Miss Beatrice both tried to get it and that's when their big fight began.

Nomsa wasn't sure if Miss Beatrice was dead or a ghost or the sister of a *tokolosh*. All she knew was that she must get this child away from her, from those clutching hands and that chicken head.

She clicked and the baby heard her. It is me, she shouted. Welcome, child of my husband. Miss Beatrice bit her ankle and it was worse than a hundred scorpions. *Ai!* She *skopped* Miss Beatrice hard and it felt like she was kicking a bag of potatoes. There was more biting and kicking and scratching until Miss Beatrice lay still on the ground.

Nomsa felt the breath of the child in her face and she picked her up with all those feathers around her. Precious stretched her arms like a baby monkey falling off a vine right into Nomsa's arms. Nomsa held her tight and it was as if September had come back to her.

Miss Beatrice was starting to move and Nomsa felt her ankle still bitten and she took that poor child and ran deeper into the hardest part of the Caves. She scrambled and crawled and her candle shivered and got small but it didn't go out.

The air got softer and the walls were streaked with the most beautiful pinks and blues and reds and there on the ceiling were stars and crystals more beautiful than anything you will ever see in the sky. She was in the Wonder Caves, where nobody had ever been before.

Precious was weak, the feathers around her hardly moving. Nomsa undid the ostrich shells that were tied around her waist. She sat down and filled her mouth with the water and the special leaves she had cooked. Then she held her head over the baby and let the water trickle slowly out of her mouth into the mouth of the child. Precious' eyes looked into hers and Nomsa saw September again, in those steady, dark honey eyes, turning up so slightly at the corners. The pleated, trembling little mouth was Miss Beatrice's and so was the chin. The baby's hair lay on her head like curling veins, and her skin was greyish brown from being left alone. Nomsa held her and soothed her and Precious melted into her arms.

The cave glowed around them, the crystals twinkling and the water in the pools soft as the moon. The colours on the ceiling were streams of blue and ochre and deep red, like the beginning of a day. Nomsa rocked Precious and then covered her eyes for a moment with her palm, so that she should not want the things other people had. She touched her mouth, so that she should not say evil things. She laid her hand on Precious' head, so that she should not have bad dreams. She held both her hands, squeezing them a little, so that Precious would be able to hold onto the things that she wanted. She held her feet, so that Precious would walk with straight, strong legs across the veld.

Then she made a nest, lined with the prime whites, inside the ostrich-skin bag and she laid Precious inside. She took off part of the wrappings of her dress and wound the bag to her back like a big bandage. The stiff part of the ostrich skin held up Precious' head and the rest of the child was covered by the bag and the thick wad of wrappings. Precious whimpered and Nomsa jiggled a little and the whimpering wavered, and then stopped. Nomsa walked through the Caves with the child on her back, her footsoles feeling the dampness on the floor. She passed the stalactites and stalagmites she had seen on the way in, this one shaped like an enormous armbone, that one like an old man leaning on two sticks. There were giant curtains of stone with many folds and Nomsa saw how they reached far above her head. But she did not stare too long because the child was still weak, and she was trying to find the same places her feet had walked on before, when Precious' voice led her on. When she came to Frikkie's name on the wall, she knew she was close to the opening Miss Beatrice had dropped into. Again, she looked at the paintings of animals hidden underneath the big, fat letters of his name, and she saw a man running, and an ostrich. A few yards further, light streamed in and you could see some branches of a dried-up tree, and a corner of sky. She climbed back into the world, and it was careful and slow with Precious on her back and the shells at her waist.

Nomsa stood by the red flag, torn into tongues, and she looked towards Meiringspoort. There was a farm between this farm and the Meirings River, and her people were there.

Nomsa walked through the veld, and finally came to a dust road. She followed the road until she got to a gate for cattle. She crossed over the gate and saw the roofs of the *pondokkies* in the distance, behind lucerne fields. The big farmhouse, pale yellow with a green corrugated iron roof and *stoep* all the way around, looked empty and hollow in the late afternoon. She turned away from it, towards the *pondokkies*. There was one line of smoke curling up, and she walked towards it, keeping it between her eyes.

Her *ouma* was there, squatting in front of the fire, cooking *mieliepap*. There was a chicken that ran into the *pondokkie* when Nomsa walked up the little path and the *ouma* looked up and saw her granddaughter. Hello, *meisiekind,* she said, and she and Nomsa held each other. Long time no see, she said, in that funny way the Coloured people have which is not like the Bantu. Then *Ouma* saw the baby and she looked at Nomsa and she laughed like a drain. Nomsa said, *Ouma, sy is honger,* and the old lady lifted her dress, and put Precious to her breast that was flat as an elephant's ear. Precious drank and the old lady laughed again and for the first time since Precious was born, Nomsa felt her arms go loose and her shoulders drop. She squatted next to *Ouma* and stared into Precious' eyes that seemed to be sucking along with her mouth. The sun warmed their heads and they sat there like that even after Precious fell asleep, her mouth still at the breast. Nomsa knew she had to go back but her feet kept her there, stuck into the ground next to *Ouma* like sticks. Right at the end, they spoke about the days that were coming, the days that belonged to Precious, and *Ouma* said she would look after the child unless there was no more *mieliepap* left. If that happened, she would send a boy to Highlands and Nomsa must come fetch her.

Nomsa walked back to Highlands and the way was long. She went past lucerne and tobacco and some ostrich farms and behind her was the shadow of the Swartberg. She saw the willow trees and the dam and the *pondokkies* and then the big house.

Miss Beatrice wasn't sitting on the front *stoep*. Nomsa came closer and she saw Miss Beatrice in one of the windows, and her hand fluttered hello or a scream. Nomsa stood and waited and waited and Miss Beatrice came out slowly and she wasn't herself anymore.

Nomsa walked up to the *stoep* and her feet slapped the ground like hands on a naughty bum. *Sy is nie dood nie,* she said, or was it the weeping willow?

Miss Beatrice didn't answer. She just poured herself another *dop*.

They looked at the sky going dark.

They blame me, Miss Beatrice said, when the sun slipped into the ground like a penny going into your purse.

Her voice was dry and hardly used.

I made the Devil in the Chimney, and now everyone is leaving because the Devil made the price of the feathers drop and the whole town is dying without any money.

That's when the Karoo seemed bigger and drier and quieter than ever before and Nomsa and Miss Beatrice sat inside its giant heart like people lost forever.

I get that feeling sometimes when you're gone and the dogs sleep around me, for hours and hours. Here where we live there is no end to the days and the nights. You can hear the crickets calling and it's always the same. Of course when Oudtshoorn was full of feather farmers and buyers and all those people who had come to fill up their pockets, it was more like a party, and people had things they don't have anymore. Now it is quiet, the same quiet that began when Nomsa and Miss Beatrice were sitting on the back *stoep*. But if you listen very hard, you can hear something underneath all that silence, which is the terrible things people carry around in their heads like that story about Pauline, and another one about Mr. Henry which is that he is still alive and living in two pieces, one piece with Nomsa, the other with Miss Beatrice. The story about Pauline is worse, I think.

Jack says he thinks the one about Mr. Henry is more frightening. I am scared of the Devil sticking his hand up inside me like with Pauline and Jack is afraid of being torn in half.

But these days the country is changing although in most ways Oudtshoorn is still the way it always was. Now you can see different things on the TV and somebody told me that what really happened to Pauline was that she wasn't really Pauline, she was Precious, the child raised by *Ouma* on the farm outside Meiringspoort. She grew up strong, her legs straight, her eyes steady like September's. When she was fourteen she went to work for the Steenkamps to clean the house and look after their baby girl, Marie-Louise. They took her to the Caves and that's when she disappeared, for the second time. I think she disappeared because she had to come back, and that coming back was finding her way to Highlands, to that big house behind the wall, to say goodbye to Nomsa and Miss Beatrice. I think that's where she still is, looking after them as they get as old as all those people in the Bible like Noah, who turn a hundred and fifty. She sits with them on the *stoep* and they look at the mountains and talk about what Oudtshoorn was like when everybody had fancy taps and Irish linen. They tell her about Mr. Jacobs and a breath of hot air blows over them, which is his spirit passing through because he's dead and buried in the Jewish cemetery.

I still think Miss Beatrice was wrong to lose Precious in the Caves like that, but Precious did live, not like my poor baby.

I tell this to Jack and I'm searching his face for the rest of the lie. I see only my own pain. Suddenly I know they gave him the baby when the breath was gone, when there was nothing left. No wonder he dug under that lemon tree.

Ag, rubbish woman, he says to me, when I tell him that Pauline was really Precious. How can that be? Dammit, woman, you can't even count properly.

The old Jack is back. I'll never tell him about Gerda as long as I live.

I'm going to *donner* you, I say, and I pick up the ashtray. It doesn't even matter whether Pauline was fourteen or forty when she got lost. I don't care.

I nearly say, They didn't even want you at the Railways, but I hold my tongue and put down the ashtray.

I get up and trip over one of the dogs onto the floor. I can feel the tears on my face as if they belong to someone else.

Cry baby, Jack says, and his head gets very red. Get up yourself. I'm sick of picking you up. I'm sick of your booze and your crying.

He takes a *sluk* of something on the table and I'm not sure if it's a cooldrink or *witblits* or a Castle. I wish I had a real baby. I wish he lived, he said.

He? The word holds me and I see the baby's face and his *piel* and I look at Jack and for the first time in my life I say I'm sorry. He isn't shouting for once and he looks at me and I see his eyes fill up with water and his mouth break open and we hold each other. We are at the aerodrome again with the windsock above our heads but this time it is pure sadness that passes between us. I wipe his nose on my sleeve. I don't even have a tissue. I'm glad, I say, and he knows what I mean.

I saw all those Bantu people on the TV standing in long lines to vote and then I saw a film on the TV about Robben Island, where they tortured people and of course we didn't know anything. Now I am sorry for the prisoners, but I am also sorry for myself and Jack and my baby, and for Miss Beatrice and Nomsa and September and even Mr. Henry. I once went shopping at Pick 'n Pay and I thought I saw Pauline or Precious sitting in a *bakkie* next to a white farmer with curlers in her hair and I got such a *skrik* because the world is really changing if you can see something like that and it's not the maid. Was it her skin or just a shadow?

I come home and I have to have a *dop*. I was going to walk out on the veld with the dogs, but I got as far as the first *koppie* and then I got scared and came home. I'm not sure if the *koppies* and bushes are for me anymore. Maybe it's the blood pressure or maybe it's all the changes, I don't know. When you go to the beach in Cape Town, they say it's like Seal Island with all the black people lying down in the sun. I don't mind seals so much. Maybe Jack can teach me how to swim and then I can go see this for myself. Jack laughs and says, You're *poep-scared* of getting your head under the waves, my girl, and look at you, you're a *dron-klap* on top of it. I don't care, I say, I am going to learn to swim.

Glossary

aandblommetjie	evening flower
assegaais	spears
aasvoëls	vultures
babbelas	hung over
bakkie	pickup truck
bakoorjakkals	kind of jackal
bedonnerd	crazy
bek	mouth
biltong	salted, dried meat
blerrie	corruption of 'bloody'
bobbejaan	baboon
bobotie	traditional dish of curried mince
Boerejood	Afrikaner Jew
Boerevrou	Afrikaner woman
boerewors	traditional sausage
Boesman	Bushman
boet	brother
bokkie	little antelope
bokmakierie	kind of bird
bolla	bun
boomslang	tree snake
bossies	mad
braai/braaivleis	barbeque
brakbos	salinaceous plant
broekies	panties
buk	bend

chommies	friends
chorrie	a dilapidated car
dagga	marijuana
dammetjie	small dam
dassie	rock rabbit
derms	intestines
deurmekaar	confused
doek	head scarf
donner	to beat up
dop	a drink
dronkie/dronklap	drunkard
Duitsland	Germany
dunsa	push
ganna	kind of bush; see **brakbos**
goggas	insects
grils	chills
hotnot	someone of mixed race
iqanda	egg
ixesha	time
jakkals	jackal
kaffir	black African (derog.)
kappie	sunbonnet
klap	to slap
klonkie	patronizing name for a black youth
knobkierie	knobbed stock
koeksuster	deep-fried doughnut
koppie	small hill
korhaan	kind of bird
kraal	pen for animals
kriek	tight muscle
kroes	frizzy
laager	defensive encampment
lam	lame
lappie	cloth
lekkerlyf	drunk
loskop	scatterbrain
meisiekind	a young girl
melktert	baked custard tart
mielie/mielepap	maize/maize porridge
miggie	gnat
moeg	tired
moffie	homosexual (derog.)
morgen	unit for measuring land
muti	medicine
naar	queasy
naartjie	tangerine
nogal	into the bargain
oom	uncle
opslag	short-lived vegetation
ouma	grandmother
oupa	grandfather
padkos	food for a journey

peri-peri	hot sauce
piel	penis
poep-scared	scared shitless
pomping	fucking
pondokkie	crude hut
potjiekos	traditional stew prepared in a cast-iron pot
riempie	thin leather strip
rooibos	kind of tea
Rooinekke	the English (derog. slang); red-necks
shebeen	illegal drinking establishment
sjambok	a heavy whip
skaam	shy
skande/skandaal	shame; scandal
skeef	crooked
skel	to scold
skollies	thugs
skop	kick
skrik	fright
sluk	a gulp
smous	peddler
spanspek	musk melon
spekboom	type of succulent shrub
stoksielalleen	all alone
suip	to drink immoderately
tannie	auntie
Tassies	brand of cheap wine
tickey	a coin
tjoepstil	very quiet
tokolosh	goblin
uxolo	peace
veldskoen	rough shoe made of ox hide
voertsek	go away
volkies	mixed race farm labourers
vrot	rotten
vrou	woman
vry	to neck
vygies	succulent flowering plants
witblits	moonshine